THE FAIRY BOOK

by Dinah Maria Mulock
illustrated by Warwick Goble

a facsimile edition published by
MAYFLOWER BOOKS · NEW YORK
in association with
Macmillan · London

Facsimile Classics Series

ENGLISH FAIRY TALES
by Flora Annie Steel
illustrated by Arthur Rackham

THE WATER-BABIES
by Charles Kingsley
illustrated by Linley Sambourne

THE HEROES OF ASGARD
by A. and E. Keary
illustrated by Charles E. Brock

THE MIKADO
by Sir W. S. Gilbert
illustrated by W. Russell Flint and
Charles E. Brock

THE YEOMEN OF THE
GUARD
by Sir W. S. Gilbert
illustrated by W. Russell Flint and
Charles E. Brock

THE FABLES OF AESOP
edited by Joseph Jacobs
illustrated by Richard Heighway

THE ROMANCE OF KING
ARTHUR
by Alfred W. Pollard abridged
from Malory
illustrated by Arthur Rackham

OLD CHRISTMAS
by Washington Irving
illustrated by Randolph Caldecott

GRIMM'S HOUSEHOLD
STORIES
translated by Lucy Crane
illustrated by Walter Crane

THE FAIRY BOOK
by Dinah Maria Mulock
illustrated by Warwick Goble

JAPANESE FAIRY TALES
by Grace James
illustrated by Warwick Goble

THE NURSERY "ALICE"
by Lewis Carroll
illustrated by Sir John Tenniel

"'Is it very far from hence?' asked the wolf. . . ." (p. 134).

THE
FAIRY BOOK

THE BEST POPULAR FAIRY STORIES
SELECTED AND RENDERED ANEW

BY THE AUTHOR OF

'JOHN HALIFAX, GENTLEMAN'

WITH 16 ILLUSTRATIONS IN COLOUR
BY WARWICK GOBLE

MACMILLAN AND CO., LIMITED
ST. MARTIN'S STREET, LONDON

First published by Macmillan & Co. 1923
First published in this edition 1979 by
MAYFLOWER BOOKS INC.
575 Lexington Avenue New York City 10022

Illustrations © Macmillan Publishers Ltd

Library of Congress Cataloging in Publication Data
Craik, Dinah Maria Mulock, 1826-1887.
  The fairy book.

  (Mayflower facsimile classics)
  Photoreprint of the 1923 ed. published by Macmillan,
London.
  SUMMARY: A collection of classic tales, some English,
and some from Perrault, d'Aulnois, and Grimm.
  1. Fairy tales. [1. Fairy tales. 2. Folklore]
I. Goble, Warwick. II. Title.
PZ8.C845Fai   1979   398.2'1   79-14514
ISBN 0-8317-3163-X

Printed in Hong Kong

DEDICATED

TO

LITTLE OLIVE

PREFACE

A PREFACE is usually an excrescence on a good book, and a vain apology for a worthless one; but in the present instance a few explanatory words seem necessary.

This is meant to be the best collection attainable of that delight of all children, and of many grown people who retain the child-heart still—the old-fashioned, time-honoured classic Fairy-tale. It has been compiled from all sources—far-off and familiar; when familiar, the stories have been traced with care to their original form, which, if foreign, has been re-translated, condensed, and in any other needful way made suitable for modern British children. Perrault, Madame d'Aulnois, and Grimm have thus been laid under contribution. Where it was not possible to get at the original of a tale, its various versions have been collated, compared, and combined; and in some instances, where this still proved unsatisfactory, the whole story has been written afresh. The few real old English fairy tales, such as *Jack the Giant-Killer*, *Tom Thumb*, etc., whose authorship is lost in obscurity, but whose charming Saxon simplicity of style, and intense realism of narration, make for them an ever-green immortality—these have been left intact; for no later touch would improve them. All modern stories have been excluded.

Of course, in fairy tales instruction is not expected—we find there only the rude moral of virtue rewarded and vice punished. But children will soon discover for themselves that in real life all beautiful people are not good, nor all ugly ones wicked; that every elder sister is not ungenerous, nor every stepmother cruel. The tender young heart is often reached as soon by the imagination as by the intellect: and without attempting any direct appeal to either reason or conscience, the Editor of this Collection has been especially careful that it should contain nothing which could really harm a child.

She therefore trusts that, whatever its defects, this Fairy Book will not deserve a criticism, almost the sharpest that can be given to any work—" that it would have been better if the author had taken more pains."

CONTENTS

LIST OF ILLUSTRATIONS

By WARWICK GOBLE

THE SLEEPING BEAUTY IN THE WOOD

ONCE there was a royal couple who grieved excessively because they had no children. When at last, after long waiting, the queen presented her husband with a little daughter, his majesty showed his joy by giving a christening feast, so grand that the like of it was never known. He invited all the fairies in the land—there were seven altogether—to stand godmothers to the little princess ; hoping that each might bestow on her some good gift, as was the custom of good fairies in those days.

After the ceremony, all the guests returned to the palace, where there was set before each fairy-godmother a magnificent covered dish, with an embroidered table-napkin, and a knife and fork of pure gold, studded with diamonds and rubies. But alas ! as they placed themselves at table, there entered an old fairy who had never been invited, because more than fifty years since she had left the king's dominion on a tour of pleasure, and had not been heard of until this day. His majesty, much troubled, desired a cover to be placed for her, but it was of common delf, for he had ordered from his jeweller only seven gold dishes for the seven fairies aforesaid. The elderly fairy thought herself neglected, and muttered angry menaces, which were overheard by one of the younger fairies, who chanced to sit beside her. This good godmother, afraid of harm to the pretty baby, hastened to hide herself behind the tapestry in the hall. She did this, because she wished all the others to speak first—so that if any ill gift were bestowed on the child, she might be able to counteract it.

The six now offered their good wishes—which, unlike most wishes, were sure to come true. The fortunate little princess was to grow up the fairest woman in the world; to have a temper sweet as an angel; to be perfectly graceful and gracious; to sing like a nightingale; to dance like a leaf on a tree; and to possess every accomplishment under the sun. Then the old fairy's turn came. Shaking her head spitefully, she uttered the wish that when the baby grew up into a young lady, and learned to spin, she might prick her finger with the spindle and die of the wound.

At this terrible prophecy, all the guests shuddered; and some of the more tender-hearted began to weep. The lately happy parents were almost out of their wits with grief. Upon which the wise young fairy appeared from behind the tapestry, saying cheerfully, "Your majesties may comfort yourselves; the princess shall not die. I have no power to alter the ill-fortune just wished her by my ancient sister—her finger must be pierced; and she shall then sink, not into the sleep of death, but into a sleep that will last a hundred years. After that time is ended, the son of a king will find her, awaken her, and marry her."

Immediately all the fairies vanished.

The king, in the hope of avoiding his daughter's doom, issued an edict, forbidding all persons to spin, and even to have spinning-wheels in their houses, on pain of instant death. But it was in vain. One day, when she was just fifteen years of age, the king and queen left their daughter alone in one of their castles, when, wandering about at her will, she came to an ancient donjon tower, climbed to the top of it, and there found a very old woman—so old and deaf that she had never heard of the king's edict—busy with her wheel.

THE SLEEPING BEAUTY IN THE WOOD

"What are you doing, good old woman?" said the princess.

"I'm spinning, my pretty child."

"Ah, how charming! Let me try if I can spin also."

She had no sooner taken up the spindle than, being lively and obstinate, she handled it so awkwardly and carelessly that the point pierced her finger. Though it was so small a wound, she fainted away at once, and dropped silently down on the floor. The poor frightened old woman called for help; shortly came the ladies in waiting, who tried every means to restore their young mistress, but all their care was useless. She lay, beautiful as an angel, the colour still lingering in her lips and cheeks; her fair bosom softly stirred with her breath: only her eyes were fast closed. When the king her father and the queen her mother beheld her thus, they knew regret was idle—all had happened as the cruel fairy meant. But they also knew that their daughter would not sleep for ever, though after one hundred years it was not likely they would either of them behold her awakening. Until that happy hour should arrive, they determined to leave her in repose. They sent away all the physicians and attendants, and themselves sorrowfully laid her upon a bed of embroidery, in the most elegant apartment of the palace. There she slept and looked like a sleeping angel still.

When this misfortune happened, the kindly young fairy who had saved the princess by changing her sleep of death into this sleep of a hundred years, was twelve thousand leagues away in the kingdom of Mataquin. But being informed of everything, she arrived speedily, in a chariot of fire drawn by dragons. The king was somewhat startled by the sight, but nevertheless went to the door of his palace, and, with a mournful countenance, presented her his hand to descend.

The fairy condoled with his majesty, and approved

3

of all he had done.   Then, being a fairy of great common sense and foresight, she suggested that the princess, awakening after a hundred years in this ancient castle, might be a good deal embarrassed, especially with a young prince by her side, to find herself alone.   Accordingly, without asking any one's leave, she touched with her magic wand the entire population of the palace—except the king and queen ; governesses, ladies of honour, waiting-maids, gentlemen ushers, cooks, kitchen-girls, pages, footmen—down to the horses that were in the stables, and the grooms that attended them, she touched each and all.   Nay, with kind consideration for the feelings of the princess, she even touched the little fat lap-dog, Puffy, who had laid himself down beside his mistress on her splendid bed.   He, like all the rest, fell fast asleep in a moment.   The very spits that were before the kitchen-fire ceased turning, and the fire itself went out, and everything became as silent as if it were the middle of the night, or as if the palace were a palace of the dead.

The king and queen—having kissed their daughter and wept over her a little, but not much, she looked so sweet and content—departed from the castle, giving orders that it was to be approached no more.   The command was unnecessary ; for in one quarter of an hour there sprung up around it a wood so thick and thorny that neither beasts nor men could attempt to penetrate there. Above this dense mass of forest could only be perceived the top of the high tower where the lovely princess slept.

A great many changes happen in a hundred years. The king, who never had a second child, died, and his throne passed into another royal family.   So entirely was the story of the poor princess forgotten, that when the reigning king's son, being one day out hunting and stopped in the chase by this formidable wood, inquired what wood it was and what were those towers which he saw appearing out of the midst of it, no one could answer him. At length an old peasant was found who remembered having heard his grandfather say to his father, that in this tower was a princess, beautiful as the day, who was doomed to sleep there for one hundred years, until awakened by a king's son, her destined bridegroom.

At this, the young prince, who had the spirit of a hero, determined to find out the truth for himself. Spurred on by both generosity and curiosity, he leaped from his horse and began to force his way through the thick wood. To his amazement the stiff branches all gave way, and the ugly thorns sheathed themselves of their own accord, and the brambles buried themselves in the earth to let him pass. This done, they closed behind him, allowing none of his suite to follow : but, ardent and young, he went boldly on alone.

The first thing he saw was enough to smite him with fear. Bodies of men and horses lay extended on the ground ; but the men had faces, not death-white, but red as peonies, and beside them were glasses half filled with wine, showing that they had gone to sleep drinking. Next he entered a large court, paved with marble, where stood rows of guards presenting arms, but motionless as if cut out of stone ; then he passed through many chambers where gentlemen and ladies, all in the costume of the past century, slept at their ease, some standing, some sitting. The pages were lurking in corners, the ladies of honour were stooping over their embroidery frames, or listening apparently with polite attention to the gentlemen of the court, but all were as silent as statues and as immovable. Their clothes, strange to say, were fresh and new as ever : and not a particle of dust or spider-web had gathered over the furniture, though it had not known a broom for a hundred years. Finally the astonished prince came to an inner chamber, where was the fairest sight his eyes had ever beheld.

A young girl of wonderful beauty lay asleep on an embroidered bed, and she looked as if she had only just closed her eyes. Trembling, the prince approached and knelt beside her. Some say he kissed her, but as nobody saw it, and she never told, we cannot be quite sure of the fact. However, as the end of the enchantment had come, the princess awakened at once, and looking at him with eyes of the tenderest regard, said drowsily, "Is it you, my prince? I have waited for you very long."

Charmed with these words, and still more with the tone in which they were uttered, the prince assured her that he loved her more than his life. Nevertheless, he was the most embarrassed of the two; for, thanks to the kind fairy, the princess had plenty of time to dream of him during her century of slumber, while he had never even heard of her till an hour before. For a long time did they sit conversing, and yet had not said half enough. Their only interruption was the little dog Puffy, who had awakened with his mistress, and now began to be exceedingly jealous that the princess did not notice him as much as she was wont to do.

Meantime all the attendants, whose enchantment was also broken, not being in love, were ready to die of hunger after their fast of a hundred years. A lady of honour ventured to intimate that dinner was served; whereupon the prince handed his beloved princess at once to the great hall. She did not wait to dress for dinner, being already perfectly and magnificently attired, though in a fashion somewhat out of date. However, her lover had the politeness not to notice this, nor to remind her that she was dressed exactly like her royal grandmother, whose portrait still hung on the palace walls.

During the banquet a concert took place by the attendant musicians, and considering they had not touched their instruments for a century, they played extremely well. They ended with a wedding march : for that very evening the marriage of the prince and princess was celebrated, and though the bride was nearly one hundred years older than the bridegroom, it is remarkable that the fact would never have been discovered by any one unacquainted therewith.

After a few days they went together out of the castle and enchanted wood, both of which immediately vanished, and were never more beheld by mortal eyes. The princess was restored to her ancestral kingdom, but it was not generally declared who she was, as during a hundred years people had grown so very much cleverer that nobody then living would ever have believed the story. So nothing was explained, and nobody presumed to ask any questions about her, for ought not a prince to be able to marry whomsoever he pleases ?

Nor—whether or not the day of fairies was over—did the princess ever see anything further of her seven godmothers. She lived a long and happy life, like any other ordinary woman, and died at length, beloved, regretted, but, the prince being already no more, perfectly contented.

HOP-O'-MY-THUMB

THERE once lived in a village a faggot-maker and his wife, who had seven children, all boys; the eldest was no more than ten years old, and the youngest was only seven. It was odd enough, to be sure, that they should have so many children in such a short time; but the truth is, the wife always brought him two and once three at a time. This made him very poor, for not one of these boys was old enough to get a living: and what was still worse, the youngest was a puny little fellow who hardly ever spoke a word. Now this, indeed, was a mark of his good sense, but it made his father and mother suppose him to be silly, and they thought that at last he would turn out quite a fool. This boy was the least size ever seen; for when he was born he was no bigger than a man's thumb, which made him be christened by the name of Hop-o'-my-thumb. The poor child was the drudge of the whole house, and always bore the blame of everything that was done wrong. For all this, Hop-o'-my-thumb was far more clever than any of his brothers; and though he spoke but little, he heard and knew more than people thought. It happened just at this time, that for want of rain the fields had grown but half as much corn and potatoes as they used to grow; so that the faggot-maker and his wife could not give the boys the food they had before, which was always either bread or potatoes.

After the father and mother had grieved some time, they thought that as they could contrive no other way to

" A young girl of wonderful beauty lay asleep on an embroidered bed."

live, they must somehow get rid of their children. One night when the boys were gone to bed, and the faggot-maker and his wife were sitting over a few lighted sticks, to warm themselves, the husband sighed deeply, and said, "You see, my dear, we cannot maintain our children any longer, and to see them die of hunger before my eyes is what I could never bear. I will, therefore, to-morrow morning take them to the forest, and leave them in the thickest part of it, so that they will not be able to find their way back : this will be very easy ; for while they amuse themselves with tying up the faggots, we need only slip away when they are looking some other way."

"Ah ! husband," cried the poor wife, "you cannot, no, you never can consent to be the death of your own children."

The husband in vain told her to think how very poor they were.

The wife replied " that this was true, to be sure ; but if she was poor, she was still their mother " ; and then she cried as if her heart would break. At last she thought how shocking it would be to see them starved to death before their eyes ; so she agreed to what her husband had said, and then went sobbing to bed.

Hop-o'-my-thumb had been awake all the time ; and when he heard his father talk very seriously, he slipped away from his brothers' side, and crept under his father's bed, to hear all that was said without being seen.

When his father and mother had left off talking, he got back to his own place, and passed the night in thinking what he should do the next morning.

He rose early, and ran to the river's side, where he filled his pockets with small white pebbles, and then went back home. In the morning they all set out, as their father and mother had agreed on ; and Hop-o'-my-thumb did not say a word to any of his brothers about what he had heard. They came to a forest that was so very thick,

9

that they could not see each other a few yards off. The faggot-maker set to work cutting down wood ; and the children began to gather the twigs, to make faggots of them.

When the father and mother saw that the young ones were all very busy, they slipped away without being seen. The children soon found themselves alone, and began to cry as loud as they could. Hop-o'-my-thumb let them cry on, for he knew well enough how to lead them safe home, as he had taken care to drop the white pebbles he had in his pocket along all the way he had come. He only said to them, "Never mind it, my lads ; father and mother have left us here by ourselves, but only take care to follow me, and I will lead you back again."

When they heard this, they left off crying, and followed Hop-o'-my-thumb, who soon brought them to their father's house by the very same path which they had come along. At first they had not the courage to go in ; but stood at the door to hear what their parents were talking about. Just as the faggot-maker and his wife had come home without their children, a great gentleman of the village sent to pay them two guineas, for work they had done for him, which he had owed them so long that they never thought of getting a farthing of it. This money made them quite happy ; for the poor creatures were very hungry, and had no other way of getting anything to eat.

The faggot-maker sent his wife out immediately to buy some meat ; and as it was a long time since she had made a hearty meal, she bought as much meat as would have been enough for six or eight persons. The truth was, when she was thinking what would be enough for dinner, she forgot that her children were not at home ; but as soon as she and her husband had done eating, she cried out, "Alas ! where are our poor children ? how they would feast on what we have left ! It was all your fault, husband ! I told you we should repent leaving them to starve in the forest !—Oh mercy ! perhaps they have already been eaten by the hungry wolves ! " The poor woman shed plenty of tears : " Alas ! alas ! " said she, over and over again, "what is become of my dear children?"

The children, who were all at the door, cried out together, " Here we are, mother, here we are ! "

She flew like lightning to let them in, and kissed every one of them.

The faggot-maker and his wife were charmed at having their children once more with them, and their joy for this lasted till their money was all spent ; but then they found themselves quite as ill off as before. So by degrees they again thought of leaving them in the forest : and that the young ones might not come back a second time, they said they would take them a great deal farther than they did at first. They could not talk this matter so slily but that Hop-o'-my-thumb found means to hear all that passed between them ; but he cared very little about it, for he thought it would be easy for him to do just the same as he had done before. But though he got up very early the next morning to go to the river's side to get the pebbles, a thing which he had not thought of hindered him ; for he found that the house door was double-locked. Hop-o'-my-thumb was now quite at a loss what to do ; but soon after this, his mother gave each of the children a piece of bread for breakfast, and then it came into his head that he could make his share do as well as the pebbles, by dropping crumbs of it all the way as he went. So he did not eat his piece, but put it into his pocket.

It was not long before they all set out, and their parents took care to lead them into the very thickest and darkest part of the forest. They then slipped away by a by-path as before, and left the children by themselves again. All this did not give Hop-o'-my-thumb any concern, for he thought himself quite sure of getting back by means of the crumbs that he had dropped by the way; but when he came to look for them he found that not a crumb was left, for the birds had eaten them all up.

The poor children were now sadly off, for the farther they went, the harder it was for them to get out of the forest. At last, night came on, and the noise of the wind among the trees seemed to them like the howling of wolves, so that every moment they thought they should be eaten up. They hardly dared to speak a word, or to move a limb, for fear. Soon after there came a heavy rain, which wetted them to the very skin, and made the ground so slippery, that they fell down almost at every step, and got dirty all over.

Before it was quite dark, Hop-o'-my-thumb climbed up to the top of a tree, and looked round on all sides to see if he could find any way of getting help. He saw a small light, like that of a candle, but it was a very great way off, and beyond the forest. He then came down from the tree, to try to find the way to it; but he could not see it when he was on the ground, and he was in the utmost trouble what to do next. They walked on towards the place where he had seen the light, and at last reached the end of the forest, and got sight of it again. They now walked faster; and after being much tired and vexed (for every time they got into lower ground they lost sight of the light), came to the house it was in. They knocked at the door, which was opened by a very good-natured-looking lady, who asked what brought them there. Hop-o'-my-thumb told her that they were poor children, who had lost their way in the forest, and begged that she would give them a bed till morning. When the lady saw that they had such pretty faces, she began to shed tears and said, " Ah! my poor children, you do not know what place you are come to. This is the house of an Ogre, who eats up little boys and girls."

" Alas ! madam," replied Hop-o'-my-thumb, who trembled from head to foot, " what shall we do ? If we go back to the forest, we are sure of being torn to pieces by the wolves ; we would rather, therefore, be eaten by the gentleman : besides, when he sees us, perhaps he may take pity on us and spare our lives."

The Ogre's wife thought she could contrive to hide them from her husband till morning ; so she let them go in and warm themselves by a good fire, before which there was a whole sheep roasting for the Ogre's supper. When they had stood a short time by the fire, there came a loud knocking at the door : this was the Ogre come home. His wife hurried the children under the bed, and told them to lie still, and she then let her husband in.

The Ogre asked if supper were ready, and if the wine were fetched from the cellar ; and then he sat down at the table. The sheep was not quite done, but he liked it much better half raw. In a minute or two the Ogre began to snuff to his right and left, and said he smelt child's flesh.

" It must be this calf which has just been killed," said his wife.

" I smell child's flesh, I tell thee once more," cried the Ogre, looking all about the room ; " I smell child's flesh ; there is something going on that I do not know of."

As soon as he had spoken these words, he rose from his chair and went towards the bed.

" Ah ! madam," said he, " you thought to cheat me, did you ? Wretch ! thou art old and tough thyself, or else I would eat thee up too ! But come, come, this is lucky enough ; for the brats will make a nice dish for three Ogres, who are my particular friends, and who are to dine with me to-morrow."

He then drew them out one by one from under the bed. The poor children fell on their knees and begged

13

his pardon as humbly as they could ; but this Ogre was the most cruel of all Ogres, and instead of feeling any pity, he only began to think how sweet and tender their flesh would be ; so he told his wife they would be nice morsels, if she served them up with plenty of sauce. He then fetched a large knife, and began to sharpen it on a long whetstone that he held in his left hand ; and all the while he came nearer and nearer to the bed. The Ogre took up one of the children, and was going to set about cutting him to pieces ; but his wife said to him, " What in the world makes you take the trouble of killing them to-night ? Will it not be time enough to-morrow morning ? "

" Hold your prating," replied the Ogre ; "they will grow tender by being kept a little while after they are killed."

" But," said his wife, " you have got so much meat in the house already ; here is a calf, two sheep, and half a pig."

" True," said the Ogre, "so give them all a good supper, that they may not get lean, and then send them to bed."

The good creature was quite glad at this. She gave them plenty for their supper, but the poor children were so terrified that they could not eat a bit.

The Ogre sat down to his wine, very much pleased with the thought of giving his friends such a dainty dish : this made him drink rather more than common, and he was soon obliged to go to bed himself. Now the Ogre had seven daughters, who were all very young like Hop-o'-my-thumb and his brothers. These young Ogresses had fair skins, because they fed on raw meat like their father ; but they had small grey eyes, quite round, and sunk in their heads, hooked noses, wide mouths, and very long sharp teeth standing a great way off each other. They were too young as yet to do much mischief ; but they showed that if they lived to be as old as their father, they would grow quite as cruel as he was, for they took pleasure already in biting young children, and sucking their blood. The Ogresses had been put to bed very early that night : they were all in one bed, which was very large, and every one of them had a crown of gold on her head. There was another bed of the same size in the room, and in this the Ogre's wife put the seven little boys, and then went to bed herself along with her husband.

Now Hop-o'-my-thumb was afraid that the Ogre would wake in the night and kill him and his brothers while they were asleep. So he got out of bed in the middle of the night as softly as he could, took off all his brothers' nightcaps and his own, and crept with them to the bed that the Ogre's daughters were in : he then took off their crowns, and put the night-caps on their heads instead : next he put the crowns on his brothers' heads and his own, and got into bed again ; expecting, after this, that, if the Ogre should come, he would take him and his brothers for his own children. Everything turned out as he wished. The Ogre waked soon after mid-night, and began to be very sorry that he had put off killing the boys till the morning : so he jumped out of bed, and took hold of his large knife. "Let us see," said he, "what the young rogues are about, and do the business at once !" He then walked softly to the room where they all slept, and went up to the bed the boys were in, who were all asleep except Hop-o'-my-thumb. He touched their heads one at a time, and feeling the crowns of gold, said to himself, "Oh, oh ! I had like to have made such a mistake. I must have drunk too much wine last night."

He went next to the bed that his own little Ogresses were in, and when he felt the night-caps, he said, "Ah ! here you are, my lads " : and so in a moment he cut the throats of all his daughters.

He was very much pleased when he had done this, and then went back to his own bed. As soon as Hop-o'-my-thumb heard him snore, he awoke his brothers, and told them to put on their clothes quickly, and follow him. They stole down softly into the garden, and then jumped from the wall into the road : they ran as fast as their legs could carry them, but were so much afraid all the while, that they hardly knew which way to take. When the Ogre waked in the morning, he said to his wife, grinning, "My dear, go and dress the young rogues I saw last night."

The wife was quite surprised at hearing her husband speak so kindly, and did not dream of the real meaning of his words. She supposed he wanted her to help them to put on their clothes ; so she went upstairs, and the first thing she saw was her seven daughters with their throats cut, and all over blood. This threw her into a fainting fit. The Ogre was afraid his wife might be too long in doing what he had set her about, so he went himself to help her ; but he was as much shocked as she had been at the dreadful sight of his bleeding children. "Ah! what have I done?" he cried ; "but the little rascals shall pay for it, I warrant them."

He first threw some water on his wife's face ; and, as soon as she came to herself, he said to her : "Bring me quickly my seven-league boots, that I may go and catch the little vipers."

The Ogre then put on these boots, and set out with all speed. He strided over many parts of the country, and at last turned into the very road in which the poor children were. For they had set off towards the faggot-maker's cottage, which they had almost reached. They watched the Ogre stepping from mountain to mountain at one step, and crossing rivers as if they had been tiny brooks. At this Hop-o'-my-thumb thought a little what was to be done ; and spying a hollow place under a large

16

rock, he made his brothers get into it. He then crept in himself, but kept his eye fixed on the Ogre, to see what he would do next.

The Ogre found himself quite weary with the journey he had gone, for seven-league boots are very tiresome to the person who wears them; so he now began to think of resting, and happened to sit down on the very rock where the poor children were hid. As he was so tired, and it was a very hot day, he fell fast asleep, and soon began to snore so loud, that the little fellows were terrified.

When Hop-o'-my-thumb saw this he said to his brothers, "Courage, my lads! never fear! you have nothing to do but to steal away and get home while the Ogre is fast asleep, and leave me to shift for myself."

The brothers now were very glad to do whatever he told them, and so they soon came to their father's house. In the meantime Hop-o'-my-thumb went up to the Ogre softly, pulled off his seven-league boots very gently, and put them on his own legs: for though the boots were very large, yet being fairy-boots, they could make themselves small enough to fit any leg they pleased.

As soon as ever Hop-o'-my-thumb had made sure of the Ogre's seven-league boots, he went at once to the palace, and offered his services to carry orders from the king to his army, which was a great way off, and to bring back the quickest accounts of the battle they were just at that time fighting with the enemy. In short, he thought he could be of more use to the king than all his mail coaches, and so should make his fortune in this manner. He succeeded so well, that in a short time he made money enough to keep himself, his father, mother, and six brothers, without the trouble of working, for the rest of their lives. Having done this, he went back to his father's cottage, where all the family were delighted to see him again. As the great fame of his boots had been talked of at court in this time, the king sent for

him, and indeed employed him very often in the greatest
affairs of the state, so that he became one of the richest
men in the kingdom.

And now let us see what became of the wicked Ogre.
He slept so soundly that he never discovered the loss of
his boots ; but having an evil conscience and bad dreams,
he fell in his sleep from the corner of the rock where
Hop-o'-my-thumb and his brothers had left him, and
bruised himself so much from head to foot, that he could
not stir : so he was forced to stretch himself out at full
length, and wait for some one to come and help him.

Now a good many faggot-makers passed near the
place where the Ogre lay ; and, when they heard him
groan, they went up to ask him what was the matter.
But the Ogre had eaten such a great number of children
in his life-time, that he had grown so very big and fat
that these men could not even have carried one of his
legs ; so they were forced to leave him there.   At last
night came on, and then a large serpent came out of a
wood just by and stung him, so that he died in great pain.

By and by, Hop-o'-my-thumb, who had become the
king's first favourite, heard of the Ogre's death ; and the
first thing he did was to tell his majesty all that the good-
natured Ogress had done to save the lives of himself and
brothers.   The king was so much pleased at what he
heard, that he asked Hop-o'-my-thumb if there was any
favour he could bestow upon her.   Hop-o'-my-thumb
thanked the king, and desired that the Ogress might
have the noble title of Duchess of Draggletail given to
her ; which was no sooner asked than granted.   The
Ogress then came to court, and lived very happily for
many years, enjoying the vast fortune she had found in
the Ogre's chests.   As for Hop-o'-my-thumb, he every
day grew more witty and brave ; till at last the king
made him the greatest lord in the kingdom, and set him
over all his affairs.

CINDERELLA

OR

THE LITTLE GLASS SLIPPER

THERE was once an honest gentleman who took for his second wife a lady, the proudest and most disagreeable in the whole country. She had two daughters exactly like herself in all things. He also had one little girl, who resembled her dead mother, the best woman in all the world. Scarcely had the second marriage taken place, than the step-mother became jealous of the good qualities of the little girl, who was so great a contrast to her own two daughters. She gave her all the menial occupations of the house; compelled her to wash the floors and staircases to dust the bedrooms, and clean the grates; and while her sisters occupied carpeted chambers hung with mirrors, where they could see themselves from head to foot, this poor little damsel was sent to sleep in an attic, on an old straw mattress, with only one chair and not a looking-glass in the room.

She suffered all in silence, not daring to complain to her father, who was entirely ruled by his new wife. When her daily work was done, she used to sit down in the chimney-corner among the ashes; from which the two sisters gave her the nick-name of *Cinderella*. But Cinderella, however shabbily clad, was handsomer than they were with all their fine clothes.

It happened that the king's son gave a series of balls,

to which were invited all the rank and fashion of the city, and among the rest the two elder sisters. They were very proud and happy, and occupied their whole time in deciding what they should wear ; a source of new trouble to Cinderella, whose duty it was to get up their fine linen and laces, and who never could please them however much she tried. They talked of nothing but their clothes.

"I," said the elder, "shall wear my velvet gown and my trimmings of English lace."

"And I," added the younger, "will have but my ordinary silk petticoat, but I shall adorn it with an upper skirt of flowered brocade, and shall put on my diamond tiara, which is a great deal finer than anything of yours."

Here the elder sister grew angry, and the dispute began to run so high, that Cinderella, who was known to have excellent taste, was called upon to decide between them. She gave them the best advice she could, and gently and submissively offered to dress them herself, and especially to arrange their hair, an accomplishment in which she excelled many a noted coiffeur. The important evening came, and she exercised all her skill to adorn the two young ladies. While she was combing out the elder's hair, this ill-natured girl said sharply, "Cinderella, do you not wish you were going to the ball?"

"Ah, madam" (they obliged her always to say madam), "you are only mocking me ; it is not my fortune to have any such pleasure."

"You are right ; people would only laugh to see a little cinder-wench at a ball."

Any other than Cinderella would have dressed the hair all awry, but she was good, and dressed it perfectly even and smooth, and as prettily as she could.

The sisters had scarcely eaten for two days, and had broken a dozen stay-laces a-day in trying to make themselves slender ; but to-night they broke a dozen more, and lost their tempers over and over again before they had completed their toilette. When at last the happy moment arrived, Cinderella followed them to the coach ; after it had whirled them away, she sat down by the kitchen fire and cried.

Immediately her godmother, who was a fairy, appeared beside her. " What are you crying for, my little maid ? "

" Oh, I wish—I wish——" Her sobs stopped her.

" You wish to go to the ball ; isn't it so ? "

Cinderella nodded.

" Well, then, be a good girl, and you shall go. First run into the garden and fetch me the largest pumpkin you can find."

Cinderella did not comprehend what this had to do with her going to the ball, but being obedient and obliging, she went. Her godmother took the pumpkin, and having scooped out all its inside, struck it with her wand ; it became a splendid gilt coach, lined with rose-coloured satin.

" Now fetch me the mouse-trap out of the pantry, my dear."

Cinderella brought it ; it contained six of the fattest, sleekest mice. The fairy lifted up the wire door, and as each mouse ran out, she struck it and changed it into a beautiful black horse.

" But what shall I do for your coachman, Cinderella ? "

Cinderella suggested that she had seen a large black rat in the rat-trap, and he might do for want of better.

" You are right ; go and look again for him."

He was found, and the fairy made him into a most respectable coachman, with the finest whiskers imaginable. She afterwards took six lizards from behind the pumpkin frame, and changed them into six footmen, all in splendid livery, who immediately jumped up behind the carriage, as if they had been footmen all their days. " Well, Cinderella, now you can go to the ball."

"What, in these clothes?" said Cinderella piteously, looking down on her ragged frock.

Her godmother laughed, and touched her also with the wand; at which her wretched threadbare jacket became stiff with gold, and sparkling with jewels; her woollen petticoat lengthened into a gown of sweeping satin, from underneath which peeped out her little feet, no longer bare, but covered with silk stockings and the prettiest glass slippers in the world. "Now, Cinderella, depart; but remember, if you stay one instant after midnight, your carriage will become a pumpkin, your coachman a rat, your horses mice, and your footmen lizards; while you yourself will be the little cinder-wench you were an hour ago."

Cinderella promised without fear, her heart was so full of joy.

Arrived at the palace, the king's son, whom some one, probably the fairy, had told to await the coming of an uninvited princess whom nobody knew, was standing at the entrance, ready to receive her. He offered her his hand and led her with the utmost courtesy through the assembled guests, who stood aside to let her pass, whispering to one another, "Oh, how beautiful she is!" It might have turned the head of any one but poor Cinderella, who was so used to be despised, that she took it all as if it were something happening in a dream.

Her triumph was complete; even the old king said to the queen, that never since her majesty's young days had he seen so charming and elegant a person. All the court ladies scanned her eagerly, clothes and all, determining to have theirs made next day of exactly the same pattern. The king's son himself led her out to dance, and she danced so gracefully that he admired her more and more. Indeed, at supper, which was fortunately early, his admiration quite took away his appetite. For Cinderella herself, with an involuntary shyness she sought out her sisters ; placed herself beside them and offered them all sorts of civil attentions, which, coming as they supposed from a stranger, and so magnificent a lady, almost overwhelmed them with delight.

While she was talking with them, she heard the clock strike a quarter to twelve, and making a courteous adieu to the royal family, she re-entered her carriage, escorted tenderly by the king's son, and arrived in safety at her own door. There she found her godmother, who smiled approval ; and of whom she begged permission to go to a second ball, the following night, to which the queen had earnestly invited her.

While she was talking, the two sisters were heard knocking at the gate, and the fairy godmother vanished, leaving Cinderella sitting in the chimney-corner, rubbing her eyes and pretending to be very sleepy.

" Ah," cried the eldest sister maliciously, " it has been the most delightful ball, and there was present the most beautiful princess I ever saw, who was so exceedingly polite to us both."

" Was she ? " said Cinderella indifferently ; " and who might she be ? "

" Nobody knows, though everybody would give their eyes to know, especially the king's son."

" Indeed ! " replied Cinderella, a little more interested ; " I should like to see her. Miss Javotte "—that was the elder sister's name—" will you not let me go to-morrow, and lend me your yellow gown that you wear on Sundays ? "

" What, lend my yellow gown to a cinder-wench ! I am not so mad as that " ; at which refusal Cinderella did not complain, for if her sister really had lent her the gown she would have been considerably embarrassed.

The next night came, and the two young ladies, richly dressed in different toilettes, went to the ball. Cinderella, more splendidly attired and beautiful than ever, followed them shortly after. "Now remember twelve o'clock," was her godmother's parting speech; and she thought she certainly should. But the prince's attentions to her were greater even than the first evening, and in the delight of listening to his pleasant conversation, time slipped by unperceived. While she was sitting beside him in a lovely alcove, and looking at the moon from under a bower of orange blossoms, she heard a clock strike the first stroke of twelve. She started up, and fled away as lightly as a deer.

Amazed, the prince followed, but could not catch her. Indeed he missed his lovely princess altogether, and only saw running out of the palace doors a little dirty lass whom he had never beheld before, and of whom he certainly would never have taken the least notice. Cinderella arrived at home breathless and weary, ragged and cold, without carriage, or footmen, or coachmen ; the only remnant of her past magnificence being one of her little glass slippers ;—the other she had dropped in the ball-room as she ran away.

When the two sisters returned they were full of this strange adventure, how the beautiful lady had appeared at the ball more beautiful than ever, and enchanted every one who looked at her ; and how as the clock was striking twelve she had suddenly risen up and fled through the ball-room, disappearing no one knew how or where, and dropping one of her glass slippers behind her in her flight. How the king's son had remained inconsolable until he chanced to pick up the little glass slipper, which he carried away in his pocket, and was seen to take it out continually, and look at it affectionately, with the air of a man very much in love ; in fact, from his behaviour during the remainder of the evening, all the court and royal family were convinced that he had become desperately enamoured of the wearer of the little glass slipper.

Cinderella listened in silence, turning her face to the

"The only remnant of her past magnificence being one of her little glass slippers."

kitchen fire, and perhaps it was that which made her look so rosy ; but nobody ever noticed or admired her at home, so it did not signify, and the next morning she went to her weary work again just as before.

A few days after, the whole city was attracted by the sight of a herald going round with a little glass slipper in his hand, publishing, with a flourish of trumpets, that the king's son ordered this to be fitted on the foot of every lady in the kingdom, and that he wished to marry the lady whom it fitted best, or to whom it and the fellow slipper belonged. Princesses, duchesses, countesses, and simple gentlewomen all tried it on, but being a fairy slipper, it fitted nobody ; and beside, nobody could produce its fellow slipper, which lay all the time safely in the pocket of Cinderella's old linsey gown.

At last the herald came to the house of the two sisters, and though they well knew neither of themselves was the beautiful lady, they made every attempt to get their clumsy feet into the glass slipper, but in vain.

" Let me try it on," said Cinderella from the chimney corner.

" What, you ? " cried the others, bursting into shouts of laughter ; but Cinderella only smiled, and held out her hand.

Her sisters could not prevent her, since the command was that every young maiden in the city should try on the slipper, in order that no chance might be left untried, for the prince was nearly breaking his heart ; and his father and mother were afraid that though a prince, he would actually die for love of the beautiful unknown lady.

So the herald bade Cinderella sit down on a three-legged stool in the kitchen, and himself put the slipper on her pretty little foot, which it fitted exactly ; she then drew from her pocket the fellow slipper, which she also put on, and stood up—for with the touch of the magic shoes all her dress was changed likewise—no longer the poor despised cinder-wench, but the beautiful lady whom the king's son loved.

Her sisters recognised her at once. Filled with astonishment, mingled with no little alarm, they threw themselves at her feet, begging her pardon for all their former unkindness. She raised and embraced them ; told them she forgave them with all her heart, and only hoped they would love her always. Then she departed with the herald to the king's palace, and told her whole story to his majesty and the royal family, who were not in the least surprised, for everybody believed in fairies, and everybody longed to have a fairy godmother.

For the young prince, he found her more lovely and lovable than ever, and insisted upon marrying her immediately. Cinderella never went home again, but she sent for her two sisters to the palace, and with the consent of all parties married them shortly after to two rich gentlemen of the court.

ADVENTURES OF JOHN DIETRICH

THERE once lived in Rambin, a town near the Baltic Sea, an honest, industrious man named James Dietrich. He had several children, all of a good disposition, especially the youngest, whose name was John. John Dietrich was a handsome, smart boy, diligent at school, and obedient at home. His great passion was for hearing stories, and whenever he met any one who was well stored with such, he never let him go till he had heard them all.

When John was about eight years old he was sent to spend a summer with his uncle, a farmer in Rodenkirchen. Here he had to keep cows with other boys, and they used to drive them to graze about the Nine-hills, where an old cowherd, one Klas Starkwolt, frequently came to join the lads, and then they would sit down all together and tell stories. Consequently Klas became John's best friend, for he knew stories without end. He could tell all about the Nine-hills, and the underground folk who inhabited them; how the giants disappeared from the country, and the dwarfs or little people came in their stead. These tales John swallowed so eagerly that he thought of nothing else, and was for ever talking of golden cups, and crowns, and glass shoes, and pockets full of ducats, and gold rings, and diamond coronets, and snow-white brides, and the like. Old Klas used often to shake his head at him and say, " John ! John ! what are you about ? The spade and scythe will be your sceptre

27

and crown, and your bride will wear a garland of rosemary and a gown of striped drill."

Still John almost longed to get into the Nine-hills, for Klas had told him that any one who by luck or cunning should get the cap of one of the little people might go down with safety, and instead of becoming their slave, he would be their master. The fairy whose cap he got would be his servant, and obey all his commands.

Midsummer-eve, when the days are longest and the nights shortest, was now come. In the village of Rambin old and young kept the holiday, had all sorts of plays, and told all kinds of stories. John, who knew that this season was the time for all fairy-people to come abroad, could now no longer contain himself, but the day after the festival he slipped away to the Nine-hills, and when it grew dark laid himself down on the top of the highest of them, which Klas had told him was the principal dancing-ground of the underground people. John lay there quite still from ten till twelve at night. At last it struck twelve. Immediately there was a ringing and a singing in the hills, and then a whispering and a lisping and a whiz and a buzz all about him, for the little people were now come out, some whirling round and round in the dance, and others sporting and tumbling about in the moonshine, and playing a thousand merry pranks. He felt a secret dread creep over him at this whispering and buzzing, for he could see nothing of them, as the caps they wore made them invisible ; but he lay quite still, with his face in the grass and his eyes fast shut, snoring a little just as if he was asleep. Yet now and then he ventured to open his eyes a little and peep out, but not the slightest trace of them could he see, though it was bright moon-light.

It was not long before three of the underground people came jumping up to where he was lying ; but they took no heed of him, and flung their brown caps up into the air, and caught them from one another. At length one snatched the cap out of the hand of another and flung it away. It flew direct, and fell upon John's head. He could feel, though he could not see it ; and the moment he did feel it, he caught hold of it. Starting up, he swung it about for joy, and made the little silver bell of it tingle, then set it upon his head, and—O wonderful to relate !— that instant he saw the countless and merry swarm of the little people.

The three little men came slily up to him, and thought by their nimbleness to get back the cap, but he held his prize fast, and they saw clearly that nothing was to be done in this way with him, for in size and strength John was a giant in comparison of these little fellows, who hardly reached his knee. The owner of the cap now came up very humbly to the finder, and begged, in as supplicating a tone as if his life depended upon it, that he would give him back his cap. "No," said John, "you sly little rogue, you'll get the cap no more. That's not the sort of thing : I should be in a nice perplexity if I had not something of yours ; now you have no power over me, but must do what I please. And I will go down with you, and see how you live below, and you shall be my servant.—Nay, no grumbling, you know you must. And I know it too, just as well as you do, for Klas Starkwolt told it to me often and often."

The little man made as if he had not heard or understood one word of all this ; he began all his crying and whining over again, and wept, and screamed, and howled most piteously for his little cap. But John cut the matter short by saying to him, "Have done ; you are my servant, and I intend to take a trip with you." So the underground man gave up the point ; especially as he well knew there was no remedy.

John now flung away his old hat and put on the cap, and set it firmly on his head, lest it should slip off or fly away, for all his power lay in it. He lost no time in trying its virtues, but commanded his new servant to fetch him food and drink. The servant ran away like the wind, and in a second was there again with bottles of wine, and bread, and rich fruits. So John ate and drank, and looked on at the sports and the dancing of the little people, and it pleased him right well, and he behaved himself stoutly and wisely, as if he was a born master.

When the cock had now crowed for the third time, and the little larks had made their first flutter in the sky, and the daybreak appeared in slender white streaks in the east, then there went a whisper, hush, hush, hush, through the bushes, and flowers, and trees; and the hills rang again, and opened up, and the little men stole down and disappeared. John gave close attention to everything, and found that it was exactly as he had been told. And behold! on the top of the hill where they had just been dancing, and which was now full of grass and flowers, as people see it by day, there rose, of a sudden, a small glass door. Whosoever wanted to go in stepped upon this; it opened, and he glided gently in, the glass closing again after him; and when they had all entered it vanished, and there was no further trace of it to be seen. Those who descended through the glass door sank quite gently into a wide silver tun or barrel, which held them all, and could easily have harboured a thousand such little people. John and his man went down also, along with several others, all of whom screamed out and prayed him not to tread on them, for if his weight came on them, they were dead men. He was, however, careful, and acted in a very friendly way towards them. Several barrels of this kind went up and down after each other, until all were in. They hung by long silver chains, which were drawn and guided from below.

In his descent John was amazed at the wonderful brilliancy of the walls between which the tun glided down.

They seemed all studded with pearls and diamonds, glittering and sparkling brightly, while below him he heard the most beautiful music tinkling at a distance, so that he did not know what he was about, and from excess of pleasure he fell fast asleep.

He slept a long time, and when he awoke he found himself in the most beautiful bed that could be, such as he had never seen in his father's or any other house. It was also the prettiest little chamber in the world, and his servant was beside him with a fan to keep away the flies and gnats. He had hardly opened his eyes when his little servant brought him a basin and towel, and held ready for him to put on the nicest new clothes of brown silk, most beautifully made ; with these was a pair of new black shoes with red ribbons, such as John had never beheld in Rambin or in Rodenkirchen either. There were also there several pairs of glittering glass shoes, such as are only used on great occasions. John was, we may well suppose, delighted to have such clothes to wear, and he put them on joyfully. His servant then flew like lightning and returned with a fine breakfast of wine and milk, and delicate white bread and fruits, and such other things as little boys are fond of. He now perceived, every moment, more and more, that Klas Starkwolt, the old cowherd, knew what he was talking about, for the splendour and magnificence here surpassed anything John had ever dreamt of. His servant, too, was the most obedient one possible ; a nod or a sign was enough for him, for he was as wise as a bee, as all these little people are by nature.

John's bedroom was all covered with emeralds and other precious stones, and in the ceiling was a diamond as big as a nine-pin bowl, that gave light to the whole chamber. In this place they have neither sun, nor moon, nor stars to give them light ; neither do they use lamps or candles of any kind ; but they live in the midst of precious stones, and have the purest of gold and silver in abundance, from which they manage to obtain light both by day and by night, though indeed, properly speaking, as there is no sun here, there is no distinction of day and night, and they reckon only by weeks. They set the brightest and clearest precious stones in their dwellings, and in the ways and passages leading under the ground, and in the places where they have their large halls, and their dances and feasts ; and the sparkle of these jewels makes a sort of silvery twilight which is far more beautiful than common day.

When John had finished his breakfast, his servant opened a little door in the wall, where was a closet with silver and gold cups and dishes and other vessels, and baskets filled with ducats, and boxes of jewels and precious stones. There were also charming pictures, and the most delightful story-books he had seen in the whole course of his life.

John spent the morning looking at these things ; and, when it was mid-day, a bell rung, and his servant said, " Will you dine alone, sir, or with the large company ? "

" With the large company, to be sure," replied John. So his servant led him out. John, however, saw nothing but solitary halls, lighted up with precious stones, and here and there little men and women, who appeared to him to glide out of the clefts and fissures of the rocks. Wondering what it was the bells rang for, he said to his servant— " But where is the company ? " And scarcely had he spoken when the hall they were in opened out to a great extent, and a canopy set with diamonds and precious stones was drawn over it. At the same moment he saw an immense throng of nicely dressed little men and women pouring in through several open doors ; the floor opened in several places, and tables, covered with the most beautiful ware, and the most luscious meats, and fruits, and wines, arranged themselves in rows, and the chairs

" When the cock had now crowed for the third time, . . . the little men stole down and disappeared."

arranged themselves along beside the tables, and then the men and women took their seats.

The principal persons now came forward, bowed to John, and led him to their table, where they placed him among their most beautiful maidens, a distinction which pleased John well. The party too was very merry, for the underground people are extremely lively and cheerful, and can never stay long quiet. Then the most charming music sounded over their heads ; and beautiful birds, flying about, sang sweetly : these were not real but artificial birds, which the little men make so ingeniously that they can fly about and sing like natural ones.

The servants of both sexes, who waited at table, and handed about the gold cups, and the silver and crystal baskets with fruit, were mortal children, whom some misfortune had thrown among the underground people, and who, having come down without securing any pledge, such as John's cap, had fallen into their power. These were differently clad from their masters. The boys and girls were dressed in snow-white coats and jackets, and wore glass shoes, so thin that their steps could never be heard, with blue caps on their heads, and silver belts round their waists.

John at first pitied them, seeing how they were forced to run about and wait on the little people ; but as they looked cheerful and happy, and were handsomely dressed, and had such rosy cheeks, he said to himself, "After all, they are not so badly off, and I was myself much worse when I had to be running after the cows and bullocks. To be sure, I am now a master here, and they are servants ; but there is no help for it : why were they so foolish as to let themselves be taken and not get some pledge before-hand ? At any rate, the time must come when they shall be set at liberty, and they will certainly not be longer than fifty years here." With these thoughts he consoled himself, and sported and played away with his little play-

D

fellows, and ate, and drank, and made his servant and the others tell him stories, for he always liked to hear something strange, and to get to the bottom of everything.

They sat at table about two hours : the principal person then rang a little bell, and the tables and chairs all vanished in a whiff, leaving the company standing on their feet. The birds now struck up a most lively air, and the little people began to dance, jumping and leaping and whirling round and round, as if the world were grown dizzy. And the pretty little girls that sat next John caught hold of him and whirled him about ; and, without making any resistance, he danced with them for two good hours. Every afternoon while he remained there he used to do the same ; and, to the last hour of his life, he always spoke of it with the greatest glee.

When the music and dancing were over it might be about four o'clock. The little people then disappeared, and went each about their work or their pleasure. After supper they sported and danced in the same way ; and at midnight, especially on starlight nights, they slipped out of their hills to dance in the open air. John used then, like a good boy, to say his prayers and go to sleep, a duty he never neglected either in the evening or in the morning.

For the first week that John was in the glass-hill he only went from his chamber to the great hall and back again. After then, however, he began to walk about, making his servant show and explain everything to him. He found that there were here most beautiful walks, in which he might ramble along for miles, in all directions, without ever finding an end of them, so immensely large was the hill that the little people lived in, and yet outwardly it seemed but a little hill, with a few bushes and trees growing on it.

He found also meadows and lanes, islands and lakes, where the birds sang sweeter, and the flowers were more

34

brilliant and fragrant than anything he had ever seen on earth. There was a breeze, and yet one did not feel the wind; it was quite clear and bright, but there was no heat; the waves were dashing, still there was no danger; and the most beautiful little barks and canoes came, like white swans, when one wanted to cross the water, and went backwards and forwards of their own accord. Whence all this came nobody knew, nor could his servant tell anything about it.

These lovely meads and plains were, for the most part, all solitary. Few of the underground people were to be seen upon them, and those that were just glided across them, as if in the greatest hurry. It very rarely happened that any of them danced out here in the open air; sometimes about three of them did so; at the most half a dozen : John never saw a greater number together. The meadows never seemed cheerful, except when the earth-children, who were kept as servants, were let out to walk. This, however, happened but twice a week, for they were mostly kept employed in the great hall and adjoining apartments, or at school.

For John soon found they had schools there also; he had been there about ten months, when one day he saw something snow-white gliding into a rock, and disappearing. " What! " said he to his servant, " are there some of you too that wear white, like the servants? " He was informed that there were; but they were few in number, and never appeared at the large tables or the dances, except once a year, on the birthday of the great Hill-king, who dwelt many thousand miles below in the great deep. These were the oldest men among them, some being many thousand years old; they knew all things, and could tell of the beginning of the world, and were called the Wise. They lived all alone, and only left their chambers to instruct the underground children and the attendants of both sexes.

John was greatly interested by this news, and he determined to take advantage of it ; so next morning he made his servant conduct him to the school, and was so well pleased with it that he never missed a day. The scholars were taught reading, writing, and accounts, to compose and relate histories and stories, and many elegant kinds of work ; so that many came out of the hills very prudent and learned. The biggest, and those of best capacity, received instruction in natural science and astronomy, and in poetry and riddle-making, arts highly esteemed by the little people. John was very diligent, and soon became a clever painter ; he wrought, too, most ingeniously in gold, and silver, and stones ; and in verse and riddle-making he had no fellow.

John had spent many a happy year here without ever thinking of the upper world, or of those he had left behind, so pleasantly passed the time—so many an agreeable playfellow had he among the children.

Of all his playfellows there was none of whom he was so fond as of a little fair-haired girl, named Elizabeth Krabbin. She was from his own village, and was the daughter of Frederick Krabbe, the minister of Rambin. She was but four years old when she was taken away, and John had often heard tell of her. She was not, however, stolen by the little people, but came into their power in this manner. One day in summer, she, with other children, ran out into the fields : in their rambles they went to the Nine-hills, where little Elizabeth fell asleep, and was forgotten by the rest. At night, when she awoke, she found herself under the ground among the little people. It was not merely because she was from his own village that John was so fond of Elizabeth, but she was a most beautiful child, with clear blue eyes and ringlets of fair hair, and a most angelic smile.

Time flew away unperceived : John was now eighteen, and Elizabeth sixteen. Their childish fondness was now become love, and the little people were pleased to see it, thinking that by means of her they might get John to renounce his power, and become their servant ; for they were fond of him, and would willingly have had him to wait upon them ; the love of dominion is their vice. But they were mistaken ; John had learned too much from his servant to be caught in that way.

John's chief delight was walking about alone with Elizabeth; for he now knew every place so well that he could dispense with the attendance of his servant. In these rambles he was always gay and lively, but his companion was frequently sad and melancholy, thinking of the land above, where men lived, and where the sun, moon, and stars shine. Now it happened in one of their walks, that as they talked of their love, and it was after midnight, they passed under the place where the tops of the glass hills used to open and let the underground people in and out. As they went along they heard of a sudden the crowing of several cocks above. At this sound, which she had not heard for twelve years, little Elizabeth felt her heart so affected that she could contain herself no longer, but throwing her arms about John's neck, she bathed his cheeks with her tears. At length she spake :

" Dearest John," said she, " everything down here is very beautiful, and the little people are kind, and do nothing to injure me, but still I have always been uneasy, nor ever felt any pleasure till I began to love you ; and yet that is not pure pleasure, for this is not a right way of living, such as it should be for human beings. Every night I dream of my dear father and mother, and of our churchyard, where the people stand so piously at the church-door waiting for my father, and I could weep tears of blood that I cannot go into the church with them, and worship God as a human being should ; for this is no Christian life we lead down here, but a delusive half heathen one. And only think, dear John, that we can

37

never marry, as there is no priest to join us. Do, then, plan some way for us to leave this place ; for I cannot tell you how I long to get once more to my father, and among pious Christians."

John too had not been unaffected by the crowing of the cocks, and he felt what he had never felt here before, a longing after the land where the sun shines. He replied :

"Dear Elizabeth, all you say is true, and I now feel that it is a sin for Christians to stay here ; and it seems to me as if our Lord said to us in that cry of the cocks, 'Come up, ye Christian children, out of those abodes of illusion and magic ; come to the light of the stars, and act as children of light.' I now feel that it was a great sin for me to come down here, but I trust I shall be forgiven on account of my youth ; for I was a child and knew not what I did. But now I will not stay a day longer. They cannot keep *me* here."

At these last words, Elizabeth turned pale, for she recollected that she was a servant, and must serve her fifty years. "And what will it avail me," cried she, "that I shall continue young and be but as twenty years old when I go out, for my father and mother will be dead, and all my companions old and gray ; and you, dearest John, will be old and gray also," cried she, throwing herself on his bosom.

John was thunderstruck at this, for it had never before occurred to him ; he, however, comforted her as well as he could, and declared he would never leave the place without her. He spent the whole night in forming various plans ; at last he fixed on one, and in the morning he despatched his servant to summon to his apartment six of the principal of the little people. When they came, John thus mildly addressed them :

"My friends, you know how I came here, not as a prisoner or servant, but as a lord and master over one of you, and consequently, over all. You have now for the ten years I have been with you treated me with respect and attention, and for that I am your debtor. But you are still more my debtors, for I might have given you every sort of annoyance and vexation, and you must have submitted to it. I have, however, not done so, but have behaved as your equal, and have sported and played with you rather than ruled over you. I now have one request to make. There is a girl among your servants whom I love, Elizabeth Krabbin, of Rambin, where I was born. Give her to me, and let us depart. For I will return to where the sun shines and the plough goes through the land. I ask to take nothing with me but her, and the ornaments and furniture of my chamber."

He spoke in a determined tone, and they hesitated and cast their eyes to the ground ; at last the eldest of them replied :

" Sir, you ask what we cannot grant. It is a fixed law that no servant should leave this place before the appointed time. Were we to break through this law, our whole subterranean empire would fall. Anything else you desire, for we love and respect you, but we cannot give up Elizabeth."

" You can and you shall give her up," cried John in a rage ; " go think of it till to-morrow. Return here at this hour. I will show you whether or no I can triumph over your hypocritical and cunning stratagems."

The six retired. Next morning, on their return, John addressed them in the kindest manner, but to no purpose ; they persisted in their refusal. He gave them till the following day, threatening them severely in case of their still proving refractory.

Next day, when the six little people appeared before him, John looked at them sternly, and made no reply to their salutations, but said to them shortly, " Yes or No ?" And they answered with one voice, " No." He then ordered his servant to summon twenty-four more of the principal persons, with their wives and children. When they came, they were in all five hundred, men, women, and children. John ordered them forthwith to go and fetch pickaxes, spades, and bars, which they did in a second.

He now led them out to a rock in one of the fields, and ordered them to fall to work at blasting, hewing, and dragging stones. They toiled patiently, and made as if it was only sport to them. From morning till night their taskmaster made them labour without ceasing, standing over them constantly, to prevent their resting. Still their obstinacy was inflexible ; and at the end of some weeks his pity for them was so great that he was obliged to give over.

He now thought of a new species of punishment for them. He ordered them to appear before him next morning, each provided with a new whip. They obeyed, and John commanded them to strip and lash one another till the blood should run down on the ground, while he stood looking on as grim and cruel as an Eastern tyrant. Still the little people cut and slashed themselves, and mocked at John, and refused to comply with his wishes. This he did for three or four days.

Several other courses did he try, but all in vain ; his temper was too gentle to struggle with their obstinacy, and he began now to despair of ever accomplishing his dearest wish. He began to hate the little people whom he was before so fond of ; he kept away from their banquets and dances, associated only with Elizabeth, and ate and drank quite solitary in his chamber. In short, he became almost a perfect hermit, and sank into moodiness and melancholy.

While in this temper, as he was taking a solitary walk in the evening, and, to divert his melancholy, was flinging the stones that lay in his path against each other, he happened to break a tolerably large one, and out of it jumped a toad. The moment John saw the ugly animal, he caught him up in ecstasy, and put him into his pocket and ran home, crying, "Now I have her! I have my Elizabeth! Now you shall catch it, you little mischievous rascals!" And on getting home he put the toad into a costly silver casket, as if it was the greatest treasure.

To account for John's joy you must know Klas Starkwolt had often told him that the underground people could not endure any ill odour, and that the sight or even the smell of a toad made them faint and suffer the most dreadful tortures, so that, by means of these animals, one could compel them to anything. Hence there are no bad smells to be found in the whole glass empire, and a toad is a thing unheard of there ; this toad must therefore have been enclosed in the stone from the Creation, as it were for the sake of John and Elizabeth.

Resolved to try the effect of his toad, John took the casket under his arm and went out, and on the way he met two of the little people in a lonesome place. The moment he approached them they fell to the ground, and whimpered and howled most lamentably, as long as he was near them.

Satisfied now of his power, he next morning summoned the fifty principal persons, with their wives and children, to his apartment. When they came, he addressed them, reminding them once again of his kindness and gentleness towards them, and of the good terms on which they had hitherto lived together. He reproached them with their ingratitude in refusing him the only favour he had ever asked of them, but firmly declared he would not give way to their obstinacy. "Wherefore," said he, "for the last time, I warn you;—think for a minute, and if you then say No, you shall feel that pain which is to you and your children the most terrible of all sufferings."

They did not take long to deliberate, but unanimously

replied " No " ; for they thought to themselves, What new scheme has the youth hit on, with which he thinks to frighten wise ones like us? and they smiled when they said No. Their smiling enraged John above all, and he ran back to where he had laid the casket with the toad, under a bush.

He was hardly come within a hundred paces of them when they all fell to the ground as if struck with a thunderbolt, and began to howl and whimper, and to writhe, as if suffering the most excruciating pain. They stretched out their hands, and cried, " Have mercy ! have mercy ! we feel you have a toad, and there is no escape for us. Take the odious beast away, and we will do all you require." He let them kick a few seconds longer, and then took the toad away. They then stood up and felt no more pain. John let all depart but the six chief persons, to whom he said—

" This night, between twelve and one, Elizabeth and I will depart. Load then for me three waggons, with gold, and silver, and precious stones. I might, you know, take all that is in the hill, and you deserve it, but I will be merciful. Further, you must put all the furniture of my chamber in two waggons, and get ready for me the handsomest travelling-carriage that is in the hill, with six black horses. Moreover, you must set at liberty all the servants who have been so long here that on earth they would be twenty years old and upwards, and you must give them as much silver and gold as will make them rich for life, and make a law that no one shall be detained here longer than his twentieth year."

The six took the oath, and went away quite melancholy, and John buried his toad deep in the ground. The little people laboured hard according to his bidding. At midnight everything was out of the hill, and John and Elizabeth got into the silver tun and were drawn up.

It was then one o'clock, and midsummer-eve, the

very time that twelve years before John had gone down into the hill. Music sounded around them, and they saw the glass hill open, and the rays of the light of heaven shine on them for the first time after so many years; and when they got out they saw the streaks of dawn already in the east. Crowds of the underground people were around them busied about the waggons. John bade them a last farewell, waved his brown cap three times in the air, and then flung it among them. And at the same moment he ceased to see them; he beheld nothing but a green hill, and the well-known bushes and fields, and heard the church-clo *κ* of Rambin strike two. When all was still, save a few larks who were tuning their morning songs, they both fell on their knees and worshipped God, resolving henceforth to lead a pious and a Christian life.

When the sun rose, John and his Elizabeth, with the children whom they had saved from the underground people, set out for Rambin. Every well-known object that they saw awakened pleasing recollections; and as they passed by Rodenkirchen, John recognised, among the people that gazed at and followed them, his old friend Klas Starkwolt, the cowherd, and his dog Speed. It was four in the morning when they entered Rambin, and they halted in the middle of the village, about twenty paces from the house where John was born. The whole village poured out to gaze on these Asiatic princes; for such the old sexton, who had in his youth been at Moscow and Constantinople, said they were. There John saw his father and mother, and his brother Andrew, and his sister Trine. The old minister, Krabbe, stood there too, in his black slippers and white nightcap, gaping and staring with the rest.

John discovered himself to his parents, and Elizabeth to hers, and the wedding-day was soon fixed, and such a wedding was never seen before or since in the island of Rugen; for John sent to Stralsund and Greifswald for whole boat-loads of wine and sugar and coffee, and whole herds of oxen, sheep, and pigs. The quantity of harts and roes and hares that were shot on the occasion it were vain to attempt to tell, or to count the fish that were caught. There was not a musician in Rugen and Pomerania that was not engaged, for John was immensely rich, and he wished to display his wealth.

John did not neglect his old friend Klas Starkwolt, the cowherd. He gave him enough to make him comfortable for the rest of his days, and insisted on his coming and staying with him as often and as long as he wished.

After his marriage, John made a progress through the country with his beautiful Elizabeth, and they purchased towns and villages and lands until he became master of nearly half Rugen, and a very considerable portion of the country. His father, old James Dietrich, was made a nobleman, and his brothers and sisters gentlemen and ladies—for what cannot money do?

John and his wife spent their days in acts of piety and charity. They built several churches, they had the blessings of every one that knew them, and died universally lamented. It was Count John Dietrich who built and richly endowed the present church of Rambin. He built it on the site of his father's house, and presented to it several of the cups and plates made by the underground people, and his own and Elizabeth's glass shoes, in memory of what had befallen them in their youth. But they were all taken away in the time of the great Charles the Twelfth of Sweden, when the Russians came on the island, and the Cossacks plundered even the churches, and took away everything.

BEAUTY AND THE BEAST

THERE was once a very rich merchant who had six children, three boys and three girls. As he was himself a man of great sense, he spared no expense for their education. The three daughters were all handsome, but particularly the youngest ; indeed she was so very beautiful, that in her childhood every one called her the Little Beauty ; and being equally lovely when she was grown up, nobody called her by any other name, which made her sisters very jealous of her. This youngest daughter was not only more handsome than her sisters, but also was better tempered. The two eldest were vain of their wealth and position. They gave themselves a thousand airs, and refused to visit other merchants' daughters ; nor would they condescend to be seen except with persons of quality. They went every day to balls, plays, and public walks, and always made game of their youngest sister for spending her time in reading or other useful employments. As it was well known that these young ladies would have large fortunes, many great merchants wished to get them for wives ; but the two eldest always answered, that, for their parts, they had no thoughts of marrying any one below a duke or an earl at least. Beauty had quite as many offers as her sisters, but she always answered, with the greatest civility, that though she was much obliged to her lovers, she would rather live some years longer with her father, as she thought herself too young to marry.

It happened that, by some unlucky accident, the

merchant suddenly lost all his fortune, and had nothing left but a small cottage in the country. Upon this he said to his daughters, while the tears ran down his cheeks, "My children, we must now go and dwell in the cottage, and try to get a living by labour, for we have no other means of support." The two eldest replied that they did not know how to work, and would not leave town; for they had lovers enough who would be glad to marry them, though they had no longer any fortune. But in this they were mistaken; for when the lovers heard what had happened, they said, "The girls were so proud and ill-tempered, that all we wanted was their fortune: we are not sorry at all to see their pride brought down: let them show off their airs to their cows and sheep." But everybody pitied poor Beauty, because she was so sweet-tempered and kind to all, and several gentlemen offered to marry her, though she had not a penny; but Beauty still refused, and said she could not think of leaving her poor father in this trouble. At first Beauty could not help sometimes crying in secret for the hardships she was now obliged to suffer; but in a very short time she said to herself, "All the crying in the world will do me no good, so I will try to be happy without a fortune."

When they had removed to their cottage, the merchant and his three sons employed themselves in ploughing and sowing the fields, and working in the garden. Beauty also did her part, for she rose by four o'clock every morning, lighted the fires, cleaned the house, and got ready the breakfast for the whole family. At first she found all this very hard; but she soon grew quite used to it, and thought it no hardship; indeed, the work greatly benefited her health. When she had done, she used to amuse herself with reading, playing her music, or singing while she spun. But her two sisters were at a loss what to do to pass the time away: they had their breakfast in bed, and did not rise till ten o'clock. Then they commonly walked out, but always found themselves very soon tired ; when they would often sit down under a shady tree, and grieve for the loss of their carriage and fine clothes, and say to each other, " What a mean-spirited poor stupid creature our young sister is, to be so content with this low way of life !" But their father thought differently, and loved and admired his youngest child more than ever.

After they had lived in this manner about a year, the merchant received a letter, which informed him that one of his richest ships, which he thought was lost, had just come into port. This news made the two eldest sisters almost mad with joy ; for they thought they should now leave the cottage, and have all their finery again. When they found that their father must take a journey to the ship, the two eldest begged he would not fail to bring them back some new gowns, caps, rings, and all sorts of trinkets. But Beauty asked for nothing ; for she thought in herself that all the ship was worth would hardly buy everything her sisters wished for. " Beauty," said the merchant, " how comes it that you ask for nothing : what can I bring you, my child ? "

" Since you are so kind as to think of me, dear father," she answered, " I should be glad if you would bring me a rose, for we have none in our garden." Now Beauty did not indeed wish for a rose, nor anything else, but she only said this that she might not affront her sisters ; otherwise they would have said she wanted her father to praise her for desiring nothing. The merchant took his leave of them, and set out on his journey ; but when he got to the ship, some persons went to law with him about the cargo, and after a deal of trouble he came back to his cottage as poor as he had left it. When he was within thirty miles of his home, and thinking of the joy of again meeting his children, he lost his way in the midst of a dense forest. It rained and snowed very hard, and, besides, the wind was so high as to throw him twice from his

horse. Night came on, and he feared he should die of
cold and hunger, or be torn to pieces by the wolves that
he heard howling round him. All at once, he cast his
eyes towards a long avenue, and saw at the end a light,
but it seemed a great way off. He made the best of his
way towards it, and found that it came from a splendid
palace, the windows of which were all blazing with light.
It had great bronze gates, standing wide open, and fine
courtyards, through which the merchant passed ; but not
a living soul was to be seen. There were stables too,
which his poor starved horse, less scrupulous than himself,
entered at once, and took a good meal of oats and hay.
His master then tied him up, and walked towards the
entrance hall, but still without seeing a single creature.
He went on to a large dining-parlour, where he found a
good fire, and a table covered with some very nice dishes,
but only one plate with a knife and fork. As the snow
and rain had wetted him to the skin, he went up to the
fire to dry himself. " I hope," said he, " the master of
the house or his servants will excuse me, for it surely will
not be long now before I see them." He waited some
time, but still nobody came : at last the clock struck
eleven, and the merchant, being quite faint for the want
of food, helped himself to a chicken, and to a few glasses
of wine, yet all the time trembling with fear. He sat till
the clock struck twelve, and then, taking courage, began
to think he might as well look about him : so he opened
a door at the end of the hall, and went through it into a
very grand room, in which there was a fine bed ; and as
he was feeling very weary, he shut the door, took off his
clothes, and got into it.

It was ten o'clock in the morning before he awoke,
when he was amazed to see a handsome new suit of
clothes laid ready for him, instead of his own, which were
all torn and spoiled. " To be sure," said he to himself,
" this place belongs to some good fairy, who has taken

pity on my ill luck." He looked out of the window, and instead of the snow-covered wood, where he had lost himself the previous night, he saw the most charming arbours covered with all kinds of flowers. Returning to the hall where he had supped, he found a breakfast table, ready prepared. "Indeed, my good fairy," said the merchant aloud, "I am vastly obliged to you for your kind care of me." He then made a hearty breakfast, took his hat, and was going to the stable to pay his horse a visit ; but as he passed under one of the arbours, which was loaded with roses, he thought of what Beauty had asked him to bring back to her, and so he took a bunch of roses to carry home. At the same moment he heard a loud noise, and saw coming towards him a beast, so frightful to look at that he was ready to faint with fear. "Ungrateful man!" said the beast in a terrible voice, "I have saved your life by admitting you into my palace, and in return you steal my roses, which I value more than anything I possess. But you shall atone for your fault : you shall die in a quarter of an hour."

The merchant fell on his knees, and clasping his hands, said, "Sir, I humbly beg your pardon : I did not think it would offend you to gather a rose for one of my daughters, who had entreated me to bring her one home. Do not kill me, my lord!"

"I am not a lord, but a beast," replied the monster : "I hate false compliments : so do not fancy that you can coax me by any such ways. You tell me that you have daughters ; now I will suffer you to escape, if one of them will come and die in your stead. If not, promise that you will yourself return in three months, to be dealt with as I may choose."

The tender-hearted merchant had no thoughts of letting any one of his daughters die for his sake ; but he knew that if he seemed to accept the beast's terms, he should at least have the pleasure of seeing them once again. So he gave his promise, and was told he might then set off as soon as he liked. "But," said the beast, "I do not wish you to go back empty-handed. Go to the room you slept in, and you will find a chest there ; fill it with whatsoever you like best, and I will have it taken to your own house for you."

When the beast had said this, he went away. The good merchant, left to himself, began to consider that as he must die—for he had no thought of breaking a promise, made even to a beast—he might as well have the comfort of leaving his children provided for. He returned to the room he had slept in, and found there heaps of gold pieces lying about. He filled the chest with them to the very brim, locked it, and, mounting his horse, left the palace as sorrowful as he had been glad when he first beheld it. The horse took a path across the forest of his own accord, and in a few hours they reached the merchant's house. His children came running round him, but, instead of kissing them with joy, he could not help weeping as he looked at them. He held in his hand the bunch of roses, which he gave to Beauty, saying, "Take these roses, Beauty ; but little do you think how dear they have cost your poor father" ; and then he gave them an account of all that he had seen or heard in the palace of the beast.

The two eldest sisters now began to shed tears, and to lay the blame upon Beauty, who, they said, would be the cause of her father's death. "See," said they, "what happens from the pride of the little wretch : why did not she ask for such things as we did? But, to be sure, Miss must not be like other people ; and though she will be the cause of her father's death, yet she does not shed a tear."

"It would be useless," replied Beauty, "for my father shall not die. As the beast will accept of one of his daughters, I will give myself up, and be only too happy to prove my love for the best of fathers."

"No, sister," said the three brothers with one voice, "that cannot be ; we will go in search of this monster, and either he or we will perish."

"Do not hope to kill him," said the merchant, "his power is far too great. But Beauty's young life shall not be sacrificed : I am old, and cannot expect to live much longer ; so I shall but give up a few years of my life, and shall only grieve for the sake of my children."

"Never, father !" cried Beauty. "If you go back to the palace, you cannot hinder my going after you : though young, I am not over-fond of life ; and I would much rather be eaten up by the monster, than die of grief for your loss."

The merchant in vain tried to reason with Beauty, who still obstinately kept to her purpose ; which, in truth, made her two sisters glad, for they were jealous of her, because everybody loved her.

The merchant was so grieved at the thoughts of losing his child, that he never once thought of the chest filled with gold ; but at night, to his great surprise, he found it standing by his bedside. He said nothing about his riches to his eldest daughters, for he knew very well it would at once make them want to return to town : but he told Beauty his secret, and she then said, that while he was away, two gentlemen had been on a visit at their cottage, who had fallen in love with her two sisters. She entreated her father to marry them without delay, for she was so sweet-natured, she only wished them to be happy.

Three months went by, only too fast, and then the merchant and Beauty got ready to set out for the palace of the beast. Upon this, the two sisters rubbed their eyes with an onion, to make believe they were crying ; both the merchant and his sons cried in earnest. Only Beauty shed no tears. They reached the palace in a very few hours, and the horse, without bidding, went into the same stable as before. The merchant and Beauty walked towards the large hall, where they found a table covered with every dainty, and two plates laid ready. The merchant had very little appetite ; but Beauty, that she might the better hide her grief, placed herself at the table, and helped her father ; she then began to eat herself, and thought all the time that to be sure the beast had a mind to fatten her before he ate her up, since he had provided such good cheer for her. When they had done their supper, they heard a great noise, and the good old man began to bid his poor child farewell, for he knew it was the beast coming to them. When Beauty first saw that frightful form, she was very much terrified, but tried to hide her fear. The creature walked up to her, and eyed her all over—then asked her in a dreadful voice if she had come quite of her own accord.

" Yes," said Beauty.

" Then you are a good girl, and I am very much obliged to you."

This was such an astonishingly civil answer that Beauty's courage rose : but it sank again when the beast, addressing the merchant, desired him to leave the palace next morning, and never return to it again. " And so good-night, merchant. And good-night, Beauty."

" Good-night, beast," she answered, as the monster shuffled out of the room.

" Ah ! my dear child," said the merchant, kissing his daughter, " I am half dead already, at the thought of leaving you with this dreadful beast ; you shall go back and let me stay in your place."

" No," said Beauty boldly, " I will never agree to that ; you must go home to-morrow morning."

They then wished each other good-night, and went to bed, both of them thinking they should not be able to close their eyes ; but as soon as ever they had lain down, they fell into a deep sleep, and did not awake till morning. Beauty dreamed that a lady came up to her, who said, " I

am very much pleased, Beauty, with the goodness you
have shown, in being willing to give your life to save that
of your father. Do not be afraid of anything ; you shall
not go without a reward."

As soon as Beauty awoke, she told her father this
dream ; but though it gave him some comfort, he was a
long time before he could be persuaded to leave the
palace. At last Beauty succeeded in getting him safely
away.

When her father was out of sight, poor Beauty began
to weep sorely ; still, having naturally a courageous
spirit, she soon resolved not to make her sad case still
worse by sorrow, which she knew was vain, but to wait
and be patient. She walked about to take a view of all
the palace, and the elegance of every part of it much
charmed her.

But what was her surprise, when she came to a door
on which was written, BEAUTY'S ROOM ! She opened it in
haste, and her eyes were dazzled by the splendour and
taste of the apartment. What made her wonder more
than all the rest, was a large library filled with books,
a harpsichord, and many pieces of music. "The beast
surely does not mean to eat me up immediately," said
she, "since he takes care I shall not be at a loss how to
amuse myself." She opened the library, and saw these
verses written in letters of gold on the back of one of the
books :

> Beauteous lady, dry your tears,
> Here's no cause for sighs or fears ;
> Command as freely as you may,
> For you command and I obey.

"Alas !" said she, sighing, "I wish I could only
command a sight of my poor father, and to know what
he is doing at this moment." Just then, by chance, she
cast her eyes on a looking-glass that stood near her, and
in it she saw a picture of her old home, and her father

THE FAIRY BOOK

riding mournfully up to the door. Her sisters came out to meet him, and although they tried to look sorry, it was easy to see that in their hearts they were very glad. In a short time all this picture disappeared, but it caused Beauty to think that the beast, besides being very powerful, was also very kind. About the middle of the day she found a table laid ready for her, and a sweet concert of music played all the time she was dining, without her seeing anybody. But at supper, when she was going to seat herself at table, she heard the noise of the beast, and could not help trembling with fear.

"Beauty," said he, "will you give me leave to see you sup?"

"That is as you please," answered she, very much afraid.

"Not in the least," said the beast; "you alone command in this place. If you should not like my company, you need only say so, and I will leave you that moment. But tell me, Beauty, do you not think me very ugly?"

"Why, yes," said she, "for I cannot tell a falsehood; but then I think you are very good."

"Am I?" sadly replied the beast; "yet, besides being ugly, I am also very stupid: I know well enough that I am but a beast."

"Very stupid people," said Beauty, "are never aware of it themselves."

At which kindly speech the beast looked pleased, and replied, not without an awkward sort of politeness, "Pray do not let me detain you from supper, and be sure that you are well served. All you see is your own, and I should be deeply grieved if you wanted for anything."

"You are very kind—so kind that I almost forgot you are so ugly," said Beauty earnestly.

"Ah, yes!" answered the beast with a great sigh; "I hope I am good-tempered, but still I am only a monster."

54

BEAUTY AND THE BEAST

"There is many a monster who wears the form of a man; it is better of the two to have the heart of a man and the form of a monster."

"I would thank you, Beauty, for this speech, but I am too senseless to say anything that would please you," returned the beast in a melancholy voice; and altogether he seemed so gentle and so unhappy, that Beauty, who had the tenderest heart in the world, felt her fear of him gradually vanish.

She ate her supper with a good appetite, and conversed in her own sensible and charming way, till at last, when the beast rose to depart, he terrified her more than ever by saying abruptly, in his gruff voice, "Beauty, will you marry me?"

Now Beauty, frightened as she was, would speak only the exact truth; besides, her father had told her that the beast liked only to have the truth spoken to him. So she answered, in a very firm tone, "No, beast."

He did not go into a passion, or do anything but sigh deeply, and depart.

When Beauty found herself alone, she began to feel pity for the poor beast. "Oh!" said she, "what a sad thing it is that he should be so very frightful, since he is so good-tempered!"

Beauty lived three months in this palace very well pleased. The beast came to see her every night, and talked with her while she supped; and though what he said was not very clever, yet, as she saw in him every day some new goodness, instead of dreading the time of his coming, she soon began continually looking at her watch to see if it were nine o'clock; for that was the hour when he never failed to visit her. One thing only vexed her, which was that every night, before he went away, he always made it a rule to ask her if she would be his wife, and seemed very much grieved at her steadfastly replying "No." At last, one night, she said to him, "You wound

me greatly, beast, by forcing me to refuse you so often;
I wish I could take such a liking to you as to agree to
marry you: but I must tell you plainly that I do not
think it will ever happen. I shall always be your friend;
so try to let that content you."

"I must," sighed the beast, "for I know well enough
how frightful I am; but I love you better than myself.
Yet I think I am very lucky in your being pleased to stay
with me: now promise me, Beauty, that you will never
leave me."

Beauty would almost have agreed to this, so sorry
was she for him, but she had that day seen in her magic
glass, which she looked at constantly, that her father was
dying of grief for her sake.

"Alas!" she said, "I long so much to see my
father, that if you do not give me leave to visit him, I
shall break my heart."

"I would rather break mine, Beauty," answered the
beast; "I will send you to your father's cottage: you
shall stay there, and your poor beast shall die of
sorrow."

"No," said Beauty, crying, "I love you too well to
be the cause of your death; I promise to return in
a week. You have shown me that my sisters are
married, and my brothers are gone for soldiers, so that
my father is left all alone. Let me stay a week with
him."

"You shall find yourself with him to-morrow
morning," replied the beast; "but mind, do not forget
your promise. When you wish to return, you have
nothing to do but to put your ring on a table when you
go to bed. Good-bye, Beauty!" The beast sighed as
he said these words, and Beauty went to bed very sorry
to see him so much grieved. When she awoke in the
morning, she found herself in her father's cottage. She
rang a bell that was at her bedside, and a servant entered;

" At last she remembered her dream, rushed to the grass-plot, and there saw him lying apparently dead."

but as soon as she saw Beauty, the woman gave a loud shriek ; upon which the merchant ran upstairs, and when he beheld his daughter he ran to her, and kissed her a hundred times. At last Beauty began to remember that she had brought no clothes with her to put on ; but the servant told her she had just found in the next room a large chest full of dresses, trimmed all over with gold, and adorned with pearls and diamonds.

Beauty, in her own mind, thanked the beast for his kindness, and put on the plainest gown she could find among them all. She then desired the servant to lay the rest aside, for she intended to give them to her sisters ; but, as soon as she had spoken these words, the chest was gone out of sight in a moment. Her father then suggested, perhaps the beast chose for her to keep them all for herself: and as soon as he had said this, they saw the chest standing again in the same place. While Beauty was dressing herself, a servant brought word to her that her sisters were come with their husbands to pay her a visit. They both lived unhappily with the gentlemen they had married. The husband of the eldest was very handsome, but was so proud of this, that he thought of nothing else from morning till night, and did not care a pin for the beauty of his wife. The second had married a man of great learning ; but he made no use of it, except to torment and affront all his friends, and his wife more than any of them. The two sisters were ready to burst with spite when they saw Beauty dressed like a princess, and looking so very charming. All the kindness that she showed them was of no use ; for they were vexed more than ever when she told them how happy she lived at the palace of the beast. The spiteful creatures went by themselves into the garden, where they cried to think of her good fortune.

"Why should the little wretch be better off than we ? " said they. "We are much handsomer than she is."

"Sister!" said the eldest, "a thought has just come into my head : let us try to keep her here longer than the week for which the beast gave her leave ; and then he will be so angry, that perhaps when she goes back to him he will eat her up in a moment."

"That is well thought of," answered the other : "but to do this, we must pretend to be very kind."

They then went to join her in the cottage, where they showed her so much false love, that Beauty could not help crying for joy.

When the week was ended, the two sisters began to pretend such grief at the thought of her leaving them, that she agreed to stay a week more : but all that time Beauty could not help fretting for the sorrow that she knew her absence would give her poor beast ; for she tenderly loved him, and much wished for his company again. Among all the grand and clever people she saw, she found nobody who was half so sensible, so affectionate, so thoughtful, or so kind. The tenth night of her being at the cottage, she dreamed she was in the garden of the palace, that the beast lay dying on a grass-plot, and with his last breath put her in mind of her promise, and laid his death to her forsaking him. Beauty awoke in a great fright, and burst into tears : "Am not I wicked," said she, "to behave so ill to a beast who has shown me so much kindness? Why will not I marry him? I am sure I should be more happy with him than my sisters are with their husbands. He shall not be wretched any longer on my account ; for I should do nothing but blame myself all the rest of my life."

She then rose, put her ring on the table, got into bed again, and soon fell asleep. In the morning she with joy found herself in the palace of the beast. She dressed herself very carefully, that she might please him the better, and thought she had never known a day pass away so slowly. At last the clock struck nine, but the beast did

BEAUTY AND THE BEAST

not come. Beauty, dreading lest she might truly have
caused his death, ran from room to room, calling out,
" Beast, dear beast " ; but there was no answer. At last
she remembered her dream, rushed to the grass - plot,
and there saw him lying apparently dead beside the
fountain. Forgetting all his ugliness, she threw herself
upon his body, and, finding his heart still beat, she fetched
some water and sprinkled it over him, weeping and sobbing
the while.

The beast opened his eyes : " You forgot your promise,
Beauty, and so I determined to die ; for I could not live
without you. I have starved myself to death, but I shall
die content since I have seen your face once more."

" No, dear beast," cried Beauty passionately, " you
shall not die ; you shall live to be my husband. I
thought it was only friendship I felt for you, but now I
know it was love."

The moment Beauty had spoken these words, the
palace was suddenly lighted up, and all kinds of rejoicings
were heard around them, none which she noticed, but
hung over her dear beast with the utmost tenderness. At
last, unable to restrain herself, she dropped her head over
her hands, covered her eyes, and cried for joy ; and,
when she looked up again, the beast was gone. In his
stead she saw at her feet a handsome, graceful young
prince, who thanked her with the tenderest expressions
for having freed him from enchantment.

" But where is my poor beast ? I only want him and
nobody else," sobbed Beauty.

" I am he," replied the prince. " A wicked fairy
condemned me to this form, and forbade me to show that
I had any wit or sense, till a beautiful lady should consent
to marry me. You alone, dearest Beauty, judged me
neither by my looks nor by my talents, but by my heart
alone. Take it then, and all that I have besides, for all is
yours."

59

Beauty, full of surprise, but very happy, suffered the prince to lead her to his palace, where she found her father and sisters, who had been brought there by the fairy-lady whom she had seen in a dream the first night she came.

"Beauty," said the fairy, "you have chosen well, and you have your reward, for a true heart is better than either good looks or clever brains. As for you, ladies," and she turned to the two elder sisters, "I know all your ill deeds, but I have no worse punishment for you than to see your sister happy. You shall stand as statues at the door of her palace, and when you repent of and have amended your faults, you shall become women again. But, to tell you the truth, I very much fear you will remain statues for ever."

LITTLE ONE EYE, LITTLE TWO EYES, AND LITTLE THREE EYES

THERE was a woman who had three daughters, the eldest of whom was called Little One Eye, because she had only one eye in the middle of her forehead ; the second, Little Two Eyes, because she had two eyes like other people ; and the youngest, Little Three Eyes, because she had three eyes, one of them being also in the middle of the forehead. But because Little Two Eyes looked no different from other people, her sisters and mother could not bear her. They said, "You with your two eyes are no better than anybody else ; you do not belong to us." They knocked her about, and gave her shabby clothes, and food which was left over from their own meals ; in short, they vexed her whenever they could.

It happened that Little Two Eyes had to go out into the fields to look after the goat ; but she was still quite hungry, because her sisters had given her so little to eat. She sat down on a hillock and began to cry, and cried so much that two little streams ran down out of each eye. And as she looked up once in her sorrow, a woman stood near her, who asked, "Little Two Eyes, why do you cry ?"

Little Two Eyes answered, "Have I not need to cry? Because I have two eyes, like other people, my sisters and my mother cannot bear me ; they push me out of one corner into the other, give me shabby clothes, and nothing

61

to eat but what they leave. To-day they have given me so little that I am still quite hungry."

The wise woman said, "Little Two Eyes, dry your eyes, and I will tell you something which will keep you from ever being hungry more. Only say to your goat, 'Little goat, bleat; little table, rise,' and a neatly-laid table will stand before you with the most delicious food on it, so that you can eat as much as you like. And when you are satisfied and do not want the table any more, only say, 'Little goat, bleat; little table, away,' and it will all disappear before your eyes." Then the wise woman went out of sight.

Little Two Eyes thought, "I must try directly if it is true what she has said, for I am much too hungry to wait." So she said, "Little goat, bleat; little table, rise"; and scarcely had she uttered the words, when there stood before her a little table, covered with a white cloth, on which was laid a plate, knife and fork, and silver spoon. The most delicious food was there also, and smoking hot, as if just come from the kitchen. Then Little Two Eyes said the shortest grace that she knew, "Lord God, be our Guest at all times.—Amen," began to eat, and found it very good. And when she had had enough, she said as the wise woman had taught her—"Little goat, bleat; little table, away." In an instant the little table, and all that stood on it, had disappeared again. "That is a beautiful, easy way of housekeeping," thought Little Two Eyes, and was quite happy and merry.

In the evening, when she came home with her goat, she found a little earthen dish with food, which her sisters had put aside for her, but she did not touch anything— she had no need. On the next day she went out again with her goat, and let the few crusts that were given her remain uneaten. The first time and the second time the sisters took no notice; but when the same thing happened every day, they remarked it, and said, "All is not right with little Two Eyes; she always leaves her food, and she

used formerly to eat up everything that was given her ;
she must have found other ways of dining."

In order to discover the truth, they resolved that Little
One Eye should go with Little Two Eyes when she drove
the goat into the meadow, and see what she did there, and
whether anybody brought her anything to eat and drink.
So when Little Two Eyes set out again, Little One Eye
came to her and said, "I will go with you into the field,
and see that the goat is taken proper care of, and driven
to good pasture."

But Little Two Eyes saw what Little One Eye had in
her mind, and drove the goat into long grass, saying,
"Come, Little One Eye, we will sit down ; I will sing you
something." Little One Eye sat down, being tired from
the unusual walk and from the heat of the sun, and Little
Two Eyes kept on singing, "Are you awake, Little One
Eye ? Are you asleep, Little One Eye ?" Then Little
One Eye shut her one eye, and fell asleep. And when
Little Two Eyes saw that Little One Eye was fast asleep,
and could not betray anything, she said, "Little goat,
bleat ; little table, rise," and sat herself at her table, and
ate and drank till she was satisfied ; then she called out
again, "Little goat, bleat ; little table, away," and instantly
everything disappeared.

Little Two Eyes now woke Little One Eye, and said,
"Little One Eye, you pretend to watch, and fall asleep
over it, and in the meantime the goat could have run all
over the world ; come, we will go home." Then they
went home, and Little Two Eyes let her little dish again
stand untouched ; and Little One Eye, who could not tell
the mother why her sister would not eat, said, as an excuse,
"Oh, I fell asleep out there."

The next day the mother said to Little Three Eyes,
"This time you shall go and see if Little Two Eyes eats
out of doors, and if any one brings her food and drink, for
she must eat and drink secretly."

Then Little Three Eyes went to Little Two Eyes, and said, " I will go with you and see whether the goat is taken proper care of, and driven to good pasture." But Little Two Eyes saw what Little Three Eyes had in her mind, and drove the goat into long grass, and said as before, " We will sit down here, Little Three Eyes ; I will sing you something." Little Three Eyes seated herself, being tired from the walk and the heat of the sun, and Little Two Eyes began the same song again, and sang, " Are you awake, Little Three Eyes ? " But instead of singing then as she should, " Are you asleep, Little *Three* Eyes ? " she sang, through carelessness, " Are you asleep, Little *Two* Eyes ? " and went on singing, " Are you awake, Little Three Eyes ? Are you asleep, Little *Two* Eyes ? " So the two eyes of Little Three Eyes fell asleep, but the third did not go to sleep, because it was not spoken to by the verse. Little Three Eyes, to be sure, shut it and made believe to go to sleep, but only through slyness ; for she winked with it, and could see everything quite well. And when Little Two Eyes thought that Little Three Eyes was fast asleep, she said her little sentence, " Little goat, bleat ; little table, rise," ate and drank heartily, and then told the little table to go away again, " Little goat, bleat ; little table, away." But Little Three Eyes had seen everything. Then Little Two Eyes came to her, woke her, and said, " Ah ! Little Three Eyes, have you been asleep ? you keep watch well ! come, we will go home." And when they got home, Little Two Eyes again did not eat, and Little Three Eyes said to the mother, " I know why the proud thing does not eat : when she says to the goat out there, ' Little goat, bleat ; little table, rise,' there stands a table before her, which is covered with the very best food, much better than we have here ; and when she is satisfied, she says, ' Little goat, bleat ; little table, away,' and everything is gone again ; I have seen it all exactly. She put two of my eyes to sleep with her little verse, but the one on my forehead luckily remained awake."

Then the envious mother cried out, " Shall she be better off than we are? " fetched a butcher's knife and stuck it into the goat's heart, so that it fell down dead.

When Little Two Eyes saw that, she went out full of grief, seated herself on a hillock, and wept bitter tears. All at once the wise woman stood near her again, and said, " Little Two Eyes, why do you cry? "

"Shall I not cry?" answered she. "The goat who every day, when I said your little verse, laid the table so beautifully, has been killed by my mother; now I must suffer hunger and thirst again."

The wise woman said, "Little Two Eyes, I will give you some good advice; beg your sisters to give you the heart of the murdered goat, and bury it in the ground before the house-door, and it will turn out lucky for you." Then she disappeared, and Little Two Eyes went home and said to her sisters, " Dear sisters, give me some part of my goat; I don't ask for anything good, only give me the heart."

Then they laughed, and said, " You can have that, if you do not want anything else." Little Two Eyes took the heart, and buried it quietly in the evening before the house-door, after the advice of the wise woman.

Next morning, when the sisters woke, and went to the house-door together, there stood a most wonderful splendid tree, with leaves of silver, and fruit of gold hanging between them. Nothing more beautiful or charming could be seen in the wide world. But they did not know how the tree had come there in the night. Little Two Eyes alone noticed that it had grown out of the heart of the goat, for it stood just where she had buried it in the ground.

Then the mother said to Little One Eye, " Climb up, my child, and gather us some fruit from the tree."

Little One Eye climbed up, but when she wanted to seize a golden apple, the branch sprang out of her hand : this happened every time, so that she could not gather a single apple, though she tried as much as she could.

Then the mother said, " Little Three Eyes, do you climb up ; you can see better about you with your three eyes than Little One Eye can."

Little One Eye scrambled down, and Little Three Eyes climbed up. But Little Three Eyes was no cleverer, and might look about her as much as she liked—the golden apples always sprang back from her grasp. At last the mother became impatient, and climbed up herself, but could touch the fruit just as little as Little One Eye or Little Three Eyes ; she always grasped the empty air.

Then Little Two Eyes said, " I will go up myself ; perhaps I shall prosper better."

" You ! " cried the sisters. " With your two eyes, what can you do ? "

But Little Two Eyes climbed up, and the golden apples did not spring away from her, but dropped of themselves into her hand, so that she could gather one after the other, and brought down a whole apron full. Her mother took them from her, and instead of her sisters, Little One Eye and Little Three Eyes, behaving better to poor Little Two Eyes for it, they were only envious because she alone could get the fruit, and behaved still more cruelly to her.

It happened, as they stood together by the tree, one day, that a young knight came by.

" Quick, Little Two Eyes," cried the two sisters, " creep under, so that we may not be ashamed of you " ; and threw over poor Little Two Eyes, in a great hurry, an empty cask that stood just by the tree, and pushed also beside her the golden apples which she had broken off.

Now, as the knight came nearer, he proved to be a

handsome prince, who stood still, admired the beautiful tree of gold and silver, and said to the two sisters :

"To whom does this beautiful tree belong ? She who gives me a branch of it shall have whatever she wishes."

Then Little One Eye and Little Three Eyes answered that the tree was theirs, and they would break off a branch for him. They both of them gave themselves a great deal of trouble, but it was no use, for the branches and fruit sprang back from them every time. Then the knight said :

"It is very wonderful that the tree belongs to you, and yet you have not the power of gathering anything from it."

They insisted, however, that the tree was their own property. But as they spoke, Little Two Eyes rolled a few golden apples from under the cask, so that they ran to the feet of the knight ; for Little Two Eyes was angry that Little One Eye and Little Three Eyes did not tell the truth.

When the knight saw the apples he was astonished, and asked where they came from. Little One Eye and Little Three Eyes answered that they had another sister, who might not, however, show herself, because she had only two eyes, like other common people. But the knight desired to see her, and called out, "Little Two Eyes, come out." Then Little Two Eyes came out of the cask quite comforted, and the knight was astonished at her great beauty, and said :

"You, Little Two Eyes, can certainly gather me a branch from the tree ? "

"Yes," answered Little Two Eyes, "I can do that, for the tree belongs to me." And she climbed up and easily broke off a branch, with its silver leaves and golden fruit, and handed it to the knight.

Then the knight said, "Little Two Eyes, what shall I give you for it ? "

"Oh," answered Little Two Eyes, "I suffer hunger and thirst, sorrow and want, from early morning till late evening; if you would take me with you and free me, I should be happy."

Then the knight lifted Little Two Eyes on to his horse, and took her home to his paternal castle; there he gave her beautiful clothes, food, and drink as much as she wanted, and because he loved her so much he married her, and the marriage was celebrated with great joy.

Now, when Little Two Eyes was taken away by the handsome knight, the two sisters envied her very much her happiness. "The wonderful tree remains for us, though," thought they; "and even though we cannot gather any fruit off it, every one will stand still before it, come to us, and praise it." But the next morning the tree had disappeared, and all their hopes with it.

Little Two Eyes lived happy a long time. Once two poor women came to her at the castle and begged alms. Then Little Two Eyes looked in their faces and recognised her sisters, Little One Eye and Little Three Eyes, who had fallen into such poverty that they had to wander about, and seek their bread from door to door. Little Two Eyes, however, bade them welcome, and was very good to them, and took care of them; for they both repented from their hearts the evil they had done to their sister in their youth.

JACK THE GIANT-KILLER

In the reign of the famous King Arthur there lived, near the Land's End of England, in the county of Cornwall, a worthy farmer, who had an only son named Jack. Jack was a boy of a bold temper ; he took pleasure in hearing or reading stories of wizards, conjurors, giants, and fairies ; and used to listen eagerly while his father talked of the great deeds of the brave knights of King Arthur's Round Table. When Jack was sent to take care of the sheep and oxen in the fields, he used to amuse himself with planning battles, sieges, and the means to conquer or surprise a foe. He was above the common sports of children, but hardly any one could equal him at wrestling ; or, if he met with a match for himself in strength, his skill and address always made him the victor. In those days there lived on St. Michael's Mount, of Cornwall, which rises out of the sea at some distance from the mainland, a huge giant. He was eighteen feet high, and three yards round ; and his fierce and savage looks were the terror of all his neighbours. He dwelt in a gloomy cavern on the very top of the mountain, and used to wade over to the mainland in search of his prey. When he came near, the people left their houses ; and, after he had glutted his appetite upon their cattle, he would throw half-a-dozen oxen upon his back, and tie three times as many sheep and hogs round his waist, and so march back to his own abode. The giant had done this for many years, and the coast of Cornwall was greatly hurt by his

69

thefts, when Jack boldly resolved to destroy him. He therefore took a horn, a shovel, a pickaxe, and a dark lantern, and, early in a long winter's evening, he swam to the Mount. There he fell to work at once, and before morning he had dug a pit twenty-two feet deep, and almost as many broad. He covered it over with sticks and straw, and strewed some of the earth over them, to make it look just like solid ground. He then put his horn to his mouth, and blew such a loud and long tantivy, that the giant awoke, and came towards Jack, roaring like thunder : " You saucy villain, you shall pay dearly for breaking my rest ; I will broil you for my breakfast." He had scarcely spoken these words, when he came advancing one step further ; but then he tumbled head-long into the pit, and his fall shook the very mountain.

"O ho, Mr. Giant ! " said Jack, looking into the pit, " have you found your way so soon to the bottom ? How is your appetite now ? Will nothing serve you for breakfast this cold morning but broiling poor Jack ? "

The giant now tried to rise, but Jack struck him a blow on the crown of the head with his pickaxe, which killed him at once. Jack then made haste back, to rejoice his friends with the news of the giant's death. When the justices of Cornwall heard of this valiant action, they sent for Jack, and declared that he should always be called Jack the Giant-Killer ; and they also gave him a sword and belt, upon which was written, in letters of gold :

> This is the valiant Cornishman
> Who slew the giant Cormoran.

The news of Jack's exploits soon spread over the western parts of England : and another giant, called Old Blunderbore, vowed to have revenge on Jack, if it should ever be his fortune to get him into his power. The giant kept an enchanted castle in the midst of a lonely wood. About four months after the death of Cormoran, as Jack was taking a journey into Wales, he passed through this wood ; and, as he was very weary, he sat down to rest by the side of a pleasant fountain, and there he fell into a deep sleep. The giant came to the fountain for water just at this time, and found Jack there ; and as the lines on Jack's belt showed who he was, the giant lifted him up and laid him gently upon his shoulder, to carry him to his castle ; but, as he passed through the thicket, the rustling of the leaves waked Jack ; and he was sadly afraid when he found himself in the clutches of Blunderbore. Yet this was nothing to his fright soon after ; for, when they reached the castle, he beheld the floor covered all over with the skulls and bones of men and women. The giant took him into a large room, where lay the hearts and limbs of persons who had been lately killed; and he told Jack, with a horrid grin, that men's hearts, eaten with pepper and vinegar, were his nicest food, and, also, that he thought he should make a dainty meal on his heart. When he had said this, he locked Jack up in that room, while he went to fetch another giant, who lived in the same wood, to enjoy a dinner off Jack's flesh with him. While he was away, Jack heard dreadful shrieks, groans, and cries from many parts of the castle ; and soon after he heard a mournful voice repeat these lines :

"Haste, valiant stranger, haste away,
Lest you become the giant's prey.
On his return he'll bring another,
Still more savage than his brother ;
A horrid, cruel monster, who,
Before he kills, will torture you.
Oh valiant stranger ! haste away,
Or you'll become these giants' prey."

This warning was so shocking to poor Jack, that he was ready to go mad. He ran to the window, and saw

71

the two giants coming along arm in arm. This window
was right over the gates of the castle. "Now," thought
Jack, "either my death or freedom is at hand."

There were two strong cords in the room. Jack
made a large noose, with a slip-knot at the ends of both
these, and, as the giants were coming through the gates,
he threw the ropes over their heads. He then made the
other ends fast to a beam in the ceiling, and pulled with all
his might, till he had almost strangled them. When he
saw that they were both quite black in the face, and had
not the least strength left, he drew his sword, and slid
down the ropes ; he then killed the giants, and thus
saved himself from a cruel death. Jack next took a great
bunch of keys from the pocket of Blunderbore, and went
into the castle again. He made a strict search through
all the rooms, and in them found three ladies tied up by
the hair of their heads, and almost starved to death.
They told him that their husbands had been killed by the
giants, who had then condemned them to be starved to
death, because they would not eat the flesh of their own
dead husbands.

"Ladies," said Jack, "I have put an end to the
monster and his wicked brother ; and I give you this
castle and all the riches it contains, to make you some
amends for the dreadful pains you have felt." He then
very politely gave them the keys of the castle, and went
farther on his journey to Wales.

As Jack had not taken any of the giant's riches for
himself, and had very little money of his own, he thought
it best to travel as fast as he could. At length he lost
his way ; and, when night came on, he was in a lonely
valley between two lofty mountains. There he walked
about for some hours, without seeing any dwelling-place,
so he thought himself very lucky at last in finding a large
and handsome house. He went up to it boldly, and
knocked loudly at the gate ; when, to his great terror and

"When the lady came she gave the handkerchief to the magician."

surprise, there came forth a monstrous giant with two heads. He spoke to Jack very civilly, for he was a Welsh giant, and all the mischief he did was by private and secret malice, under the show of friendship and kindness. Jack told him that he was a traveller who had lost his way, on which the huge monster made him welcome, and led him into a room, where there was a good bed in which to pass the night. Jack took off his clothes quickly; but though he was so weary, he could not go to sleep. Soon after this, he heard the giant walking backward and forward in the next room, and saying to himself:

> "Though here you lodge with me this night,
> You shall not see the morning light;
> My club shall dash your brains out quite."

"Say you so?" thought Jack. "Are these your tricks upon travellers? But I hope to prove as cunning as you." Then, getting out of bed, he groped about the room, and at last found a large thick billet of wood; he laid it in his own place in the bed, and hid himself in a dark corner of the room. In the middle of the night the giant came with his great club, and struck many heavy blows on the bed, in the very place where Jack had laid the billet, and then he went back to his own room, thinking he had broken all his bones. Early in the morning, Jack put a bold face upon the matter, and walked into the giant's room to thank him for his lodging.

The giant started when he saw him, and he began to stammer out, "Oh, dear me! is it you? Pray how did you sleep last night? Did you hear or see anything in the dead of the night?"

"Nothing worth speaking of," said Jack carelessly; "a rat, I believe, gave me three or four slaps with his tail, and disturbed me a little, but I soon went to sleep again."

The giant wondered more and more at this; yet he

did not answer a word, and went to bring two great bowls of hasty-pudding for their breakfast.

Jack wished to make the giant believe that he could eat as much as himself; so he contrived to button a leathern bag inside his coat, and slipped the hasty-pudding into this bag, while he seemed to put it into his mouth. When breakfast was over, he said to the giant, "Now I will show you a fine trick; I can cure all wounds with a touch; I could cut off my head one minute, and the next put it sound again on my shoulders: you shall see an example." He then took hold of the knife, ripped up the leathern bag, and all the hasty-pudding tumbled out upon the floor.

"Ods splutter hur nails," cried the Welsh giant, who was ashamed to be outdone by such a little fellow as Jack; "hur can do that hurself." So he snatched up the knife, plunged it into his stomach, and in a moment dropped down dead.

As soon as Jack had thus tricked the Welsh monster, he went farther on his journey; and, a few days after, he met with King Arthur's only son, who had got his father's leave to travel into Wales, to deliver a beautiful lady from the power of a wicked magician, by whom she was held in enchantment. When Jack found that the young prince had no servants with him, he begged leave to attend him; and the prince at once agreed to this, and gave Jack many thanks for his kindness.

King Arthur's son was a handsome, polite, and brave knight, and so good-natured, that he gave money to everybody he met. At length he gave his last penny to an old woman, and then turned to Jack, "How shall we be able to get food for ourselves the rest of our journey?"

"Leave that to me, sir," replied Jack; "I will provide for my prince."

Night now came on, and the prince began to grow uneasy at thinking where they should lodge.

JACK THE GIANT-KILLER

"Sir," said Jack, "be of good heart; two miles farther there lives a large giant, whom I know well; he has three heads, and will fight five hundred men, and make them fly before him."

"Alas!" cried the king's son, "we had better never have been born than meet with such a monster."

"My lord, leave me to manage him, and wait here in quiet till I return."

The prince now stayed behind, while Jack rode on at full speed; and when he came to the gates of the castle, he gave a loud knock. The giant, with a voice like thunder, roared out, "Who is there?"

Jack made answer, and said, "No one but your poor cousin Jack."

"Well," said the giant, "what news, cousin Jack?"

"Dear uncle," said Jack, "I have heavy news."

"Pooh!" said the giant, "what heavy news can come to me? I am a giant with three heads, and can fight five hundred men, and make them fly before me."

"Alas!" said Jack, "here is the king's son coming with two thousand men to kill you, and to destroy the castle and all that you have."

"Oh, cousin Jack," said the giant, "this is heavy news indeed! But I have a large cellar underground, where I will hide myself, and you shall lock, bolt, and bar me in, and keep the keys till the king's son is gone."

Now, when Jack had barred the giant fast in the vault, he went back and fetched the prince to the castle; they both made themselves merry with the wine and other dainties that were in the house. So that night they rested very pleasantly, while the poor giant lay trembling and shaking with fear in the cellar underground. Early in the morning, Jack gave the king's son gold and silver out of the giant's treasure, and accompanied him three miles forward on his journey. The prince then sent Jack to let his uncle out of the

75

hole, who asked him what he should give him as a reward for saving his castle.

"Why, good uncle," said Jack, "I desire nothing but the old coat and cap, with the old rusty sword and slippers, which are hanging at your bed's head."

"Then," said the giant, "you shall have them; and pray keep them for my sake, for they are things of great use. The coat will keep you invisible, the cap will give you knowledge, the sword will cut through anything, and the shoes are of vast swiftness; they may be useful to you in all times of danger, so take them with all my heart."

Jack gave many thanks to the giant, and then set off to the prince. When he had come up with the king's son, they soon arrived at the dwelling of the beautiful lady, who was under the power of a wicked magician. She received the prince very politely, and made a noble feast for him : when it was ended, she rose, and, wiping her mouth with a fine handkerchief, said, "My lord, you must submit to the custom of my palace; to-morrow morning I command you to tell me on whom I bestow this handkerchief, or lose your head." She then left the room.

The young prince went to bed very mournful, but Jack put on his cap of knowledge, which told him that the lady was forced, by the power of enchantment, to meet the wicked magician every night in the middle of the forest. Jack now put on his coat of darkness, and his shoes of swiftness, and was there before her. When the lady came she gave the handkerchief to the magician. Jack, with his sword of sharpness, at one blow cut off his head; the enchantment was then ended in a moment, and the lady was restored to her former virtue and goodness. She was married to the prince on the next day, and soon after went back, with her royal husband and a great company, to the court of King Arthur, where they were

76

received with loud and joyful welcomes; and the valiant hero Jack, for the many great exploits he had done for the good of his country, was made one of the Knights of the Round Table.

As Jack had been so lucky in all his adventures, he resolved not to be idle for the future, but still to do what services he could for the honour of the king and the nation. He therefore humbly begged his majesty to furnish him with a horse and money, that he might travel in search of new and strange exploits. "For," said he to the king, "there are many giants yet living in the remote parts of Wales, to the great terror and distress of your majesty's subjects; therefore, if it please you, sire, to favour me in my design, I will soon rid your kingdom of these giants and monsters in human shape."

Now when the king heard this offer, and began to think of the cruel deeds of these bloodthirsty giants and savage monsters, he gave Jack everything proper for such a journey. After this, Jack took leave of the king, the prince, and all the knights, and set off, taking with him his cap of knowledge, his sword of sharpness, his shoes of swiftness, and his invisible coat, the better to perform the great exploits that might fall in his way. He went along over hills and mountains; and on the third day he came to a wide forest. He had hardly entered it, when on a sudden he heard dreadful shrieks and cries; and forcing his way through the trees, saw a monstrous giant dragging along, by the hair of their heads, a handsome knight and a beautiful lady. Their tears and cries melted the heart of honest Jack; he alighted from his horse, and, tying him to an oak-tree, put on his invisible coat, under which he carried his sword of sharpness.

When he came up to the giant he made several strokes at him, but could not reach his body, on account of the enormous height of the terrible creature; but he wounded his thighs in several places; and at length, putting both hands to his sword, and aiming with all his might, he cut off both the giant's legs just below the garter ; and the trunk of his body, tumbling to the ground, made not only the trees shake, but the earth itself tremble with the force of his fall. Then Jack, setting his foot upon his neck, exclaimed, " Thou barbarous and savage wretch, behold, I come to execute upon thee the just reward for all thy crimes " ; and instantly plunged his sword into the giant's body. The huge monster gave a groan, and yielded up his life into the hands of the victorious Jack the Giant-Killer, whilst the noble knight and the virtuous lady were both joyful spectators of his sudden death. They not only returned Jack hearty thanks for their deliverance, but also invited him to their house, to refresh himself after his dreadful encounter, as likewise to receive a reward for his good services.

"No," said Jack, "I cannot be at ease till I find out the den that was the monster's habitation."

The knight, on hearing this, grew very sorrowful, and replied, "Noble stranger, it is too much to run a second hazard ; this monster lived in a den under yonder mountain, with a brother of his, more fierce and cruel than himself ; therefore, if you should go thither, and perish in the attempt, it would be a heart-breaking thing to me and my lady ; so let me persuade you to go back with us, and desist from any farther pursuit."

"Nay," answered Jack, "if there be another, even if there were twenty, I would shed the last drop of blood in my body before one of them should escape. When I have finished this task, I will come and pay my respects to you."

So when they had told him where to find them again, he got on his horse and went after the dead giant's brother.

Jack had not ridden a mile and a half before he came

in sight of the mouth of the cavern ; and, nigh the entrance of it, he saw the other giant sitting on a huge block of timber, with a knotted iron club lying by his side, waiting for his brother. His eyes looked like flames of fire, his face was grim and ugly, and his cheeks were like two flitches of bacon ; the bristles of his beard seemed to be thick rods of iron wire ; and his long locks of hair hung down upon his broad shoulders like curling snakes. Jack got down from his horse, and turned him into a thicket ; then he put on his coat of darkness, and drew a little nearer to behold this figure, and said softly, "Oh, monster ! are you there ? It will not be long before I shall take you fast by the beard."

The giant all this while could not see him, by reason of his invisible coat ; so Jack came quite close to him, and struck a blow at his head with his sword of sharpness ; but he missed his aim, and only cut off his nose, which made him roar like loud claps of thunder. He rolled his glaring eyes round on every side, but could not see who had given him the blow ; so he took up his iron club, and began to lay about him like one that was mad with pain and fury.

"Nay," said Jack, "if this be the case, I will kill you at once." So saying, he slipped nimbly behind him, and jumping upon the block of timber, as the giant rose from it, he stabbed him in the back ; when, after a few howls, he dropped down dead. Jack cut off his head, and sent it, with the head of his brother, to King Arthur, by a waggon which he had hired for that purpose. When Jack had thus killed these two monsters, he went into their cave in search of their treasure. He passed through many turnings and windings, which led him to a room paved with freestone ; at the end of it was a boiling cauldron, and on the right hand stood a large table, where the giants used to dine. He then came to a window that was secured with iron bars, through which he saw a number of wretched captives, who cried out when they saw Jack, "Alas! alas! young man, you are come to be one among us in this horrid den."

"I hope," said Jack, "you will not stay here long; but pray tell me what is the meaning of your being here at all?"

"Alas!" said one poor old man, "I will tell you, sir. We are persons that have been taken by the giants who hold this cave, and are kept till they choose to have a feast; then one of us is to be killed, and cooked to please their taste. It is not long since they took three for the same purpose."

"Well," said Jack, "I have given them such a dinner, that it will be long enough before they have any more."

The captives were amazed at his words.

"You may believe me," said Jack, "for I have killed them both with the edge of this sword, and have sent their large heads to the court of King Arthur, as marks of my great success."

To show that what he said was true, he unlocked the gate, and set the captives all free. Then he led them to the great room, placed them round the table, and placed before them two quarters of beef, with bread and wine; upon which they feasted their fill. When supper was over, they searched the giant's coffers, and Jack divided among them all the treasures. The next morning they set off to their homes, and Jack to the knight's house, whom he had left with his lady not long before.

He was received with the greatest joy by the thankful knight and his lady, who, in honour of Jack's exploits, gave a grand feast, to which all the nobles and gentry were invited. When the company were assembled, the knight declared to them the great actions of Jack, and gave him, as a mark of respect, a fine ring, on which was engraved the picture of the giant dragging the knight and the lady by the hair, with this motto round it:

JACK THE GIANT-KILLER

Behold in dire distress were we,
   Under a giant's fierce command ;
But gain'd our lives and liberty
   From valiant Jack's victorious hand.

Among the guests then present were five aged gentlemen, who were fathers to some of those captives who had been freed by Jack from the dungeon of the giants. As soon as they heard that he was the person who had done such wonders, they pressed round him with tears of joy, to return him thanks for the happiness he had caused them. After this the bowl went round, and every one drank the health and long life of the gallant hero. Mirth increased, and the hall was filled with peals of laughter. But, on a sudden, a herald, pale and breathless, rushed into the midst of the company, and told them that Thundel, a savage giant with two heads, had heard of the death of his two kinsmen, and was come to take his revenge on Jack ; and that he was now within a mile of the house, the people flying before him like chaff before the wind. At this news the very boldest of the guests trembled ; but Jack drew his sword, and said, " Let him come, I have a rod for him also. Pray, ladies and gentlemen, do me the favour to walk into the garden, and you shall soon behold the giant's defeat and death."

To this they all agreed, and heartily wished him success in his dangerous attempt.

The knight's house stood in the middle of a moat, thirty feet deep and twenty wide, over which lay a drawbridge. Jack set men to work, to cut the bridge on both sides, almost to the middle, and then dressed himself in his coat of darkness, and went against the giant with his sword of sharpness. As he came close to him, though the giant could not see him for his invisible coat, yet he found some danger was near, which made him cry out :

"Fa, fe, fi, fo, fum,
I smell the blood of an Englishman ;
Let him be alive, or let him be dead,
I'll grind his bones to make me bread."

"Say you so, my friend?" said Jack ; "you are a monstrous miller, indeed !"

"Art thou," cried the giant, "the villain that killed my kinsmen ? Then I will tear thee with my teeth, and grind thy bones to powder."

"You must catch me first," said Jack ; and throwing off his coat of darkness, and putting on his shoes of swiftness, he began to run, the giant following him like a walking castle, making the earth shake at every step.

Jack led him round and round the walls of the house, that the company might see the monster ; then, to finish the work, he ran over the drawbridge, the giant going after him with his club ; but when he came to the middle, where the bridge had been cut on both sides, the great weight of his body made it break, and he tumbled into the water, where he rolled about like a large whale. Jack now stood by the side of the moat, and laughed and jeered at him, saying, "I think you told me you would grind my bones to powder ; when will you begin ?"

The giant foamed at both his horrid mouths with fury, and plunged from side to side of the moat ; but he could not get out to have revenge on his little foe. At last Jack ordered a cart-rope to be brought to him ; he then drew it over his two heads, and by the help of a team of horses, dragged him to the edge of the moat, where he cut off his heads, and before he either ate or drank, sent them both to the court of King Arthur. He then went back to the table with the company, and the rest of the day was spent in mirth and good cheer.

After staying with the knight for some time, Jack grew weary of such an idle life, and set out again in search of new adventures. He went over hills and dales without meeting any, till he came to the foot of a very high mountain. Here he knocked at the door of a small and lonely house, and an old man, with a head as white as snow, let him in.

"Good father," said Jack, "can you lodge a traveller who has lost his way?"

"Yes," said the hermit, "I can, if you will accept such fare as my poor house affords."

Jack entered, and the old man set before him some bread and fruit for his supper. When Jack had eaten as much as he chose, the hermit said, "My son, I know you are the famous conqueror of giants; now, at the top of this mountain is an enchanted castle, kept by a giant named Galligantus, who, by the help of a vile magician, gets many knights into his castle, where he changes them into the shape of beasts. Above all, I lament the hard fate of a duke's daughter, whom they seized as she was walking in her father's garden, and brought hither through the air in a chariot drawn by two fiery dragons, and turned her into the shape of a deer. Many knights have tried to destroy the enchantment and deliver her, yet none have been able to do it, by reason of two fiery griffins, who guard the gate of the castle, and destroy all who come nigh; but as you, my son, have an invisible coat, you may pass by them without being seen; and on the gates of the castle you will find engraved by what means the enchantment may be broken."

Jack promised that in the morning, at the risk of his life, he would break the enchantment; and after a sound sleep, he arose early, put on his invisible coat, and got ready for the attempt. When he had climbed to the top of the mountain, he saw the two fiery griffins; but he passed between them without the least fear of danger, for they could not see him because of his invisible coat. On the castle-gate he found a golden trumpet, under which were written these lines:

THE FAIRY BOOK

Whoever can this trumpet blow
Shall cause the giant's overthrow.

As soon as Jack had read this, he seized the trumpet, and blew a shrill blast, which made the gates fly open, and the very castle itself tremble. The giant and the conjuror now knew that their wicked course was at an end, and they stood biting their thumbs and shaking with fear. Jack, with his sword of sharpness, soon killed the giant, and the magician was then carried away by a whirlwind. All the knights and beautiful ladies, who had been changed into birds and beasts, returned to their proper shapes. The castle vanished away like smoke, and the head of the giant Galligantus was sent to King Arthur. The knights and ladies rested that night at the old man's hermitage, and next day they set out for the court. Jack then went up to the king, and gave his majesty an account of all his fierce battles. Jack's fame had spread through the whole country ; and at the king's desire, the duke gave him his daughter in marriage, to the joy of all the kingdom. After this, the king gave him a large estate, on which he and his lady lived the rest of their days in joy and content.

TOM THUMB

In the days of King Arthur, Merlin, the most learned enchanter of his time, was on a journey; and being very weary, stopped one day at the cottage of an honest ploughman to ask for refreshment. The ploughman's wife, with great civility, immediately brought him some milk in a wooden bowl, and some brown bread on a wooden platter. Merlin could not help observing, that although everything within the cottage was particularly neat and clean, and in good order, the ploughman and his wife had the most sorrowful air imaginable; so he questioned them on the cause of their melancholy, and learned that they were very miserable because they had no children. The poor woman declared, with tears in her eyes, that she should be the happiest creature in the world, if she had a son, although he were no bigger than his father's thumb. Merlin was much amused with the notion of a boy no bigger than a man's thumb; and as soon as he returned home, he sent for the queen of the fairies (with whom he was very intimate), and related to her the desire of the ploughman and his wife to have a son the size of his father's thumb. She liked the plan exceedingly, and declared their wish should be speedily granted. Accordingly, the ploughman's wife had a son, who in a few minutes grew as tall as his father's thumb. The queen of the fairies came in at the window as the mother was sitting up in bed admiring the child. Her majesty kissed the infant, and, giving it the name of

Tom Thumb, immediately summoned several fairies from Fairyland, to clothe her new little favourite :

> An oak-leaf hat he had for his crown,
> His shirt it was by spiders spun :
> With doublet wove of thistledown,
> His trousers up with points were done :
> His stockings, of apple-rind, they tie
> With eye-lash pluck'd from his mother's eye :
> His shoes were made of a mouse's skin,
> Nicely tann'd with hair within.

Tom was never any bigger than his father's thumb, which was not a large thumb either ; but as he grew older, he became very cunning, for which his mother did not sufficiently correct him ; and by this ill quality he was often brought into difficulties. For instance, when he had learned to play with other boys for cherry-stones, and had lost all his own, he used to creep into the boys' bags, fill his pockets, and come out again to play. But one day as he was getting out of a bag of cherry-stones, the boy to whom it belonged chanced to see him.

"Ah, ha, my little Tom Thumb!" said he, "have I caught you at your bad tricks at last ? Now I will reward you for thieving." Then drawing the string tight round his neck, and shaking the bag, the cherry-stones bruised Tom's legs, thighs, and body sadly ; which made him beg to be let out, and promise never to be guilty of such things any more.

Shortly afterwards, Tom's mother was making a batter-pudding, and that he might see how she mixed it, he climbed on the edge of the bowl ; but his foot happening to slip, he fell over head and ears into the batter, and his mother, not observing him, stirred him into the pudding, and popped him into the pot to boil. The hot water made Tom kick and struggle ; and his mother, seeing the pudding jump up and down in such a furious manner, thought it was bewitched ; and a tinker coming by just at the time, she quickly gave him the pudding ; he put it into his budget, and walked on.

As soon as Tom could get the batter out of his mouth, he began to cry aloud, which so frightened the poor tinker, that he flung the pudding over the hedge, and ran away from it as fast as he could. The pudding being broken to pieces by the fall, Tom was released, and walked home to his mother, who gave him a kiss and put him to bed.

Tom Thumb's mother once took him with her when she went to milk the cow ; and it being a very windy day, she tied him with a needleful of thread to a thistle, that he might not be blown away. The cow, liking his oak-leaf hat, took him and the thistle up at one mouthful. While the cow chewed the thistle, Tom, terrified at her great teeth, which seemed ready to crush him to pieces, roared, " Mother, mother ! " as loud as he could bawl.

" Where are you, Tommy, my dear Tommy ? " said the mother.

" Here, mother, here in the red cow's mouth."

The mother began to cry and wring her hands ; but the cow, surprised at such odd noises in her throat, opened her mouth and let him drop out. His mother clapped him into her apron, and ran home with him. Tom's father made him a whip of a barley straw to drive the cattle with, and being one day in the field he slipped into a deep furrow. A raven flying over picked him up with a grain of corn, and flew with him to the top of a giant's castle by the seaside, where he left him ; and old Grumbo, the giant, coming soon after to walk upon his terrace, swallowed Tom like a pill, clothes and all. Tom presently made the giant very uncomfortable, and he threw him up into the sea. A great fish then swallowed him. This fish was soon after caught, and sent as a present to King Arthur. When it was cut open, everybody was delighted with little Tom Thumb. The king made him his dwarf ;

he was the favourite of the whole court ; and, by his merry pranks, often amused the queen and the knights of the Round Table. The king, when he rode on horseback, frequently took Tom in his hand ; and if a shower of rain came on, he used to creep into the king's waistcoat-pocket, and sleep till the rain was over. The king also sometimes questioned Tom concerning his parents ; and when Tom informed his majesty they were very poor people, the king led him into his treasury, and told him he should pay his friends a visit, and take with him as much money as he could carry. Tom procured a little purse, and putting a threepenny piece into it, with much labour and difficulty got it upon his back ; and, after travelling two days and nights, arrived at his father's house. His mother met him at the door, almost tired to death, having in forty-eight hours travelled almost half a mile with a huge silver threepence upon his back. Both his parents were glad to see him, especially when he had brought such an amazing sum of money with him. They placed him in a walnut-shell by the fireside, and feasted him for three days upon a hazel-nut, which made him sick, for a whole nut usually served him for a month. Tom got well, but could not travel because it had rained ; therefore his mother took him in her hand, and with one puff blew him into King Arthur's court ; where Tom entertained the king, queen, and nobility at tilts and tournaments, at which he exerted himself so much that he brought on a fit of sickness, and his life was despaired of. At this juncture the queen of the fairies came in a chariot, drawn by flying mice, placed Tom by her side, and drove through the air without stopping till they arrived at her palace ; when, after restoring him to health and permitting him to enjoy all the gay diversions of Fairyland, she commanded a fair wind, and, placing Tom before it, blew him straight to the court of King Arthur. But just as Tom should have alighted in the courtyard of

"The butterfly took wing, and mounted into the air with little Tom on his back."

the palace, the cook happened to pass along with the king's great bowl of furmenty (King Arthur loved furmenty), and poor Tom Thumb fell plump into the middle of it, and splashed the hot furmenty into the cook's eyes. Down went the bowl.

"Oh dear! oh dear!" cried Tom.

"Murder! murder!" bellowed the cook; and away poured the king's nice furmenty into the kennel.

The cook was a red-faced, cross fellow, and swore to the king that Tom had done it out of mere mischief; so he was taken up, tried, and sentenced to be beheaded. Tom, hearing this dreadful sentence, and seeing a miller stand by with his mouth wide open, took a good spring, and jumped down the miller's throat, unperceived by all, even by the miller himself.

Tom being lost, the court broke up, and away went the miller to his mill. But Tom did not leave him long at rest; he began to roll and tumble about, so that the miller thought himself bewitched, and sent for a doctor. When the doctor came, Tom began to dance and sing; the doctor was as much frightened as the miller, and sent in great haste for five more doctors and twenty learned men. While all these were debating upon the affair, the miller (for they were very tedious) happened to yawn, and Tom, taking the opportunity, made another jump, and alighted on his feet in the middle of the table. The miller, provoked to be thus tormented by such a little creature, fell into a great passion, caught hold of Tom, and threw him out of the window into the river. A large salmon swimming by snapped him up in a minute. The salmon was soon caught and sold in the market to a steward of a lord. The lord, thinking it an uncommon fine fish, made a present of it to the king, who ordered it to be dressed immediately. When the cook cut open the salmon, he found poor Tom, and ran with him directly to the king; but the king, being busy with state

affairs, desired that he might be brought another day.
The cook resolving to keep him safely this time, as he
had so lately given him the slip, clapped him into a
mouse-trap, and left him to amuse himself by peeping
through the wires for a whole week ; when the king sent
for him, he forgave him for throwing down the furmenty,
ordered him new clothes, and knighted him :

> His shirt was made of butterflies' wings,
> His boots were made of chicken skins ;
> His coat and breeches were made with pride ;
> A tailor's needle hung by his side ;
> A mouse for a horse he used to ride.

Thus dressed and mounted, he rode a-hunting with the
king and nobility, who all laughed heartily at Tom and
his fine prancing steed. As they rode by a farmhouse
one day, a cat jumped from behind the door, seized the
mouse and little Tom, and began to devour the mouse ;
however, Tom boldly drew his sword and attacked the cat,
who then let him fall. The king and his nobles, seeing
Tom falling, went to his assistance, and one of the lords
caught him in his hat, but poor Tom was sadly scratched,
and his clothes were torn by the claws of the cat. In
this condition he was carried home, when a bed of down
was made for him in a little ivory cabinet. The queen
of the fairies came and took him again to Fairyland,
where she kept him for some years ; and then, dressing
him in bright green, sent him flying once more through
the air to the earth, in the days of King Thunstone. The
people flocked far and near to look at him ; and the king,
before whom he was carried, asked him who he was,
whence he came, and where he lived. Tom answered :

> "My name is Tom Thumb,
> From the Fairies I come ;
> When King Arthur shone,
> This court was my home.

TOM THUMB

In me he delighted,
By him I was knighted;
Did you never hear of
Sir Thomas Thumb?"

The king was so charmed with this address that he ordered a little chair to be made, in order that Tom might sit on his table, and also a palace of gold a span high, with a door an inch wide, for little Tom to live in. He also gave him a coach drawn by six small mice. This made the queen angry, because she had not a new coach too ; therefore, resolving to ruin Tom, she complained to the king that he had behaved very insolently to her. The king sent for him in a rage. Tom, to escape his fury, crept into an empty snail-shell, and there lay till he was almost starved ; when, peeping out of the hole, he saw a fine butterfly settle on the ground : he now ventured out, and, getting astride, the butterfly took wing, and mounted into the air with little Tom on his back. Away he flew from field to field, from tree to tree, till at last he flew to the king's court. The king, queen, and nobles all strove to catch the butterfly, but could not. At length poor Tom, having neither bridle nor saddle, slipped from his seat, and fell into a watering-pot, where he was found almost drowned. The queen vowed he should be guillotined ; but while the guillotine was getting ready, he was secured once more in a mouse-trap ; when the cat, seeing something stir, and supposing it to be a mouse, patted the trap about till she broke it, and set Tom at liberty. Soon afterwards a spider, taking him for a fly, made at him. Tom drew his sword and fought valiantly, but the spider's poisonous breath overcame him :

He fell dead on the ground where late he had stood,
And the spider suck'd up the last drop of his blood.

King Thunstone and his whole court went into mourning for little Tom Thumb. They buried him under a rosebush, and raised a nice white marble monument over his grave, with the following epitaph :

> Here lies Tom Thumb, King Arthur's knight,
> Who died by a spider's cruel bite.
> He was well known in Arthur's court,
> Where he afforded gallant sport ;
> He rode at tilt and tournament,
> And on a mouse a-hunting went ;
> Alive he fill'd the court with mirth,
> His death to sorrow soon gave birth.
> Wipe, wipe your eyes, and shake your head,
> And cry, " Alas ! Tom Thumb is dead."

RUMPELSTILZCHEN

THERE was once a miller who was very poor, but he had a beautiful daughter. Now, it happened that he came to speak to the king, and, to give himself importance, he said to him, " I have a daughter who can spin straw into gold."

The king said to the miller, " That is a talent that pleases me well ; if she be as skilful as you say, bring her to-morrow to the palace, and I will put her to the proof."

When the maiden was brought to him, he led her to a room full of straw, gave her a wheel and spindle, and said, " Now set to work, and if by the morrow this straw be not spun into gold, you shall die." He locked the door, and left the maiden alone.

The poor girl sat down disconsolate, and could not for her life think what she was to do ; for she knew not— how could she ?—the way to spin straw into gold ; and her distress increased so much that at last she began to weep. All at once the door opened, and a little man entered and said, " Good evening, my pretty miller's daughter ; why are you weeping so bitterly ? "

" Ah ! " answered the maiden, " I must spin straw into gold, and know not how to do it."

The little man said, " What will you give me if I do it for you ? "

" My neckerchief," said the maiden.

He took the kerchief, sat down before the wheel, and grind, grind, grind—three times did he grind—and the spindle was full; then he put another thread on, and grind, grind, grind, the second was full; so he spun on till morning; when all the straw was spun, and all the spindles were full of gold.

The king came at sunrise, and was greatly astonished and overjoyed at the sight; but it only made his heart the more greedy of gold. He put the miller's daughter into another much larger room, full of straw, and ordered her to spin it all in one night, if life were dear to her. The poor helpless maiden began to weep, when once more the door flew open, the little man appeared, and said, "What will you give me if I spin this straw into gold?"

"My ring from my finger," answered the maiden.

The little man took the ring, began to turn the wheel, and, by the morning, all the straw was spun into shining gold.

The king was highly delighted when he saw it, but was not yet satisfied with the quantity of gold; so he put the damsel into a still larger room full of straw, and said, "Spin this during the night; and if you do it you shall be my wife." "For," he thought, "if she's only a miller's daughter, I shall never find a richer wife in the whole world."

As soon as the damsel was alone the little man came the third time and said, "What will you give me if I again spin all this straw for you?"

"I have nothing more to give you," answered the girl.

"Then promise, if you become queen, to give me your first child."

"Who knows how that may be, or how things may turn out between now and then?" thought the girl, but in her perplexity she could not help herself; so she promised the little man what he desired, and he spun all the straw into gold.

When the king came in the morning and saw that

his orders had been obeyed, he married the maiden, and the beautiful miller's daughter became a queen. After a year had passed she brought a lovely baby into the world, but quite forgot the little man, till he walked suddenly into her chamber, and said, " Give me what you promised me." The queen was frightened, and offered the dwarf all the riches of the kingdom if he would only leave her her child ; but he answered, " No ; something living is dearer to me than all the treasures of the world."

Then the queen began to grieve and to weep so bitterly, that the little man took pity upon her and said, " I will give you three days ; if in that time you can find out my name, you shall keep the child."

All night long the queen thought over every name she had ever heard, and sent a messenger through the kingdom, to inquire what names were usually given to people in that country. When, next day, the little man came again, she began with Caspar, Melchior, Balthazar, and repeated, each after each, all the names she knew or had heard of ; but at each one the little man said, " That is not my name."

The second day she again sent round about in all directions, to ask how the people were called, and repeated to the little man the strangest names she could hear of or imagine : to each he answered always, " That is not my name."

The third day the messenger returned and said, " I have not been able to find a single new name ; but as I came over a high mountain by a wood, where the fox and the hare bid each other good-night, I saw a little house, and before the house was burning a little fire, and round the fire danced a very funny little man, who hopped upon one leg, and cried out :

> " To-day I brew, to-morrow I bake,
> Next day the queen's child I shall take ;
> How glad I am that nobody knows
> My name is Rumpelstilzchen ! "

You may guess how joyful the queen was at hearing this ; and when, soon after, the little man entered and said, "Queen, what is my name ? " she asked him mischievously, " Is your name Kunz ? "

" No."

" Is your name Carl ? "

" No."

" Are you not sometimes called Rumpelstilzchen ? "

" A witch has told you that—a witch has told you ! " shrieked the poor little man, and stamped so furiously with his right foot that it sank into the earth up to the hip ; then he seized his left foot with both hands with such violence that he tore himself right in two.

THE BREMEN TOWN MUSICIANS

THERE was a man who owned a donkey, which had carried his sacks to the mill industriously for many years, but whose strength had come to an end, so that the poor beast grew more and more unfit for work. The master determined to stop his food, but the donkey, discovering that there was no good intended to him, ran away and took the road to Bremen. "There," thought he, "I can turn Town Musician."

When he had gone a little way, he found a hound lying on the road and panting, like one who was tired with running. "Hollo! what are you panting so for, worthy Seize 'em?" asked the donkey.

"Oh!" said the dog, "just because I am old, and get weaker every day, and cannot go out hunting, my master wanted to kill me, so I have taken leave of him; but how shall I gain my living now?"

"I'll tell you what," said the donkey, "I am going to Bremen to be Town Musician, come with me and take to music too. I will play the lute, and you shall beat the drum."

The dog liked the idea, and they travelled on. It was not long before they saw a cat sitting by the road, making a face like three rainy days.

"Now then, what has gone wrong with you, old Whiskers?" said the donkey.

"Who can be merry when his neck is in danger?" answered the cat. "Because I am advanced in years, and my teeth are blunt, and I like sitting before the fire and purring better than chasing the mice about, my mistress wanted to drown me. I have managed to escape, but good advice is scarce ; tell me where I shall go to ? "

" Come with us two to Bremen ; you understand serenading ; you also can become a Town Musician."

The cat thought it a capital idea, and went with them. Soon after the three runaways came to a farmyard, and there sat a cock on the gate, crowing with might and main.

" You crow loud enough to deafen one," said the donkey, " what is the matter with you ? "

" I prophesied fair weather," said the cock, " because it is our good mistress's washing-day, and she wants to dry the clothes ; but because to-morrow is Sunday, and company is coming, the mistress has no pity on me, and has told the cook to put me into the soup to-morrow, and I must have my head cut off to-night, so now I am crowing with all my might as long as I can."

" Oh you old Redhead," said the donkey, " you had better come with us ; we are going to Bremen, where you will certainly find something better than having your head cut off ; you have a good voice, and if we all make music together, it will be something striking."

The cock liked the proposal, and they went on, all four together.

But they could not reach the city of Bremen in one day, and they came in the evening to a wood, where they agreed to spend the night. The donkey and the dog laid themselves down under a great tree, but the cat and the cock went higher—the cock flying up to the topmost branch, where he was safest. Before he went to sleep he looked round towards all the four points of the compass, and he thought he saw a spark shining in the distance. He called to his companions that there must be a house not far off, for he could see a light. The donkey said,

"Then we must rise and go to it, for the lodgings here are very bad"; and the dog said, "Yes, a few bones with a little flesh on them would do me good." So they took the road in the direction where the light was, and soon saw it shine brighter; and it got larger and larger till they came to a brilliantly-illumined robbers' house. The donkey, being the biggest, got up at the window and looked in.

"What do you see, Greybeard?" said the cock.

"What do I see?" answered the donkey, "a table covered with beautiful food and drink, and robbers are sitting round it and enjoying themselves."

"That would do nicely for us," said the cock.

"Yes, indeed, if we were only there," replied the donkey.

The animals then consulted together how they should manage to drive out the robbers, till at last they settled on a plan. The donkey was to place himself with his fore-feet on the window-sill, the dog to climb on the donkey's back, and the cat on the dog's, and, at last, the cock was to fly up and perch himself on the cat's head. When that was done, at a signal they began their music all together: the donkey brayed, the dog barked, the cat mewed, and the cock crowed; then, with one great smash, they dashed through the window into the room, so that the glass clattered down. The robbers jumped up at this dreadful noise, thinking that nothing less than a ghost was coming in, and ran away into the wood in a great fright. The four companions then sat down at the table, quite content with what was left there, and ate as if they were expecting to fast for a month to come.

When the four musicians had finished, they put out the light, and each one looked out for a suitable and comfortable sleeping-place. The donkey lay down on the dunghill, the dog behind the door, the cat on the hearth near the warm ashes, and the cock set himself on the hen-roost; and, as they were all tired with their long journey, they soon went to sleep. Soon after midnight, as the robbers in the distance could see that no more lights were burning in the house, and as all seemed quiet, the captain said, "We ought not to have let ourselves be scared so easily," and sent one of them to examine the house. The messenger found everything quiet, went into the kitchen to light a candle, and, thinking the cat's shining fiery eyes were live coals, he held a match to them to light it. But the cat did not understand the joke, flew in his face, spat at him, and scratched. He was dreadfully frightened, ran away, and was going out of the back door, when the dog, who was lying there, jumped up and bit him in the leg. As he ran through the yard, past the dunghill, the donkey gave him a good kick with his hind-foot; and the cock being awakened, and made quite lively by the noise, called out from the hen-roost, "Cock-a-doodle-doo!"

The robber ran as hard as he could, back to the captain, and said, "Oh, dear! in the house sits a horrid old witch, who flew at me, and scratched my face with her long fingers; and by the door stands a man with a knife, who stabbed me in the leg; and in the yard lies a black monster, who hit me with a club; and up on the roof there sits the judge, who called out, 'Bring the rascal up here'—so I made the best of my way off."

From that time the robbers never trusted themselves again in the house; but the four musicians liked it so well that they could not make up their minds to leave it, and spent there the remainder of their days, as the last person who told the story is ready to avouch for a fact.

SNOW-WHITE AND ROSE-RED

A poor widow lived alone in a little cottage, in front of which was a garden, where stood two little rose trees : one bore white roses, the other red. The widow had two children, who resembled the two rose trees : one was called Snow-white, and the other Rose-red. They were two of the best children that ever lived ; but Snow-white was quieter and more gentle than Rose-red. Rose-red liked best to jump about in the meadows, to look for flowers and catch butterflies ; but Snow-white sat at home with her mother, helped her in the house, or read to her when there was nothing else to do. The two children loved one another so much, that they always walked hand in hand ; and when Snow-white said, "We will not forsake one another," Rose-red answered, "Never as long as we live"; and the mother added, "Yes, my children, whatever one has, let her divide with the other." They often ran about in solitary places, and gathered red berries ; and the wild creatures of the wood never hurt them, but came confidingly up to them. The little hare ate cabbage-leaves out of their hands, the doe grazed at their side, the stag sprang merrily past them, and the birds remained sitting on the boughs, and never ceased their songs. They met with no accident if they loitered in the wood and night came on ; they lay down together on the moss, and slept till morning ; and the mother knew this, and was in no anxiety about them. Once, when they had spent the night in the wood, and the red

morning awoke them, they saw a beautiful child in a
shining white dress, sitting by the place where they had
slept, who, arising, and looking at them kindly, said
nothing, but went into the wood.   And when they looked
round, they found out that they had been sleeping close to
a precipice, and would certainly have fallen down it if
they had gone a few steps farther in the dark.   Their
mother told them it must have been the angel that takes
care of good children who had sat by them all night long.

Snow-white and Rose-red kept their mother's cottage
so clean, that it was a pleasure to look into it.   In the
summer, Rose-red managed the house, and every morning
she gathered a nosegay in which was a rose off each tree,
and set it by her mother's bed before she awoke.   In
winter Snow-white lighted the fire, and hung the kettle
on the hook ; and though it was only copper, it shone
like gold, it was rubbed so clean.   In the evening, when
the snow fell, the mother said, "Go, Snow-white, and
bolt the door" ;   and then they seated themselves on
the hearth, and the mother took her spectacles, and read
aloud out of a great book, and the two girls listened, and
sat and span.   Near them lay a lamb on the floor, and
behind them, on a perch, sat a white dove, with its head
under its wing.

One evening, as they were thus happy together, some
one knocked to be let in.   The mother said, "Quick,
Rose-red, open the door ; perhaps it is a traveller, who
seeks shelter."   Rose-red went and pushed the bolt back,
and thought it was a poor man, but a bear stretched his
thick black head into the door.   Rose-red screamed and
sprang back, the little lamb bleated, the little dove
fluttered about, and Snow-white hid herself behind her
mother's bed.   However, the bear began to speak, and
said, "Do not be frightened, I will do you no harm ; I
am half frozen, and only want to warm myself a little."

"You poor bear," said the mother, "lay yourself

down before the fire, only take care your fur does not burn." Then she called out, " Snow-white and Rose-red, come out; the bear will not hurt you—he means honestly by us." Then they both came out, and, by degrees, the lamb and the dove also approached, and ceased to be afraid. The bear said, " Children, knock the snow a little out of my fur "; and they fetched a broom, and swept the bear's skin clean; and he stretched himself before the fire and growled softly, like a bear that was quite happy and comfortable. In a short time, they all became quite friendly together, and the children played tricks with the awkward guest. They pulled his hair, set their feet on his back, and rolled him here and there; or took a hazel-rod and beat him, and when he growled they laughed. The bear was very much pleased with this frolic, only, when they became too mischievous, he called out, " Children, leave me alone—

> Little Snow-white and Rose-red,
> You will strike your lover dead."

When bedtime came, and the others went to sleep, the mother said to the bear : "You can lie there on the hearth, and then you will be sheltered from the cold and the bad weather." At daybreak the two children let him out, and he trotted over the snow into the wood. Henceforward, the bear came every evening at the same hour, laid himself on the hearth, and allowed the children to play with him as much as they liked; and they became so used to him, that the door was never bolted until their black companion had arrived. When spring came, and everything was green out of doors, the bear said one morning to Snow-white : " Now I must go away, and may not come again the whole summer."

" Where are you going, dear Bear?" asked Snow-white.

" I must go into the wood, and guard my treasures

from the bad dwarfs ; in winter, when the ground is
frozen hard, they have to stay underneath, and cannot
work their way through, but now that the sun has thawed
and warmed the earth, they break through, come up,
seek, and steal : what is once in their hands, and lies in
their caverns, does not come so easily into daylight again."
Snow-white was quite sorrowful at parting, and as she
unbolted the door for him, and the bear ran out, the
hook of the door caught him, and a piece of his skin
tore off ; it seemed to Snow-white as if she had seen
gold shining through, but she was not sure. But the
bear ran quickly away, and soon disappeared behind the
trees.

After some time, their mother sent the children into
the wood to collect faggots. They found there a large
tree, which had been cut down and lay on the ground,
and by the trunk something was jumping up and down,
but they could not tell what it was. As they came
nearer, they saw that it was a dwarf, with an old withered
face, and a snow-white beard a yard long. The end of
the beard was stuck fast in a cleft in the tree, and the
little fellow jumped about like a dog on a rope, and did
not know how to help himself. He stared at the girls
with his fiery red eyes, and screamed out, "Why do you
stand there ? Can't you come and render me some
assistance ? "

"What is the matter with you, little man ? " asked
Rose-red.

"Stupid little goose !" answered the dwarf; "I
wanted to chop the tree, so as to have some small pieces
of wood for the kitchen ; we only want little bits ; with
thick logs, the small quantity of food that we cook for
ourselves—we are not, like you, great greedy people—
burns directly. I had driven the wedge well in, and it
was all going on right, but the detestable wood was too
smooth, and sprang out unexpectedly ; and the tree

" The compassionate children instantly seized hold of the little man, held him fast,
and struggled so long that the eagle let his prey go."

closed up so quickly, that I could not pull my beautiful white beard out : now it is sticking there, and I can't get away. There you foolish, soft, milk-faces ! you are laughing and crying out, ' How ugly you are ! how ugly you are ! ' "

The children took a great deal of trouble, but they could not pull the beard out ; it stuck too fast.

" I will run and fetch somebody," said Rose-red.

" You great ninny ! " snarled the dwarf, " to want to call more people ; you are two too many for me now. Can't you think of anything better ? "

" Only don't be impatient," said Snow-white, " I have thought of something " ; and she took her little scissors out of her pocket, and cut the end of the beard off.

As soon as the dwarf felt himself free, he seized a sack filled with gold that was sticking between the roots of the tree ; pulling it out, he growled to himself, " You rude people, to cut off a piece of my beautiful beard ! May evil reward you ! " Then he threw his sack over his shoulders and walked away, without once looking at the children.

Some time afterwards, Snow-white and Rose-red wished to catch some fish for dinner. As they came near to the stream, they saw that something like a grasshopper was jumping towards the water, as if it were going to spring in. They ran on and recognised the dwarf.

" Where are you going ? " asked Rose-red. " You don't want to go into the water ? "

" I am not such a fool as that," cried the dwarf. " Don't you see the detestable fish wants to pull me in ? "

The little fellow had been sitting there fishing, and, unluckily, the wind had entangled his beard with the line. When directly afterwards a great fish bit at his hook, the weak creature could not pull him out, so the fish was pulling the dwarf into the water. It is true he caught hold of all the reeds and rushes, but that did not help him much ; he had to follow all the movements of the fish, and was in imminent danger of being drowned. The girls, coming at the right time, held him fast and tried to get the beard loose from the line, but in vain—beard and line were entangled fast together. There was nothing to do but to pull out the scissors and to cut off the beard, in doing which a little piece of it was lost. When the dwarf saw that, he cried out : "Is that manners, you goose ! to disfigure one's face so ? Is it not enough that you once cut my beard shorter ? But now you have cut the best part of it off. I dare not be seen by my people. I wish you had had to run, and had lost the soles of your shoes !" Then he fetched a sack of pearls that lay among the rushes, and, without saying a word more, he dragged it away and disappeared behind a stone.

Soon after, the mother sent the two girls to the town to buy cotton, needles, cord, and tape. The road led them by a heath, scattered over which lay great masses of rock. There they saw a large bird hovering in the air ; it flew round and round just above them, always sinking lower and lower, and at last it settled down by a rock not far distant. Directly after, they heard a piercing, wailing cry. They ran up, and saw with horror that the eagle had seized their old acquaintance the dwarf, and was going to carry him off. The compassionate children instantly seized hold of the little man, held him fast, and struggled so long that the eagle let his prey go.

When the dwarf had recovered from his first fright, he called out, in his shrill voice : "Could not you deal rather more gently with me ? You have torn my thin coat all in tatters, awkward, clumsy creatures that you are !" Then he took a sack of precious stones, and slipped behind the rock again into his den. The girls, who were used to his ingratitude, went on their way, and completed their business in the town. As they were coming home again over the heath, they surprised the dwarf, who had emptied his sack of precious stones on a little clean place, and had not thought that any one would come by there so late. The evening sun shone on the glittering stones, which looked so beautiful in all their colours, that the children could not help standing still to gaze.

"Why do you stand there gaping?" cried the dwarf, his ash-coloured face turning vermilion with anger.

With these cross words he was going away, when he heard a loud roaring, and a black bear trotted out of the wood towards them. The dwarf sprang up terrified, but he could not get to his lurking-hole again—the bear was already close upon him. Then he called out in anguish:

"Dear Mr. Bear, spare me, and you shall have all my treasures; look at the beautiful precious stones that lie there. Give me my life! for what do you want with a poor thin little fellow like me? You would scarcely feel me between your teeth. Rather seize those two wicked girls; they will be tender morsels for you, as fat as young quails; pray, eat them at once."

The bear, without troubling himself to answer, gave the malicious creature one single stroke with his paw, and he did not move again. The girls had run away, but the bear called after them, "Snow-white and Rose-red, do not be frightened; wait, I will go with you." Recognising the voice of their old friend, they stood still, and when the bear came up to them his skin suddenly fell off; and behold he was not a bear, but a handsome young man dressed all in gold.

"I am a king's son," said he; "I was changed by the wicked dwarf, who had stolen all my treasures, into a wild bear, and obliged to run about in the wood until I should be freed by his death. Now he has received his well-deserved punishment."

So they all went home together to the widow's cottage, and Snow-white was married to the prince, and Rose-red to his brother. They divided between them the great treasures which the dwarf had amassed. The old mother lived many quiet and happy years with her children ; but when she left her cottage for the palace, she took the two rose trees with her, and they stood before her window and bore every year the most beautiful roses—one white and the other red.

JACK AND THE BEAN-STALK

In the days of King Alfred there lived a poor woman, whose cottage was in a remote country village, many miles from London. She had been a widow some years, and had an only child named Jack, whom she indulged so much that he never paid the least attention to anything she said, but was indolent, careless, and extravagant. His follies were not owing to a bad disposition, but to his mother's foolish partiality. By degrees, he spent all that she had—scarcely anything remained but a cow. One day, for the first time in her life, she reproached him: " Cruel, cruel boy ! you have at last brought me to beggary. I have not money enough to purchase even a bit of bread ; nothing now remains to sell but my poor cow ! I am sorry to part with her ; it grieves me sadly, but we cannot starve." For a few minutes Jack felt remorse, but it was soon over ; and he began asking his mother to let him sell the cow at the next village ; teasing her so much that she at last consented. As he was going along he met a butcher, who inquired why he was driving the cow from home? Jack replied, he was going to sell it. The butcher held some curious beans in his hat ; they were of various colours, and attracted Jack's attention : this did not pass unnoticed by the man, who, knowing Jack's easy temper, thought now was the time to take an advantage of it ; and, determined not to let slip so good an opportunity, asked what was the price of the cow, offering at the same time all the beans in his hat for her. The silly boy could not conceal the pleasure he felt at what he supposed so great an offer : the bargain was struck instantly, and the cow exchanged for a few paltry beans. Jack made the best of his way home, calling aloud to his mother before he reached the door, thinking to surprise her.

When she saw the beans, and heard Jack's account, her patience quite forsook her : she tossed the beans out of the window, where they fell on the garden-bed below. Then she threw her apron over her head, and cried bitterly. Jack attempted to console her, but in vain, and, not having anything to eat, they both went supperless to bed. Jack awoke early in the morning, and seeing something uncommon darkening the window of his bedchamber, ran downstairs into the garden, where he found some of the beans had taken root, and sprung up surprisingly : the stalks were of an immense thickness, and had twined together until they formed a ladder like a chain, and so high that the top appeared to be lost in the clouds. Jack was an adventurous lad ; he determined to climb up to the top, and ran to tell his mother, not doubting but that she would be equally pleased with himself. She declared he should not go ; said it would break her heart if he did —entreated and threatened, but all in vain. Jack set out, and after climbing for some hours, reached the top of the bean-stalk, quite exhausted. Looking around, he found himself in a strange country ; it appeared to be a barren desert—not a tree, shrub, house, or living creature was to be seen ; here and there were scattered fragments of stone ; and at unequal distances, small heaps of earth were loosely thrown together.

Jack seated himself pensively upon a block of stone, and thought of his mother ; he reflected with sorrow upon his disobedience in climbing the bean-stalk against her will, and concluded that he must die of hunger. However, he walked on, hoping to see a house, where he might beg something to eat and drink. He did not find it ;

but he saw at a distance a beautiful lady, walking all alone. She was elegantly clad, and carried a white wand, at the top of which sat a peacock of pure gold.

Jack, who was a gallant fellow, went straight up to her ; when, with a bewitching smile, she asked him how he came there. He told her all about the bean-stalk. The lady answered him by a question, " Do you remember your father, young man ?"

" No, madam ; but I am sure there is some mystery about him, for when I name him to my mother she always begins to weep, and will tell me nothing."

" She dare not," replied the lady, " but I can and will. For know, young man, that I am a fairy, and was your father's guardian. But fairies are bound by laws as well as mortals ; and by an error of mine I lost my power for a term of years, so that I was unable to succour your father when he most needed it, and he died." Here the fairy looked so sorrowful that Jack's heart warmed to her, and he begged her earnestly to tell him more.

" I will ; only you must promise to obey me in everything, or you will perish yourself."

Jack was brave, and, besides, his fortunes were so bad they could not well be worse—so he promised.

The fairy continued : " Your father, Jack, was a most excellent, amiable, generous man. He had a good wife, faithful servants, plenty of money ; but he had one misfortune—a false friend. This was a giant, whom he had succoured in misfortune, and who returned his kindness by murdering him, and seizing on all his property ; also making your mother take a solemn oath that she would never tell you anything about your father, or he would murder both her and you. Then he turned her off with you in her arms, to wander about the wide world as she might. I could not help her, as my power only returned on the day you went to sell your cow."

" It was I," added the fairy, " who impelled you to

take the beans, who made the bean-stalk grow, and inspired you with the desire to climb up it to this strange country ; for it is here the wicked giant lives who was your father's destroyer. It is you who must avenge him, and rid the world of a monster who never will do anything but evil. I will assist you. You may lawfully take possession of his house and all his riches, for everything he has belonged to your father, and is therefore yours. Now farewell ! Do not let your mother know you are acquainted with your father's history : this is my command, and if you disobey me you will suffer for it. Now go."

Jack asked where he was to go.

"Along the direct road, till you see the house where the giant lives. You must then act according to your own just judgment, and I will guide you if any difficulty arises. Farewell ! "

She bestowed on the youth a benignant smile, and vanished.

Jack pursued his journey. He walked on till after sunset, when, to his great joy, he espied a large mansion. A plain-looking woman was at the door : he accosted her, begging she would give him a morsel of bread and a night's lodging. She expressed the greatest surprise, and said it was quite uncommon to see a human being near their house ; for it was well known that her husband was a powerful giant, who would never eat anything but human flesh, if he could possibly get it ; that he would walk fifty miles to procure it, usually being out the whole day for that purpose.

This account greatly terrified Jack, but still he hoped to elude the giant, and therefore he again entreated the woman to take him in for one night only, and hide him where she thought proper. She at last suffered herself to be persuaded, for she was of a compassionate and generous disposition, and took him into the house. First, they entered a fine large hall, magnificently furnished ; they

"Jack . . . seized the hen, and ran off with her, . . . reached the top of the bean-stalk, which he descended in safety."

then passed through several spacious rooms, in the same style of grandeur ; but all appeared forsaken and desolate. A long gallery came next ; it was very dark—just light enough to show that, instead of a wall on one side, there was a grating of iron which parted off a dismal dungeon, from whence issued the groans of those victims whom the cruel giant reserved in confinement for his own voracious appetite. Poor Jack was half dead with fear, and would have given the world to have been with his mother again, for he now began to doubt if he should ever see her more ; he even mistrusted the good woman, and thought she had let him into the house for no other purpose than to lock him up among the unfortunate people in the dungeon. However, she bade Jack sit down, and gave him plenty to eat and drink ; and he, not seeing anything to make him uncomfortable, soon forgot his fear, and was just beginning to enjoy himself, when he was startled by a loud knocking at the outer door, which made the whole house shake.

"Ah ! that's the giant ; and if he sees you he will kill you and me too," cried the poor woman, trembling all over. "What shall I do ? "

"Hide me in the oven," cried Jack, now as bold as a lion at the thought of being face to face with his father's cruel murderer. So he crept into the oven—for there was no fire near it—and listened to the giant's loud voice and heavy step as he went up and down the kitchen scolding his wife. At last he seated himself at table, and Jack, peeping through a crevice in the oven, was amazed to see what a quantity of food he devoured. It seemed as if he never would have done eating and drinking ; but he did at last, and, leaning back, called to his wife in a voice like thunder :

"Bring me my hen ! "

She obeyed, and placed upon the table a very beautiful live hen.

"Lay !" roared the giant, and the hen laid immediately an egg of solid gold.

"Lay another !" and every time the giant said this the hen laid a larger egg than before.

He amused himself a long time with his hen, and then sent his wife to bed, while he fell asleep by the fireside, and snored like the roaring of cannon.

As soon as he was asleep, Jack crept out of the oven, seized the hen, and ran off with her. He got safely out of the house, and finding his way along the road he came, reached the top of the bean-stalk, which he descended in safety.

His mother was overjoyed to see him. She thought he had come to some ill end.

"Not a bit of it, mother. Look here !" and he showed her the hen. "Now lay"; and the hen obeyed him as readily as the giant, and laid as many golden eggs as he desired.

These eggs being sold, Jack and his mother got plenty of money, and for some months lived very happily together; till Jack got another great longing to climb the bean-stalk, and carry away some more of the giant's riches. He had told his mother of his adventure, but had been very careful not to say a word about his father. He thought of his journey again and again, but still he could not summon resolution enough to break it to his mother, being well assured that she would endeavour to prevent his going. However, one day he told her boldly, that he must take another journey up the bean-stalk ; she begged and prayed him not to think of it, and tried all in her power to dissuade him. She told him that the giant's wife would certainly know him again, and that the giant would desire nothing better than to get him into his power, that he might put him to a cruel death, in order to be revenged for the loss of his hen. Jack, finding that all his arguments were useless, ceased speaking, though resolved to go at all events. He had a dress prepared which would disguise him, and something to colour his skin ; he thought it impossible for any one to recollect him in this dress.

A few mornings after, he rose very early, and, unperceived by any one, climbed the bean-stalk a second time. He was greatly fatigued when he reached the top, and very hungry. Having rested some time on one of the stones, he pursued his journey to the giant's mansion, which he reached late in the evening : the woman was at the door as before. Jack addressed her, at the same time telling her a pitiful tale, and requesting that she would give him some victuals and drink, and also a night's lodging.

She told him (what he knew before very well) about her husband's being a powerful and cruel giant, and also that she had one night admitted a poor, hungry, friendless boy ; that the little ungrateful fellow had stolen one of the giant's treasures ; and ever since that her husband had been worse than before, using her very cruelly, and continually upbraiding her with being the cause of his misfortune. Jack felt sorry for her, but confessed nothing, and did his best to persuade her to admit him, but found it a very hard task. At last she consented, and as she led the way, Jack observed that everything was just as he had found it before : she took him into the kitchen, and after he had done eating and drinking, she hid him in an old lumber-closet. The giant returned at the usual time, and walked in so heavily, that the house was shaken to its foundation. He seated himself by the fire, and soon after exclaimed : " Wife, I smell fresh meat ! "

The wife replied it was the crows, which had brought a piece of raw meat, and left it at the top of the house. While supper was preparing, the giant was very illtempered and impatient, frequently lifting up his hand to strike his wife for not being quick enough. He was also continually upbraiding her with the loss of his wonderful hen.

At last, having ended his supper, he cried, "Give me something to amuse me—my harp or my money-bags."

"Which will you have, my dear?" said the wife humbly.

"My money-bags, because they are the heaviest to carry," thundered he.

She brought them, staggering under the weight; two bags—one filled with new guineas, and the other with new shillings; she emptied them out on the table, and the giant began counting them in great glee. "Now you may go to bed, you old fool." So the wife crept away.

Jack from his hiding-place watched the counting of the money, which he knew was his poor father's, and wished it was his own; it would give him much less trouble than going about selling the golden eggs. The giant, little thinking he was so narrowly observed, reckoned it all up, and then replaced it in the two bags, which he tied up very carefully and put beside his chair, with his little dog to guard them. At last he fell asleep as before, and snored so loud, that Jack compared his noise to the roaring of the sea in a high wind, when the tide is coming in. At last Jack, concluding all secure, stole out, in order to carry off the two bags of money; but just as he laid his hand upon one of them, the little dog, which he had not perceived before, started from under the giant's chair and barked most furiously. Instead of endeavouring to escape, Jack stood still, though expecting his enemy to awake every instant. Contrary, however, to his expectation, the giant continued in a sound sleep, and Jack, seeing a piece of meat, threw it to the dog, who at once ceased barking, and began to devour it. So Jack carried off the bags, one on each shoulder, but they were so heavy that it took him two whole days to descend the beanstalk and get back to his mother's door.

JACK AND THE BEAN-STALK

When he came he found the cottage deserted. He ran from one room to another, without being able to find any one ; he then hastened into the village, hoping to see some of the neighbours, who could inform him where he could find his mother. An old woman at last directed him to a neighbouring house, where she was ill of a fever. He was greatly shocked at finding her apparently dying, and blamed himself bitterly as the cause of it all. However, at sight of her dear son, the poor woman revived, and slowly recovered health. Jack gave her his two money-bags : they had the cottage rebuilt and well furnished, and lived happier than they had ever done before.

For three years Jack heard no more of the bean-stalk, but he could not forget it, though he feared making his mother unhappy. It was in vain endeavouring to amuse himself ; he became thoughtful, and would arise at the first dawn of day, and sit looking at the bean-stalk for hours together. His mother saw that something preyed upon his mind, and endeavoured to discover the cause ; but Jack knew too well what the consequence would be should she succeed. He did his utmost, therefore, to conquer the great desire he had for another journey up the bean-stalk. Finding, however, that his inclination grew too powerful for him, he began to make secret preparations for his journey. He got ready a new disguise, better and more complete than the former ; and when summer came, on the longest day he woke as soon as it was light, and without telling his mother, ascended the bean-stalk. He found the road, journey, etc., much as it was on the two former times. He arrived at the giant's mansion in the evening, and found the wife standing, as usual, at the door. Jack had disguised himself so completely, that she did not appear to have the least recollection of him ; however, when he pleaded hunger and poverty, in order to gain admittance, he found it very difficult indeed to persuade her. At last he prevailed, and was concealed in the copper. When the giant returned, he said furiously, "I smell fresh meat!" But Jack felt quite composed, as he had said so before, and had been soon satisfied. However, the giant started up suddenly, and, notwithstanding all his wife could say, he searched all round the room. Whilst this was going forward, Jack was exceedingly terrified, wishing himself at home a thousand times; but when the giant approached the copper, and put his hand upon the lid, Jack thought his death was certain. However, nothing happened; for the giant did not take the trouble to lift up the lid, but sat down shortly by the fireside, and began to eat his enormous supper. When he had finished, he commanded his wife to fetch down his harp. Jack peeped under the copper-lid, and saw a most beautiful harp. The giant placed it on the table, said "Play!" and it played of its own accord, without anybody touching it, the most exquisite music imaginable. Jack, who was a very good musician, was delighted, and more anxious to get this than any other of his enemy's treasures. But the giant not being particularly fond of music, the harp had only the effect of lulling him to sleep earlier than usual. As for the wife, she had gone to bed as soon as ever she could.

As soon as he thought all was safe, Jack got out of the copper, and seizing the harp, was eagerly running off with it. But the harp was enchanted by a fairy, and as soon as it found itself in strange hands, it called out loudly, just as if it had been alive, "Master! Master!"

The giant awoke, started up, and saw Jack scampering away as fast as his legs could carry him.

"Oh, you villain! it is you who have robbed me of my hen and my money-bags, and now you are stealing my harp also. Wait till I catch you, and I'll eat you up alive!"

"Very well; try!" shouted Jack, who was not a bit afraid, for he saw the giant was so tipsy he could hardly stand, much less run ; and he himself had young legs and a clear conscience, which carry a man a long way. So, after leading the giant a considerable race, he contrived to be first at the top of the bean-stalk, and then scrambled down it as fast as he could, the harp playing all the while the most melancholy music, till he said, " Stop," and it stopped.

Arrived at the bottom, he found his mother sitting at her cottage-door, weeping silently.

" Here, mother, don't cry ; just give me a hatchet ; make haste." For he knew there was not a moment to spare ; he saw the giant beginning to descend the bean-stalk.

However, it was too late—the monster's ill deeds had come to an end. Jack with his hatchet cut the bean-stalk close off at the root ; the giant fell headlong into the garden, and was killed on the spot.

Instantly the fairy appeared, and explained everything to Jack's mother, begging her to forgive Jack, who was his father's own son for bravery and generosity, and who would be sure to make her happy for the rest of her days.

So all ended well, and nothing was ever more heard or seen of the wonderful Bean-stalk.

THE IRON STOVE

In the days when magic was still of some avail, a king's
son was enchanted by an old witch, and compelled to
spend his life sitting inside a great Iron Stove in a wood.
There he passed many years, and nobody could release
him.

Once a king's daughter came into the wood. She had
gone astray, and could not find her father's kingdom
again ; and having wandered about for nine days, at last
she stood before the Iron Stove. Then a voice came out
of it, and said, " Whence do you come, and where do you
want to go ? "

She answered, " I have wandered from my father's
kingdom, and lost myself, and cannot get home again."

Then the voice spoke out of the Iron Stove : " I will
help you home again, and that, too, in a short time, if
you will promise to do what I desire. I am a greater
prince than you are a princess, and I wish to marry you."

She was very much frightened, and thought, " Oh,
what shall I do ? How can I marry an Iron Stove ? "

However, as she wanted very much to go home to
her father, she promised what was demanded of her.
" Very well," said the voice ; " you must come again, and
bring a knife with you, and scrape a hole in the iron."

And the Iron Stove gave her for a companion something, or somebody—she was not quite sure what—who
walked by her side and did not speak, but took her safe
home within two hours. Then there was great joy in her

"At evening-tide she climbed up into a little tree, and purposed spending the night there, for fear of the wild beasts."

father's palace, and the old king fell on her neck, and kissed her many times. But she was very sorrowful, and said, "Dear father, you little know what has happened to me; I should never have come home again out of the great wild wood, if I had not passed by an Iron Stove. But I had to promise faithfully that I would return back to it, and marry it."

The old king was so terrified that he nearly fell into a swoon; for he had only this one child. They therefore consulted together, and decided to send, not the princess, but a miller's daughter, who was very beautiful; and leading her out, they gave her a knife, and told her how she was to scrape the Iron Stove. When she reached the wood, she scraped away for four-and-twenty hours, but could not make the slightest impression. But when day began to break, a voice in the Iron Stove called out, "It seems to me that it is day out there."

She answered, "It seems so to me too; I think I hear my father's mill turning."

"Oh, then, you are a miller's daughter; go straight back and send the king's daughter here!"

Then she returned and told the old king that the Iron Stove would not have her; he wanted the princess only. The old king was greatly frightened, and the princess wept. But they had still a swineherd's daughter, who was still more beautiful than the miller's girl; so they gave her a piece of gold, in order that she might be persuaded to go, instead of the king's daughter, to the Iron Stove. She was taken to the wood as before, and had also to scrape for four-and-twenty hours; but she could make no impression.

Now when dawn broke, a voice called out of the Stove, "It seems to me it is day out there."

Then she answered, "It seems so to me too; I think I hear my father's little horn sounding."

"So you are the swineherd's daughter: go away

directly, and bid the king's daughter come, and tell her it shall happen to her as I forewarned her ; if she does not come, everything in the kingdom shall fall to pieces and tumble down, and no stone remain upon another."

When the king's daughter heard this, she began to cry ; but there was nothing else to be done—she must keep her promise. She took leave of her father, put a knife in her pocket, and went out to the Iron Stove in the wood. When she arrived there, she began to scrape and scrape ; the iron yielded, and in two hours she had already scraped a little hole. She looked in and saw a most beautiful youth : oh ! he shone so with gold and precious stones, that he pleased her to the very bottom of her heart. She scraped away faster than ever, till she made the hole so large that he was able to get out.

Then he said, "You are mine, and I am yours ; you have freed me, and you are my bride."

He wished to take her home to his kingdom, but she begged that she might go once more to see her father ; and the prince gave her leave, on condition that she should speak no more than three words with him, and come back again. So she went home ; but, alas ! being a little chatterbox, she spoke more than three words. The Iron Stove disappeared instantly, and was removed far away, over glass mountains and sharp swords ; but the king's son, being now freed, was not shut up in it.

The princess took leave of her father, and took some money with her, but not much, and went again into the great wood. There she looked everywhere for the Iron Stove, but it was not to be found.

She sought it for nine days, until her hunger was so great that she did not know what to do ; for she had eaten all the food she could find, and had nothing left to keep her alive. At evening-tide she climbed up into a little tree, and purposed spending the night there, for fear of the wild beasts. But when midnight came she saw afar off a little glimmering light, and thinking, " Oh! there I should be safe," climbed down and went towards it.

Then she came to a little old house, overgrown with grass, with a little heap of wood before the door. Wondering how it came there, she looked in through the window, and saw nothing inside but a number of fat little frogs, and a table beautifully spread. There were on it roast meats and wines, and the plates and cups were all of silver. So she took heart, and knocked. Immediately the fattest frog called out :

> " Maiden sweet and small,
> Hutzelbein I call;
> Hutzelbein's little dog,
> Creep about and see
> Who this can be."

Then a little frog came and opened the door for her ; and as soon as she came in, the frogs all bade her welcome, and persuaded her to sit down. They asked—" Whence do you come ? where do you want to go?"

Then she told them all that had happened to her, and how, because she had disobeyed the command not to speak to her father more than three words, the Stove had disappeared, as well as the king's son ; now she was determined to seek him, and to wander over mountain and valley till she found him.

The old fat frog said :

> " Maiden sweet and small,
> Hutzelbein I call ;
> Hutzelbein's little dog,
> Creep about and see ;
> Bring the great box to me."

Then the little frog went and brought the box. Afterwards they gave the princess food and drink, and took her to a beautifully-made bed, all of silk and velvet ; she laid herself in it, and slept peacefully.

When day came she arose, and the old frog gave her

three needles out of the great box, and told her to take them with her. They would be very necessary to her, for she would have to go over a high glass mountain, and three sharp swords, and a great sea ; if she passed all those, she would recover her dearest prince. The frog also gave her, besides the three needles, other gifts, which she was to take great care of—namely, a plough-wheel, and three nuts.

With these she set off, and when she came to the slippery glass mountain, she stuck the three needles into it as she walked—some before her feet, and some behind —and so managed to get across. When she was on the other side, she hid the needles, in a place which she had noticed particularly, and went on her way. Afterwards she came to the sharp-cutting swords, but she set herself on her plough-wheel and rolled safely over them. At last she came before a great lake, which she had to sail across, and when she had done so she saw a great castle. She went in and said she was a poor maiden, who wished very much to hire herself out, if she might be taken in there as a servant. For the frogs had told her that the king's son, whom she had released out of the Iron Stove in the great wood, dwelt there ; so she was content to be taken as kitchen-maid, for very small pay.

Now the king's son had thought the princess was dead ; and there was now with him another maiden, whom he had been persuaded he ought to marry, which grieved the poor kitchen-maid very much.

In the evening, when she had washed up the dishes, and had done all her work, she felt in her pocket, and found the three nuts which the old frog had given her. She bit one open, and was going to eat the kernel, when, behold, inside it was the most beautiful dress imaginable —so beautiful that the bride soon heard of it, came and asked to see it, and wanted to buy it, saying it was no dress for a kitchen-maid. But the kitchen-maid thought differently, and refused to sell it, but offered to give it as a present, if the bride would grant her one favour—namely, to sleep one night on the mat outside the bridegroom's door. The bride gave her leave, because the dress was so beautiful, and she had none like it.

Now when it was evening, she said to her bridegroom : "The foolish kitchen-maid wants to sleep on the mat outside your door."

"If you are content, I am," said he.

But the bride gave him a glass of wine, in which she had put a sleeping-draught ; so that he slept so soundly, nothing could wake him. While, outside the door, the princess wept the whole night, saying : "I have released you out of the wild wood — out of an Iron Stove ; in seeking you, I have gone over a glass mountain, over three sharp swords, and over a great lake ; yet, now that I find you, you will not hear me."

Next evening, when she had washed up everything, she bit the second nut open ; and inside it was a far more beautiful dress than the first, which, when the bride saw, she wished to buy also. But the girl again refused to take money, and again begged that she might spend the night outside the bridegroom's door. Once more the bride gave him a sleeping-draught, and he slept so soundly, that he could hear nothing. But the kitchen-maid wept the whole night long, crying, "I have released you out of a wild wood, and out of an Iron Stove ; and have gone over a glass mountain, over three sharp swords, and over a great lake, before I found you ; and yet, when I find you, you will not hear me."

The third evening, she bit open the third nut ; and there was in it a still more beautiful dress, which shone stiff with pure gold. When the bride saw it, she wished more earnestly than ever to have it; but the kitchen-maid would only give it to her on condition that she might sleep, for the third time, on the mat at the bridegroom's door. But this time the prince was cautious, and left the sleeping-draught untouched. Now, when she began to weep, and to call out, "Dearest treasure, I have released you out of the horrible wild wood, and out of an Iron Stove," the king's son sprang up, crying out, "This is my right true love—she is mine, and I am hers." Then he declared he would not marry the other bride, whom he did not love; and so, still in the middle of the night, he got into a carriage with the kitchen-maid, and drove away.

When they came to the great lake, they sailed over; and at the three sharp swords, they seated themselves on the plough-wheel; and at the glass mountain, they found the three needles, and stuck them in step by step. So they came at last to the little old house; but, as they went in, lo! it changed to a great castle; the frogs turned to princes and princesses, all kings' children, and received them both with great joy. There the wedding was celebrated, and they remained in the castle, which was much larger than that which belonged to the princess's father. But as the old man lamented very much his daughter's loss, and his own loneliness, they soon went and fetched him home to themselves. So they had two kingdoms, instead of one, and live happily together all their days.

BROTHER AND SISTER

A BROTHER took his sister by the hand and said, "Since our mother is dead we have no more happy hours: our stepmother beats us every day, and whenever we come near her she kicks us away. She gives us hard crusts and nasty scraps to eat, and the dog under the table fares better than we do, for he does sometimes get a nice bit thrown to him. It would break our mother's heart if she knew it! Come, we will go out into the wide world together."

They went along the whole day through meadows, over rocks and stones, and when it rained the little sister said, "Heaven and our hearts are crying together." In the evening they came to a great wood, and were so worn out with grief, hunger, and weariness, that they sat down in a hollow tree and went to sleep.

The next morning, when they awoke, the sun was already high in the heavens, and shone down very hot on the tree. Upon which said the brother: "Sister, I am thirsty; I would go and have a drink if I knew where there was a spring: I think I can hear one trickling." He got up, took his sister by the hand, and they went to look for the spring.

The wicked stepmother, however, who was a witch and well knew how the children had run away, had crept after them secretly, in the way witches do, and had bewitched all the springs in the wood. When they had found a spring that was dancing brightly over the stones, the brother stooped down to drink ; but his sister heard a voice in its murmur, which said, " Whoever drinks of me will become a tiger." Eagerly the little sister cried, " I pray thee, brother, do not drink, lest thou become a wild beast and tear me to pieces."

The brother did not drink, although he was so thirsty, but said, " I will wait for the next spring." When they came to the next, the little sister heard it say, " Who drinks of me will become a wolf ; who drinks of me will become a wolf!" and cried out, " O brother, I pray thee do not drink, lest thou become a wolf and eat me up."

The brother did not drink, but said : " I will wait till I come to the next spring, but then I must drink, say what you will, for my thirst is getting unbearable."

And when they came to the third spring, the little sister heard a voice in its murmur, saying, " Whoever drinks of me will become a roe," and she cried, " O brother, do not drink, I pray thee, lest thou become a roe and run away from me." But the brother had already knelt down by the stream, stooped down, and drank of the water ; and as soon as the first drop touched his lips, there he lay—a white roe.

The little sister cried over her poor bewitched brother, and the roe cried also as he rested mournfully beside her. At last the maiden said, " Never mind, dear Roe, I will never forsake you." So she took off her golden garter and put it round the roe's neck, then pulled some rushes and wove them into a cord. To this she tied the little animal and led him on, and they both went still deeper into the wood. When they had gone a long, long way, they came at last to a little house, into which the maiden peeped ; and as it was empty, she thought, " Here we may stay and live." So she made a pretty bed of leaves and moss for the roe ; and every morning she went out and gathered roots, berries, and nuts for herself ; and for the roe she brought tender grass, which he ate out of her hand, and played about and was very happy. In the evening, when the little sister was tired and had said her prayers, she laid her head upon the roe, who was her pillow, and went sweetly to sleep ; and if her brother had only kept his proper shape, they would have led a very happy life.

They had lived alone in this way during a long time, when it happened that the king of the country held a great hunt in the forest. Through the trees might be heard the blowing of horns, the barking of dogs, and the joyous cries of the hunters, which when the little roe heard he was almost beside himself with delight. " Oh," said he to his sister, " let me go and see the hunt—I can no longer refrain"; and he begged hard till she consented.

" But," said she, " when you return at evening I shall have shut my door against the wild huntsmen, and in order that I may know you, knock and say—' My little sister, let me in ' ; but if you do not say so, I shall not open the door."

Now off sprang the roe, and was so happy to find himself in the open air. The king and his huntsmen saw the beautiful beast and set off after him, but they could not catch him ; for when they thought they had certainly got him, he sprang over a bush and disappeared. When it was dark he galloped up to the little house, knocked, and cried, " My little sister, let me in." And when the door was opened he sprang in, and rested all night on his pretty little bed. Next morning the hunt began again, and when the roe heard the blast of the horns, and the " Ho ! ho ! " of the hunters, he could not rest, and cried, " Sister, open the door—I must go."

His sister opened the door and said, " But mind you must be back in the evening and make your little speech, that I may let you in."

When the king and his huntsmen saw the white roe

with the gold band once more, they all rode after him, but
he was too quick and agile for them. This chase lasted
the whole day; at last, towards evening, the hunters
surrounded him, and wounded him with an arrow in the
foot, so that he was forced to limp and go slowly. One
of the hunters creeping softly after him to the little house,
heard him say, "My sister, let me in," and saw that the
door was opened and immediately shut to again; so he
went back to the king, and told him all he had seen and
heard.

"We will have another hunt to-morrow," said the
king.

The little sister was greatly alarmed when she saw her
white roe was wounded; she washed off the blood, laid
herbs upon the place, and said, "Go now to thy bed, dear
Roe, and get well."

The wound, however, was so slight that the next
morning he felt nothing of it, and when he heard the
noise of the hunt, he said, "I cannot keep away,—I must
go, and nothing shall keep me."

His sister cried and said, "Now you will go and be
killed, and leave me here alone in the forest, forsaken by
all the world; I will not let you go out."

"Then I shall die here of grief," answered the roe :
"for when I hear the sound of the horn, I do feel as if I
could jump out of my shoes." So his sister could not do
less than open the door with a heavy heart, and the roe
sprang out joyfully into the forest.

As soon as the king saw him, he said to his huntsmen,
"Now hunt him all day till evening, but don't do
anything to hurt him."

When the sun was set the king said to his huntsman,
"Now come and show me the little house you saw in the
wood." And when he was before the door he knocked
and cried, "Dear little sister, let me in." Immediately
the door opened, the king entered, and there stood a

maiden more beautiful than any one he had ever seen.
The damsel was frightened when she found there had
come in, not her roe, but a man who wore a golden crown
on his head.   But the king looked kindly at her, took her
hand and said, "Wilt thou go with me to my castle, and
be my dear wife ? "

"Oh yes," answered the maiden, "but the roe must
come with me, for I cannot forsake him."

The king replied, "He shall remain with you as long
as you live, and shall want for nothing."

At this moment he came springing in, his sister tied
the cord of rushes round his neck, led him with her own
hand, and they all left the little house together.

The king took the beautiful maiden on his own horse
and conducted her to his castle, where the marriage was
celebrated with great pomp.   She was now queen, and
they lived a long time very happily together ; while the
roe was petted and taken care of, and played all day about
the palace-garden.

But the wicked stepmother, on whose account these
children had been driven into the wide world, thought
nothing less than that the little sister had been torn to
pieces by wild beasts in the forest, and that the brother, in
the shape of a roe, had been killed by the hunters.   When
she now heard they were so happy, and that everything
went well with them, envy and spite raged in her heart
and gave her no rest, and her only thought was how she
could do some mischief to them both.   Her own daughter,
who was as ugly as the night and had only one eye, was
continually reproaching her, and saying, "It is I who
ought to have been made queen."

"Never mind," said the old witch to console her ;
"when the time comes I will manage it."

By and by the queen gave birth to a beautiful little
boy ; and the king being away at the hunt, the old witch
took upon herself the form of the lady-in-waiting, entered

the room where the queen lay, and said to her, "Come, the bath is ready, which will do you good and give you new strength ; make haste before it gets cold." Her daughter was also at hand, and they carried the poor weak queen between them into the bath-room, and laid her in the bath : then they shut the door and ran away. But under the bath they had first lighted a great furnace-fire, so that the beautiful young queen could not save herself from being scorched alive.

When that was done the old witch took her own daughter, put a cap on her, and laid her on the bed in the queen's room. She changed her also into the shape of the young queen, all except her one eye, and she could not give her another. But in order that the king might not observe it, she was obliged to lie on that side where there was no eye. In the evening, when he was come home, and heard that he had a little son, he was very much delighted, and wished to visit his dear wife and see how she was getting on ; on which the old woman cried out in a great hurry, " As you value your life, don't touch the curtain ; the queen must not see the light, and must be left quite quiet." So the king went away, and never found out that it was a false queen in the bed.

But when it was midnight, and all the world was asleep, the nurse who was sitting beside the cradle, and who was the only person awake, saw the door open and the true queen come in. She took the baby out of the cradle, laid it in her arms, and nursed it tenderly. She then shook up the pillows, laid it down again, and covered it with the counterpane. She did not forget the roe either, but went into the corner where it lay, and stroked it gently. After this she passed out, quite silently, through the door ; and the nurse inquired next morning of the sentinels whether any one had gained entrance into the palace during the night, but they answered, " No—we have seen nobody." She continued to come in the same way for several nights, though she spoke never a word : the nurse always saw her, but never dared to mention it.

When some time had passed, the queen at last began to speak, and said :

"How is my baby ?   How is my roe ?
I can come again twice, then for ever must go."

The nurse could not answer her ; but when she had disappeared she went to the king, and told him all about it, upon which he cried, "What does it mean?   I will myself watch by the child to-night."

In the evening he came to the nursery, and there at midnight the dead queen appeared, and said :

"How is my baby ?   How is my roe ?
I can come but once more, then for ever must go ;"

and nursed and fondled the baby as before, then vanished. The king did not dare to address her, but watched again the following night.   This time she said :

"How is my baby ?   How is my roe ?
I can come but this once, then for ever must go."

Upon which the king could no longer contain himself, but sprang forward and cried, "Thou canst surely be no one but my own dear wife ! "

She replied, " Yes, I am thy dear wife " ; and as soon as she had spoken these words she was restored to life, and became once more fresh and blooming.

Then she related to the king the crime committed on her by the old witch and her ugly daughter, whom he at once commanded to be brought to judgment, and had sentence passed upon them.   The daughter was taken forth into the woods, where the wild beasts tore her in pieces, and the witch was burnt.   And behold ! as soon as there was nothing left of her but ashes, the white roe became changed again and resumed his human form ; so they all lived happily together till the end of their lives.

LITTLE RED-RIDING-HOOD

ONCE there was a little village maiden, the prettiest ever seen. Her mother was foolishly fond of her and her grandmother likewise. The old woman made for her a little hood, which became the damsel so well, that ever after she went by the name of Little Red-Riding-Hood. One day, when her mother was making cakes, she said, "My child, you shall go and see your grandmother, for I hear she is not well; and you shall take her some of these cakes, and a pot of butter."

Little Red-Riding-Hood was delighted to go, though it was a long walk; but she was a good child, and fond of her kind grandmother. Passing through a wood, she met a great wolf, who was most eager to eat her up, but dared not, because of a woodcutter who was busy hard by. So he only came and asked her politely where she was going. The poor child, who did not know how dangerous it is to stop and speak to wolves, replied, "I am going to see my grandmother, and to take her a cake and a pot of butter, which my mother has sent her."

"Is it very far from hence?" asked the wolf.

"Oh yes, it is just above the mill which you may see up there—the first house you come to in the village."

"Well," said the wolf, "I will go there also, to inquire after your excellent grandmother; I will go one way, and you the other, and we will see who can be there first."

So he ran as fast as ever he could, taking the shortest road, but the little maiden took the longest; for she stopped to pluck roses in the wood, to chase butterflies, and gather nosegays of the prettiest flowers she could find —she was such a happy and innocent little soul.

The wolf was not long in reaching the grandmother's door. He knocked, Toc—toc, and the grandmother said, " Who is there ? "

" It is your child, Little Red-Riding-Hood," replied the wicked beast, imitating the girl's voice ; " I bring you a cake and a pot of butter, which my mother has sent you."

The grandmother, who was ill in her bed, said, " Very well, my dear, pull the string and the latch will open." The wolf pulled the string—the door flew open ; he leaped in, fell upon the poor old woman, and ate her up in less than no time, tough as she was, for he had not tasted anything for more than three days. Then he carefully shut the door, and laying himself down snugly in the bed, waited for Little Red-Riding-Hood, who was not long before she came and knocked, Toc—toc, at the door.

" Who is there ? " said the wolf ; and the little maiden, hearing his gruff voice, felt sure that her poor grandmother must have caught a bad cold and be very ill indeed.

So she answered cheerfully, " It is your child, Little Red-Riding-Hood, who brings you a cake and a pot of butter that my mother has sent you."

Then the wolf, softening his voice as much as he could, said, " Pull the string, and the latch will open."

So Little Red-Riding-Hood pulled the string and the door opened. The wolf, seeing her enter, hid himself as much as he could under the coverlid of the bed, and said in a whisper, " Put the cake and the pot of butter on the shelf, and then make haste and come to bed, for it is very late."

Little Red-Riding-Hood did not think so ; but to please her grandmother, she undressed herself and began to get ready for bed, when she was very much astonished to find how different the old woman looked from ordinary.

"Grandmother, what great arms you have!"

"That is to hug you the better, my dear."

"Grandmother, what great ears you have!"

"That is to hear you the better, my dear."

"Grandmother, what great eyes you have!"

"That is to see you the better, my dear."

"Grandmother, what a great mouth you have!"

"That is to eat you up," cried the wicked wolf; and immediately he fell upon poor Little Red-Riding-Hood, and ate her up in a moment.

"'You have but to give me a sack, and a pair of boots such as gentlemen wear when they go shooting."

PUSS IN BOOTS

A MILLER, dying, divided all his property between his three children. This was a very simple matter, as he had nothing to leave but his mill, his ass, and his cat ; so he made no will, and called in no lawyer, who would, probably, have taken a large slice out of these poor possessions. The eldest son took the mill, the second the ass, while the third was obliged to content himself with the cat, at which he grumbled very much. " My brothers," said he, " by putting their property together, may gain an honest livelihood, but there is nothing left for me, except to die of hunger ; unless, indeed, I were to kill my cat and eat him, and make a coat out of his skin, which would be very scanty clothing."

The cat, who heard the young man talking to himself, sat up on his four paws, and looking at him with a grave and wise air, said, " Master, I think you had better not kill me ; I shall be much more useful to you alive."

" How so ? " asked his master.

" You have but to give me a sack, and a pair of boots such as gentlemen wear when they go shooting, and you will find you are not so ill off as you suppose."

Now, though the young miller did not much depend upon the cat's words, still he thought it rather surprising that a cat should speak at all. And he had before now seen him show so much adroitness and cleverness in catching rats and mice, that it seemed advisable to trust him a little further ; especially as, poor young fellow ! he had nobody else to trust.

When the cat got his boots, he drew them on with a grand air, and slinging his sack over his shoulder, and drawing the cords of it round his neck, he marched bravely to a rabbit-warren hard by, with which he was well acquainted. Then, putting some bran and lettuces into his bag, and stretching himself out beside it as if he were dead, he waited till some fine fat young rabbit, ignorant of the wickedness and deceit of the world, should peer into the sack to eat the food that was inside. This happened very shortly, for there are plenty of foolish young rabbits in every warren ; and when one of them, who really was a splendid fat fellow, put his head inside, Master Puss drew the cords immediately, and took him and killed him without mercy. Then, very proud of his prey, he marched direct up to the palace, and begged to speak with the king. He was desired to ascend to the apartment of his majesty, where, making a low bow, he said :

"Sire, here is a magnificent rabbit, killed in the warren which belongs to my lord the Marquis of Carabas, and which he has desired me to offer humbly to your majesty."

"Tell your master," replied the king politely, "that I accept his present, and am very much obliged to him."

Another time, Puss went and hid himself and his sack in a wheat-field, and there caught two splendid fat partridges in the same manner as he had done the rabbit. When he presented them to the king, with a similar message as before, his majesty was so pleased that he ordered the cat to be taken down into the kitchen and given something to eat and drink ; where, while enjoying himself, the faithful animal did not cease to talk in the most cunning way of the large preserves and abundant game which belonged to my lord the Marquis of Carabas.

One day, hearing that the king was intending to take

a drive along the river-side with his daughter, the most beautiful princess in the world, Puss said to his master, "Sir, if you would only follow my advice, your fortune is made."

"Be it so," said the miller's son, who was growing very disconsolate, and cared little what he did: "Say your say, cat."

"It is but little," replied Puss, looking wise, as cats can. "You have only to go and bathe in the river, at a place which I shall show you, and leave all the rest to me. Only remember that you are no longer yourself, but my lord the Marquis of Carabas."

"Just so," said the miller's son, "it's all the same to me"; but he did as the cat told him.

While he was bathing, the king and all the court passed by, and were startled to hear loud cries of "Help, help! my lord the Marquis of Carabas is drowning." The king put his head out of the carriage, and saw nobody but the cat, who had, at different times, brought him so many presents of game: however, he ordered his guards to fly quickly to the succour of my lord the Marquis of Carabas. While they were pulling the unfortunate marquis out of the water, the cat came up, bowing, to the side of the king's carriage, and told a long and pitiful story about some thieves, who, while his master was bathing, had come and carried away all his clothes, so that it would be impossible for him to appear before his majesty and the illustrious princess.

"Oh, we will soon remedy that," answered the king kindly; and immediately ordered one of the first officers of the household to ride back to the palace with all speed, and bring back the most elegant supply of clothes for the young gentleman, who kept in the background until they arrived. Then, being handsome and well-made, his new clothes became him so well, that he looked as if he had been a marquis all his days, and advanced with an air of respectful ease to offer his thanks to his majesty.

The king received him courteously, and the princess admired him very much. Indeed, so charming did he appear to her, that she hinted to her father to invite him into the carriage with them, which, you may be sure, the young man did not refuse. The cat, delighted at the success of his scheme, went away as fast as he could, and ran so swiftly that he kept a long way ahead of the royal carriage. He went on and on, till he came to some peasants who were mowing in a meadow. " Good people," said he in a very firm voice, " the king is coming past here shortly, and if you do not say that the field you are mowing belongs to my lord the Marquis of Carabas, you shall all be chopped as small as mince-meat."

So when the king drove by, and asked whose meadow it was where there was such a splendid crop of hay, the mowers all answered, trembling, that it belonged to my lord the Marquis of Carabas.

" You have very fine land, Marquis," said his majesty to the miller's son ; who bowed, and answered " that it was not a bad meadow, take it altogether."

Then the cat came to a wheat-field, where the reapers were reaping with all their might. He bounced in upon them : " The king is coming past to-day, and if you do not tell him that this wheat belongs to my lord the Marquis of Carabas, I will have you every one chopped as small as mince-meat." The reapers, very much alarmed, did as they were bid, and the king congratulated the Marquis upon possessing such beautiful fields, laden with such an abundant harvest.

They drove on—the cat always running before and saying the same thing to everybody he met, that they were to declare the whole country belonged to his master ; so that even the king was astonished at the vast estate of my lord the Marquis of Carabas.

But now the cat arrived at a great castle where dwelt an Ogre, to whom belonged all the land through which the royal equipage had been driving. He was a cruel tyrant, and his tenants and servants were terribly afraid of him, which accounted for their being so ready to say whatever they were told to say by the cat, who had taken pains to inform himself of all about the Ogre. So, putting on the boldest face he could assume, Puss marched up to the castle with his boots on, and asked to see the owner of it, saying that he was on his travels, but did not wish to pass so near the castle of such a noble gentleman, without paying his respects to him. When the Ogre heard this message, he went to the door, received the cat as civilly as an Ogre can, and begged him to walk in and repose himself.

"Thank you, sir," said the cat ; "but first I hope you will satisfy a traveller's curiosity. I have heard in far countries of your many remarkable qualities, and especially how you have the power to change yourself into any sort of beast you choose—a lion for instance, or an elephant."

"That is quite true," replied the Ogre; "and lest you should doubt it, I will immediately become a lion."

He did so ; and the cat was so frightened that he sprang up to the roof of the castle and hid himself in the gutter—a proceeding rather inconvenient on account of his boots, which were not exactly fitted to walk with upon tiles. At length, perceiving that the Ogre had resumed his original form, he came down again stealthily, and confessed that he had been very much frightened.

"But, sir," said he, "it may be easy enough for such a big gentleman as you to change himself into a large animal : I do not suppose you can become a small one—a rat or mouse for instance. I have heard that you can ; still, for my part, I consider it quite impossible."

"Impossible ? " cried the other indignantly. "You shall see ! " and immediately the cat saw the Ogre no longer, but a little mouse running along on the floor.

This was exactly what he wanted ; and he did the very best a cat could do, and the most natural under the circumstances—he sprang upon the mouse and gobbled it up in a trice. So there was an end of the Ogre.

By this time the king had arrived opposite the castle, and was seized with a strong desire to enter it. The cat, hearing the noise of the carriage-wheels, ran forward in a great hurry, and standing at the gate, said in a loud voice, " Welcome, sire, to the castle of my lord the Marquis of Carabas."

" What ! " cried his majesty, very much surprised, " does the castle also belong to you ? Truly, Marquis, you have kept your secret well up to the last minute. I have never seen anything finer than this courtyard and these battlements. Indeed, I have nothing like them in the whole of my dominions."

The Marquis, without speaking, offered his hand to the princess to assist her to descend, and, standing aside that the king might enter first—for he had already acquired all the manners of a court—followed his majesty to the great hall, where a magnificent collation was laid out, and where, without more delay, they all sat down to feast.

Before the banquet was over, the king, charmed with the good qualities of the Marquis of Carabas — and likewise with his wine, of which he had drunk six or seven cups—said, bowing across the table at which the princess and the miller's son were talking very confidentially together, " It rests with you, Marquis, whether you will not become my son-in-law."

" I shall be only too happy," said the complaisant Marquis, and the princess's cast-down eyes declared the same.

So they were married the very next day, and took possession of the Ogre's castle, and of everything that had belonged to him.

As for the cat, he became at once a grand personage, and had never more any need to run after mice, except for his own diversion.

THE WOLF AND THE SEVEN YOUNG
GOSLINGS

THERE was once an old goose who had seven young goslings, and loved them as only a mother can love her children. One day she was going into the wood to seek for provender, and before setting off she called all seven to her and said, "Dear children, I am obliged to go into the wood, so be on your guard against the wolf; for if he gets in here he will eat you up, feathers, skin, and all. The villain often disguises himself, but you can easily recognise him by his rough voice and black paws."

The children answered, "Dear mother, we will take great care; you may go without any anxiety." So the old lady was comforted, and set off cheerfully for the wood.

Before long, some one knocked at the door, and cried, "Open, open, my dear children; your mother is here, and has brought something for each of you."

But the goslings soon perceived, by the rough voice, that it was the wolf. "We will not open," said they; "you are not our mother, for she has a sweet and lovely voice; but your voice is rough—you are the wolf."

Thereupon the wolf set off to a merchant and bought a large lump of chalk; he ate it, and it made his voice sweet. Back he came, knocked at the door, and cried, "Open, open, my dear children; your mother is here, and has brought something for each of you."

But the wolf had laid his black paw on the window-sill,

and when the children saw it, they cried, " We will not open ; our mother has not black feet like you—you are the wolf."

So the wolf ran off to the baker, and said, " I have hurt my foot, put some dough on it." And when the baker had plastered it with dough, the wolf went to the miller and cried, " Strew some meal on my paws." But the miller thought to himself, " The wolf wants to deceive some one," and he hesitated to do it ; till the wolf said, " If you don't do it at once, I will eat you up." So the miller was afraid and made his paws white. Such is the way of the world !

Now came the rogue back for the third time, knocked and said, " Open the door, dear children ; your mother has come home, and has brought something for each of you out of the wood."

The little goslings cried, " Show us your paws first, that we may see whether you are indeed our mother." So he laid his paws on the window-sill, and when the goslings saw that they were white, they believed it was all right, and opened the door; and who should come in but the wolf!

They screamed out and tried to hide themselves ; one jumped under the table, another into the bed, the third into the oven ; the fourth ran into the kitchen, the fifth hopped into a chest, the sixth under the wash-tub, and the seventh got into the clock-case. But the wolf seized them, and stood on no ceremony with them ; one after another he gobbled them all up, except the youngest, who being in the clock-case he couldn't find. When the wolf had eaten his fill, he strolled forth, laid himself down in the green meadow under a tree, and went fast asleep.

Not long after, back came the old goose home from the wood ; but what, alas ! did she see ? The house-door stood wide open ; table, chairs, benches, were all overthrown ; the wash-tub lay in the ashes ; blankets and

THE WOLF AND YOUNG GOSLINGS

pillows were torn off the bed. She looked for her children, but nowhere could she find them ; she called them each by name, but nobody answered. At last, when she came to the youngest, a little squeaking voice answered, "Dear mother, I am in the clock-case." She pulled him out, and he told her how the wolf had come and had eaten up all the others. You may think how she wept for her dear children.

At last, in her grief, she went out, and the youngest gosling ran beside her. And when she came to the meadow there lay the wolf under the tree, snoring till the boughs shook. She walked round and examined him on all sides, till she perceived that something was moving and kicking about inside him.

"Can it be," thought she, "that my poor children whom he has swallowed for his supper are yet alive ? " So she sent the little gosling back to the house for scissors, needle, and thread, and began to slit up the monster's stomach. Scarcely had she given one snip, when out came the head of a gosling, and when she had cut a little further, the six jumped out one after another, not having taken the least hurt, because the greedy monster had swallowed them down whole. That was a joy ! They embraced their mother tenderly, and skipped about as lively as a tailor at his wedding.

But the old goose said, "Now go and find me six large stones, which we will put inside the greedy beast while he is still asleep." So the goslings got the stones in all haste, and they put them inside the wolf ; and the old goose sewed him up again in a great hurry, while he never once moved nor took any notice.

Now when the wolf at last woke up and got upon his legs, he found he was very thirsty, and wished to go to the spring to drink. But as soon as he began to move the stones began to shake and rattle inside him, till he cried :

145   L

"What's this rumbling and tumbling,
What's this rattling like bones?
I thought I had eaten six little geese.
But they've turn'd out only stones."

And when he came to the spring and bent down his head to drink, the heavy stones overbalanced him, and in he went head over heels. Now when the seven goslings saw this, they came running up, crying loudly, "The wolf is dead, the wolf is dead!" and danced for joy all round the spring, and their mother with them.

THE FAIR ONE WITH GOLDEN LOCKS

THERE was once a king's daughter so beautiful that they named her the Fair One with Golden Locks. These golden locks were the most remarkable in the world, soft and fine, and falling in long waves down to her very feet. She wore them always thus, loose and flowing, surmounted with a wreath of flowers ; and though such long hair was sometimes rather inconvenient, it was so exceedingly beautiful, shining in the sun like ripples of molten gold, that everybody agreed she fully deserved her name.

Now there was a young king of a neighbouring country, very handsome, very rich, and wanting nothing but a wife to make him happy. He heard so much of the various perfections of the Fair One with Golden Locks, that at last, without even seeing her, he fell in love with her so desperately that he could neither eat nor drink, and resolved to send an ambassador at once to demand her in marriage. So he ordered a magnificent equipage— more than a hundred horses and a hundred footmen—in order to bring back to him the Fair One with Golden Locks, who, he never doubted, would be only too happy to become his queen. Indeed, he felt so sure of her that he refurnished the whole palace, and had made, by all the dressmakers of the city, dresses enough to last a lady for a lifetime. But, alas ! when the ambassador arrived and delivered his message, either the princess was in a bad humour, or the offer did not appear to be to her taste ; for she returned her best thanks to his majesty, but said she had not the slightest wish or intention to be married. She also, being a prudent damsel, declined receiving any of the presents which the king had sent her ; except that, not quite to offend his majesty, she retained a box of English pins, which were in that country of considerable value.

When the ambassador returned, alone and unsuccessful, all the court was very much affected, and the king himself began to weep with all his might. Now, there was in the palace household a young gentleman named Avenant, beautiful as the sun, besides being at once so amiable and so wise that the king confided to him all his affairs ; and every one loved him, except those people—to be found in all courts—who were envious of his good fortune. These malicious folk hearing him say gaily, "If the king had sent me to fetch the Fair One with Golden Locks, I know she would have come back with me," repeated the saying in such a manner, that it appeared as if Avenant thought so much of himself and his beauty, and felt sure the princess would have followed him all over the world ; which when it came to the ears of the king, as it was meant to do, irritated him so much that he commanded Avenant to be imprisoned in a high tower, and left to die there of hunger. The guards accordingly carried off the young man, who had quite forgotten his idle speech, and had not the least idea what fault he had committed. They ill-treated him very much, and then left him, with nothing to eat and only water to drink. This, however, kept him alive for a few days, during which he did not cease to complain aloud, and to call upon the king, saying, "O king, what harm have I done ? You have no subject more faithful than I. Never have I had a thought which could offend you."

And it so befell that the king, coming by chance, or else with a sort of remorse, past the tower, was touched by the voice of the young Avenant, whom he had once so much regarded. In spite of all the courtiers could do to prevent him, he stopped to listen, and overheard these words. The tears rushed into his eyes ; he opened the door of the tower, and called, "Avenant!" Avenant came, creeping feebly along, fell at the king's knees, and kissed his feet :

"Oh, sire, what have I done that you should treat me so cruelly?"

"You have mocked me and my ambassador ; for you said, if I had sent you to fetch the Fair One with Golden Locks, you would have been successful and brought her back."

"I did say it, and it was true," replied Avenant fearlessly ; "for I should have told her so much about your majesty and your various high qualities, which no one knows so well as myself, that I am persuaded she would have returned with me."

"I believe it," said the king, with an angry look at those who had spoken ill of his favourite ; he then gave Avenant a free pardon, and took him back with him to the court.

After having supplied the famished youth with as much supper as he could eat, the king admitted him to a private audience, and said, "I am as much in love as ever with the Fair One with Golden Locks, so I will take thee at thy word, and send thee to try and win her for me."

"Very well, please your majesty," replied Avenant cheerfully ; "I will depart to-morrow."

The king, overjoyed with his willingness and hopefulness, would have furnished him with a still more magnificent equipage and suite than the first ambassador ; but Avenant refused to take anything except a good horse to ride, and letters of introduction to the princess's father. The king embraced him, and eagerly saw him depart.

It was on a Monday morning when, without any pomp or show, Avenant thus started on his mission. He rode slowly and meditatively, pondering over every possible means of persuading the Fair One with Golden Locks to marry the king ; but, even after several days' journey towards her country, no clear project had entered into his mind. One morning, when he had started at break of day, he came to a great meadow with a stream running through it, along which were planted willows and poplars. It was such a pleasant, rippling stream that he dismounted and sat down on its banks. There he perceived, gasping on the grass, a large golden carp, which, in leaping too far after gnats, had thrown itself quite out of the water, and now lay dying on the greensward. Avenant took pity on it, and though he was very hungry, and the fish was very fat, and he would well enough have liked it for his breakfast, still he lifted it gently and put it back into the stream. No sooner had the carp touched the fresh cool water than it revived and swam away ; but shortly returning, it spoke to him from the water in this wise :

" Avenant, I thank you for your good deed. I was dying, and you have saved me : I will recompense you for this one day."

After this pretty little speech, the fish popped down to the bottom of the stream, according to the habit of carp, leaving Avenant very much astonished, as was natural.

Another day he met with a raven that was in great distress, being pursued by an eagle, which would have swallowed him up in no time. "See," thought Avenant, "how the stronger oppress the weaker ! What right has an eagle to eat up a raven?" So taking his bow and arrow, which he always carried, he shot the eagle dead, and the raven, delighted, perched in safety on an opposite tree.

"Avenant," screeched he, though not in the sweetest voice in the world ; " you have generously succoured me, a poor miserable raven. I am not ungrateful, and I will recompense you one day."

"Thank you," said Avenant, and continued his road.

THE FAIR ONE WITH GOLDEN LOCKS

Entering in a thick wood, so dark with the shadows of early morning that he could scarcely find his way, he heard an owl hooting, like an owl in great tribulation. She had been caught by the nets spread by bird-catchers to entrap finches, larks, and other small birds. "What a pity," thought Avenant, "that men must always torment poor birds and beasts who have done them no harm!" So he took out his knife, cut the net, and let the owl go free. She went sailing up into the air, but immediately returned, hovering over his head on her brown wings.

"Avenant," said she, "at daylight the bird-catchers would have been here, and I should have been caught and killed. I have a grateful heart; I will recompense you one day."

These were the three principal adventures that befell Avenant on his way to the kingdom of the Fair One with Golden Locks. Arrived there, he dressed himself with the greatest care, in a habit of silver brocade, and a hat adorned with plumes of scarlet and white. He threw over all a rich mantle, and carried a little basket, in which was a lovely little dog, an offering of respect to the princess. With this he presented himself at the palace-gates, where, even though he came alone, his mien was so dignified and graceful, so altogether charming, that every one did him reverence, and was eager to run and tell the Fair One with Golden Locks that Avenant, another ambassador from the king her suitor, awaited an audience.

"Avenant!" repeated the princess, "that is a pretty name; perhaps the youth is pretty too."

"So beautiful," said the ladies of honour, "that while he stood under the palace window we could do nothing but look at him."

"How silly of you!" sharply said the princess. But she desired them to bring her robe of blue satin, to comb out her long hair, and adorn it with the freshest garland of flowers; to give her her high-heeled shoes, and her fan. " Also," added she, "take care that my audience-chamber is well swept and my throne well dusted. I wish in everything to appear as becomes the Fair One with Golden Locks."

This done, she seated herself on her throne of ivory and ebony, and gave orders for her musicians to play, but softly, so as not to disturb conversation. Thus, shining in all her beauty, she admitted Avenant to her presence.

He was so dazzled that at first he could not speak : then he began and delivered his harangue to perfection.

"Gentle Avenant," returned the princess, after listening to all his reasons for her returning with him, " your arguments are very strong, and I am inclined to listen to them ; but you must first find for me a ring, which I dropped into the river about a month ago. Until I recover it, I can listen to no propositions of marriage."

Avenant, surprised and disturbed, made her a profound reverence and retired, taking with him the basket and the little dog Cabriole, which she refused to accept. All night long he sat sighing to himself, " How can I ever find a ring which she dropped into the river a month ago ? She has set me an impossibility."

"My dear master," said Cabriole, "nothing is an impossibility to one so young and charming as you are : let us go at daybreak to the river-side."

Avenant patted him, but replied nothing : until, worn out with grief, he slept. Before dawn Cabriole wakened him, saying, " Master, dress yourself and let us go to the river."

There Avenant walked up and down, with his arms folded and his head bent, but saw nothing. At last he heard a voice, calling from a distance, "Avenant, Avenant!"

The little dog ran to the water-side—" Never believe me again, master, if it is not a golden carp, with a ring in its mouth !"

"Yes, Avenant," said the carp, " this is the ring which

the princess has lost. You saved my life in the willow meadow, and I have recompensed you. Farewell!"

Avenant took the ring gratefully and returned to the palace with Cabriole, who scampered about in great glee. Craving an audience, he presented the princess with her ring, and begged her to accompany him to his master's kingdom. She took the ring, looked at it, and thought she was surely dreaming.

"Some fairy must have assisted you, fortunate Avenant," said she.

"Madam, I am only fortunate in my desire to obey your wishes."

"Obey me still," she said graciously. "There is a prince named Galifron, whose suit I have refused. He is a giant as tall as a tower, who eats a man as a monkey eats a nut; he puts cannons into his pockets instead of pistols; and when he speaks, his voice is so loud that every one near him becomes deaf. Go and fight him, and bring me his head."

Avenant was thunderstruck; but after a time he recovered himself—"Very well, madam. I shall certainly perish, but I will perish like a brave man. I will depart at once to fight the Giant Galifron."

The princess, now in her turn, surprised and alarmed, tried every persuasion to induce him not to go, but in vain. Avenant armed himself and started, carrying his little dog in its basket. Cabriole was the only creature that gave him consolation: "Courage, master! While you attack the giant, I will bite his legs: he will stoop down to strike me, and then you can knock him on the head." Avenant smiled at the little dog's spirit, but he knew it was useless.

Arrived at the castle of Galifron, he found the road all strewn with bones and carcases of men. Soon he saw the giant walking. His head was level with the highest trees, and he sang in a terrific voice:

THE FAIRY BOOK

"Bring me babies to devour;
More—more—more—more—
Men and women, tender and tough;
All the world holds not enough."

To which Avenant replied, imitating the tune:

"Avenant you here may see,
He is come to punish thee:
Be he tender, be he tough,
To kill thee, giant, he is enough."

Hearing these words, the giant took up his massive club, looked around for the singer, and, perceiving him, would have slain him on the spot, had not a raven, sitting on a tree close by, suddenly flown out upon him and picked out both his eyes. Then Avenant easily killed him and cut off his head, while the raven, watching him, said:

"You shot the eagle who was pursuing me: I promised to recompense you, and to-day I have done it. We are quits."

"No, it is I who am your debtor, Sir Raven," replied Avenant, as, hanging the frightful head to his saddle-bow, he mounted his horse and rode back to the city of the Fair One with Golden Locks.

There everybody followed him, shouting, "Here is brave Avenant, who has killed the giant," until the princess, hearing the noise, and fearing it was Avenant himself who was killed, appeared, all trembling; and even when he appeared with Galifron's head, she trembled still, although she had nothing to fear.

"Madam," said Avenant, "your enemy is dead: so I trust you will accept the hand of the king my master."

"I cannot," replied she thoughtfully, "unless you first bring me a phial of the water in the Grotto of Darkness. It is six leagues in length, and guarded at the entrance by two fiery dragons. Within it is a pit, full of scorpions, lizards, and serpents, and at the bottom of this place flows the Fountain of Beauty and Health. All who wash in it become, if ugly, beautiful, and if beautiful, beautiful for ever ; if old, young ; and if young, young for ever.   Judge then, Avenant, if I can quit my kingdom without carrying with me some of this miraculous water."

"Madam," replied Avenant, "you are already so beautiful that you require it not ; but I am an unfortunate ambassador whose death you desire : I will obey you, though I know I shall never return."

So he departed with his only friends—his horse and his faithful dog Cabriole ; while all who met him looked at him compassionately, pitying so pretty a youth bound on such a hopeless errand.   But, however kindly they addressed him, Avenant rode on and answered nothing, for he was too sad at heart.

He reached a mountain-side, where he sat down to rest, leaving his horse to graze, and Cabriole to run after the flies.   He knew that the Grotto of Darkness was not far off, yet he looked about him like one who sees nothing.   At last he perceived a rock, as black as ink, whence came a thick smoke ; and in a moment appeared one of the two dragons, breathing out flames.   It had a yellow and green body, claws, and a long tail.   When Cabriole saw the monster, the poor little dog hid himself in terrible fright.   But Avenant resolved to die bravely ; so, taking a phial which the princess had given him, he prepared to descend into the cave.

"Cabriole," said he, "I shall soon be dead : then fill this phial with my blood, and carry it to the Fair One with Golden Locks, and afterwards to the king my master, to show him I have been faithful to the last."

While he was thus speaking, a voice called, "Avenant, Avenant ! "—and he saw an owl sitting on a hollow tree. Said the owl, "You cut the net in which I was caught, and I vowed to recompense you.   Now is the time. Give me the phial : I know every corner of the Grotto of Darkness—I will fetch you the water of beauty."

Delighted beyond words, Avenant delivered up his phial ; the owl flew with it into the grotto, and in less than half-an-hour reappeared, bringing it quite full and well corked. Avenant thanked her with all his heart, and joyfully took once more the road to the city.

The Fair One with Golden Locks had no more to say. She consented to accompany him back, with all her suite, to his master's court. On the way thither she saw so much of him, and found him so charming, that Avenant might have married her himself had he chosen ; but he would not have been false to his master for all the beauties under the sun. At length they arrived at the king's city, and the Fair One with Golden Locks became his spouse and queen. But she still loved Avenant in her heart, and often said to the king her lord—" But for Avenant I should not be here ; he has done all sorts of impossible deeds for my sake ; he has fetched me the water of beauty, and I shall never grow old—in short, I owe him everything."

And she praised him in this sort so much, that at length the king became jealous ; and though Avenant gave him not the slightest cause of offence, he shut him up in the same high tower once more—but with irons on his hands and feet, and a cruel jailer besides, who fed him with bread and water only. His sole companion was his little dog Cabriole.

When the Fair One with Golden Locks heard of this, she reproached her husband for his ingratitude, and then, throwing herself at his knees, implored that Avenant might be set free. But the king only said, " She loves him ! " and refused her prayer. The queen entreated no more, but fell into a deep melancholy.

When the king saw it, he thought she did not care for him because was not handsome enough ; and that if he could wash his face with her water of beauty, it would make her love him more. He knew that she kept it in a cabinet in her chamber, where she could find it always.

Now it happened that a waiting-maid, in cleaning out this cabinet, had, the very day before, knocked down the phial, which was broken in a thousand pieces, and all the contents were lost. Very much alarmed, she then remembered seeing, in a cabinet belonging to the king, a similar phial. This she fetched, and put in the place of the other one, in which was the water of beauty. But the king's phial contained the water of death. It was a poison, used to destroy great criminals—that is, noblemen, gentlemen, and such like. Instead of hanging them or cutting their heads off, like common people, they were compelled to wash their faces with this water ; upon which they fell asleep, and woke no more. So it happened that the king, taking up this phial, believing it to be the water of beauty, washed his face with it, fell asleep, and—died.

Cabriole heard the news, and, gliding in and out among the crowd which clustered round the young and lovely widow, whispered softly to her—" Madam, do not forget poor Avenant." If she had been disposed to do so, the sight of his little dog would have been enough to remind her of him—his many sufferings, and his great fidelity. She rose up, without speaking to anybody, and went straight to the tower where Avenant was confined. There, with her own hands, she struck off his chains, and putting a crown of gold on his head, and a purple mantle on his shoulders, said to him, " Be king—and my husband."

Avenant could not refuse ; for in his heart he had loved her all the time. He threw himself at her feet, and then took the crown and sceptre, and ruled her kingdom like a king. All the people were delighted to have him as their sovereign. The marriage was celebrated in all imaginable pomp, and Avenant and the Fair One with Golden Locks lived and reigned happily together all their days.

THE FROG-PRINCE

In times of yore, when wishes were both heard and granted, lived a king whose daughters were all beautiful, but the youngest was so lovely that the sun himself, who has seen so much, wondered at her beauty every time he looked in her face. Now, near the king's castle was a large dark forest ; and in the forest, under an old linden-tree, was a deep well. When the day was very hot, the king's daughter used to go to the wood and seat herself at the edge of the cool well ; and when she became wearied, she would take a golden ball, throw it up in the air, and catch it again. This was her favourite amusement. Once it happened that her golden ball, instead of falling back into the little hand that she stretched out for it, dropped on the ground, and immediately rolled away into the water. The king's daughter followed it with her eyes, but the ball had vanished, and the well was so deep that no one could see down to the bottom. Then she began to weep, wept louder and louder every minute, and could not console herself at all.

While she was thus lamenting some one called to her : "What is the matter with you, king's daughter ? You weep so, that you would touch the heart of a stone."

She looked around to see whence the voice came, and saw a frog stretching his thick ugly head out of the water.

"Ah ! it is you, old water-paddler ! " said she. " I am crying for my golden ball, which has fallen into the well."

158

"Be content," answered the frog, "I daresay I can give you some good advice; but what will you give me if I bring back your plaything to you?"

"Whatever you like, dear frog," said she; "my clothes, my pearls and jewels, even the golden crown I wear."

The frog answered, "Your clothes, your pearls and jewels, even your golden crown, I do not care for; but if you will love me, and let me be your companion and play-fellow; sit near you at your little table, eat from your little golden plate, drink from your little cup, and sleep in your little bed;—if you will promise me this, then I will bring you back your golden ball from the bottom of the well."

"Oh yes!" said she; "I promise you everything, if you will only bring me back my golden ball."

She thought to herself, meanwhile: "What nonsense the silly frog talks! He sits on the water with the other frogs, and croaks, and cannot be anybody's play-fellow!"

But the frog, as soon as he had received the promise, dipped his head under the water and sank down. In a little while up he came again with the ball in his mouth, and threw it on the grass. The king's daughter was overjoyed when she beheld her pretty plaything again, picked it up, and ran away with it.

"Wait! wait!" cried the frog; "take me with you. I cannot run as fast as you."

Alas! of what use was it that he croaked after her as loud as he could. She would not listen to him, but hastened home, and soon forgot the poor frog, who was obliged to plunge again to the bottom of his well.

The next day, when she was sitting at dinner with the king and all the courtiers, eating from her little gold plate, there came a sound of something creeping up the marble staircase—splish, splash; and when it had reached the top, it knocked at the door and cried, "Youngest king's daughter, open to me."

She ran, wishing to see who was outside ; but when she opened the door, and there sat the frog, she flung it hastily to again, and sat down at table, feeling very, very uncomfortable. The king saw that her heart was beating violently, and said, "How, my child, why are you afraid? Is a giant standing outside the door to carry you off?"

"Oh no!" answered she, "it is no giant, but a nasty frog, who yesterday, when I was playing in the wood near the well, fetched my golden ball out of the water. For this I promised him he should be my companion, but I never thought he could come out of his well. Now he is at the door, and wants to come in."

Again, the second time, there was a knock, and a voice cried :

"Youngest king's daughter,
 Open to me ;
Know you what yesterday
 You promised me,
By the cool water ?
Youngest king's daughter,
 Open to me."

Then said the king, "What you promised you must perform. Go and open the door."

She went and opened the door ; the frog hopped in, always following and following her till he came up to her chair. There he sat, and cried out, "Lift me up to you on the table."

She refused, till the king, her father, commanded her to do it. When the frog was on the table, he said, "Now push your little golden plate nearer to me, that we may eat together." She did as he desired, but one could easily see that she did it unwillingly. The frog seemed to enjoy his dinner very much, but every morsel she ate stuck in the throat of the poor little princess.

THE FROG-PRINCE

Then said the frog, "I have eaten enough, and am
tired ; carry me to your little room, and make your little
silken bed smooth, and we will lay ourselves down to
sleep together."

At this the daughter of the king began to weep ; for
she was afraid of the cold frog, who wanted to sleep in her
pretty clean bed.

But the king looked angrily at her, and said again :
"What you have promised you must perform. The frog
is your companion."

It was no use to complain whether she liked it or not ;
she was obliged to take the frog with her up to her little
bed. So she picked him up with two fingers, hating him
bitterly the while, and carried him upstairs ; but when she
got into bed, instead of lifting him up to her, she threw
him with all her strength against the wall, saying, " Now,
you nasty frog, there will be an end of you."

But what fell down from the wall was not a dead frog,
but a living young prince, with beautiful and loving eyes,
who at once became, by her own promise and her father's
will, her dear companion and husband. He told her how
he had been cursed by a wicked sorceress, and that no one
but the king's youngest daughter could release him from
his enchantment and take him out of the well.

The next day a carriage drove up to the palace-gates
with eight white horses, having white feathers on their
heads and golden reins. Behind it stood the servant of
the young prince, called the Faithful Henry. This faithful
Henry had been so grieved when his master was changed
into a frog, that he had been compelled to have three iron
bands fastened round his heart, lest it should break. Now
the carriage came to convey the prince to his kingdom, so
the faithful Henry lifted in the bride and bridegroom, and
mounted behind, full of joy at his lord's release. But
when they had gone a short distance, the prince heard
behind him a noise as if something was breaking. He

turned round, and cried out, " Henry, the carriage is breaking!"

But Henry replied, " No, sir, it is not the carriage, but one of the bands from my heart, with which I was forced to bind it up, or it would have broken with grief, while you sat as a frog at the bottom of the well."

Twice again this happened, and the prince always thought the carriage was breaking; but it was only the bands breaking off from the heart of the faithful Henry, out of joy that his lord the Frog-Prince was a frog no more.

THE WHITE CAT

THERE was once a king who had three sons, all handsome, brave and noble of heart. Nevertheless, some wicked courtiers made their father believe they were eager to wear his crown, which, though he was old, he had no mind to resign. He therefore invented a plan to get them out of the kingdom, and prevent their carrying out any undutiful projects. Sending for them to a private audience, he conversed with them kindly, and said : "You must be sensible, my dear children, that my great age prevents me from attending so closely as I have hitherto done to state affairs. I fear this may be injurious to my subjects; I therefore desire to place my crown on the head of one of you ; but it is no more than just that, in return for such a present, you should procure me some amusement in my retirement, before I leave the capital for ever. I cannot help thinking that a little dog, handsome, faithful, and engaging, would be the very thing to make me happy ; so that, without bestowing a preference on either of you, I declare that he who brings me the most perfect little dog shall be my successor."

The princes were much surprised at the fancy of their father to have a little dog, yet they accepted the proposition with pleasure ; and accordingly, after taking leave of the king, who presented them with abundance of money and jewels, and appointed that day twelvemonth for their return, they set off on their travels.

Before separating, however, they took some refreshment together, in an old palace about three miles out of town, where they mutually agreed to meet in the same place on that day twelvemonth, and go all together with their presents to court. They also agreed to change their names, and travel incognito.

Each took a different road ; but it is intended to relate the adventures of only the youngest, who was the most beautiful, amiable, and accomplished prince in the world. As he travelled from town to town, he bought all the handsome dogs that fell in his way ; and as soon as he saw one that was handsomer than those he had, he made a present of the rest ; for twenty servants would scarcely have been sufficient to take care of all the dogs he was continually purchasing. At length, wandering he knew not whither, he found himself in a forest ; night suddenly came on, and with it a violent storm of thunder, lightning, and rain : to add to his perplexity, he lost his way. After he had groped about for a long time, he perceived a light, which made him suppose that he was not far from some house : he accordingly pursued his way towards it, and in a short time found himself at the gates of the most magnificent palace he had ever beheld. The entrance-door was of gold, covered with sapphires, which shone so that scarcely could the strongest eyesight bear to look at it : this was the light the prince had seen from the forest. The walls were of transparent porcelain, variously coloured, and represented the history of all the fairies that had existed from the beginning of the world. The prince, coming back to the golden door, observed a deer's foot fastened to a chain of diamonds ; he could not help wondering at the magnificence he beheld, and the security in which the inhabitants seemed to live ; " For," said he to himself, " nothing could be easier than for thieves to steal this chain, and as many of the sapphire stones as would make their fortunes." He pulled the chain, and heard a bell, the sound of which was exquisite. In a few moments the door was opened ; yet he perceived nothing but twelve hands in the air, each holding a torch. The prince was so astonished that he durst not move a step— when he felt himself gently pushed on by some other hands from behind him. He walked on, in great perplexity, till he entered a vestibule inlaid with porphyry and lapis-stone, where the most melodious voice he had ever heard chanted the following words :

"Welcome, prince, no danger fear,
Mirth and love attend you here ;
You shall break the magic spell,
That on a beauteous lady fell.

Welcome, prince, no danger fear,
Mirth and love attend you here."

The prince now advanced with confidence, wondering what these words could mean ; the hands moved him forward towards a large door of coral, which opened of itself to give him admittance into a splendid apartment built of mother-o'-pearl, through which he passed into others, so richly adorned with paintings and jewels, and so resplendently lighted with thousands of lamps, girandoles, and lustres, that he imagined he must be in an enchanted palace. When he had passed through sixty apartments, all equally splendid, he was stopped by the hands, and a large easy-chair advanced of itself towards the fireplace ; then the hands, which he observed were extremely white and delicate, took off his wet clothes, and supplied their place with the finest linen imaginable, adding a comfortable wrapping-gown, embroidered with gold and pearls.

The hands next brought him an elegant dressing-table, and combed his hair so very gently that he scarcely felt their touch. They held before him a beautiful basin, filled with perfumes, for him to wash his face and hands, and afterwards took off the wrapping-gown, and dressed him in a suit of clothes of still greater splendour. When his toilet was complete, they conducted him to an apartment he had not yet seen, and which also was magnificently furnished. There was a table spread for supper, and everything upon it was of the purest gold, adorned with jewels. The prince observed there were two covers set, and was wondering who was to be his companion, when his attention was suddenly caught by a small figure not a foot high, which just then entered the room, and advanced towards him. It had on a long black veil, and was supported by two cats dressed in mourning, and with swords by their sides : they were followed by a numerous retinue of cats, some carrying cages full of rats, and others mouse-traps full of mice.

The prince was at a loss what to think. The little figure now approached, and throwing aside her veil, he beheld a most beautiful white cat : she seemed young and melancholy ; and, addressing herself to him, she said, " My prince, you are welcome ; your presence affords me the greatest pleasure."

" Madam," replied he, " I would fain thank you for your generosity, nor can I help observing that you must be an extraordinary creature to possess, with your present form, the gift of speech, and the most magnificent palace I have ever seen."

" All this is very true," answered the beautiful cat ; " but, prince, I am not fond of talking, and least of all do I like compliments ; let us therefore sit down to supper."

The trunkless hands then placed the dishes on the table, and the prince and white cat seated themselves at it. The first dish was a pie made of young pigeons, and the next was a fricassee of the fattest mice. The view of the one made the prince almost afraid to taste the other, till the white cat, who guessed his thoughts, assured him that there were certain dishes at table which had been dressed on purpose for him, in which there was not a morsel of either rat or mouse : accordingly, he ate heartily of such as she recommended. When supper was over, he perceived that the white cat had a portrait set in gold hanging to one of her feet. He begged her permission to look at it ; when, to his astonishment, he saw the portrait of a handsome young man, who exactly resembled himself ! He thought there was something most extraordinary in all this : yet, as the white cat sighed and looked very sorrowful, he did not venture to ask any questions. He conversed with her on different subjects, and found her extremely well versed in everything that was passing in the world. When night was far advanced, his hostess wished him a good night, and he was conducted by the hands to his bedchamber, which was different still from anything he had seen in the palace, being hung with the wings of butterflies mixed with the most curious feathers. His bed was of gauze, festooned with bunches of the gayest ribands, and the looking - glasses reached from the floor to the ceiling. The prince was undressed and put into bed by the hands, without speaking a word. He, however, slept little, and in the morning was awakened by a confused noise. The hands took him out of bed, and put on him a handsome hunting-jacket. He looked into the courtyard, and perceived more than five hundred cats, busily employed in preparing for the field—for this was a day of festival. Presently the white cat came to his apartment ; and having politely inquired after his health, she invited him to partake of their amusement. The prince willingly acceded, and mounted a wooden horse, richly caparisoned, which had been prepared for him, and which he was assured would gallop to admiration. The beautiful white cat mounted a monkey ; she wore a dragoon's cap, which made her look so fierce that all the rats and mice ran away in the utmost terror.

Everything being ready, the horns sounded, and away they went : no hunting was ever more agreeable. The cats ran faster than the hares and rabbits ; and when they caught any, they turned them out to be hunted in the presence of the white cat, and a thousand cunning tricks were played. Nor were the birds in safety; for the monkey made nothing of climbing up the trees, with the white cat on his back, to the nests of the young eagles. When the chase was over, the whole retinue returned to the palace; the white cat immediately exchanged her dragoon's cap for the veil, and sat down to supper with the prince, who, being very hungry, ate heartily, and afterwards partook with her of the most delicious wines. He then was conducted to his chamber as before, and wakened in the morning to renew the same sort of life, which day after day became so pleasant to him that he no longer thought of anything but of pleasing the sweet little creature who received him so courteously: accordingly, every day was spent in new amusements. The prince had almost forgotten his country and relations, and sometimes even regretted that he was not a cat, so great was his affection for his mewing companions.

"Alas!" said he to the white cat, "how will it afflict me to leave you, whom I love so much! Either make yourself a lady, or make me a cat." She smiled at the prince's wish, but offered no reply.

At length, the twelvemonth was nearly expired: the white cat, who knew the very day when the prince was to reach his father's palace, reminded him that he had but three days longer to look for a perfect little dog. The prince, astonished at his own forgetfulness, began to afflict himself; when the cat told him not to be so sorrowful, since she would not only provide him with a little dog, but also with a wooden horse, which should convey him safely home in less than twelve hours.

"Look here," said she, showing him an acorn; "this contains what you desire."

The prince put the acorn to his ear, and heard the barking of a little dog. Transported with joy, he thanked the cat a thousand times ; and the next day, bidding her tenderly adieu, he set out on his return.

The prince arrived first at the place of rendezvous, and was soon joined by his brothers : they mutually embraced, and began to give an account of their success ; when the youngest showed them only a little mongrel cur, telling them that he thought it could not fail to please the king, from its extraordinary beauty. The brothers trod on each other's toes under the table, as much as to say, "We have little to fear from this sorry-looking animal." The next day they went together to the palace. The dogs of the two elder brothers were lying on cushions, and so curiously wrapped around with embroidered quilts, that one would scarcely venture to touch them. The youngest produced his cur, and all wondered how the prince could hope to receive a crown for such a shabby present. The king examined the two little dogs of the elder princes, and declared he thought them so equally beautiful that he knew not to which, with justice, he could give the preference. They accordingly began to dispute ; when the youngest prince, taking his acorn from his pocket, soon ended their contention ; for a little dog appeared, which could with ease go through the smallest ring, and was besides a miracle of beauty. The king could not possibly hesitate in declaring his satisfaction ; yet, as he was not more inclined than the year before to part with his crown, he told his sons that he was extremely obliged to them for the pains they had taken : and since they had succeeded so well, he wished they would make a second attempt ; he therefore begged they would take another year in order to procure a piece of cambric, fine enough to be drawn through the eye of a small needle.

The three princes thought this very hard ; yet they set out, in obedience to the king's command. The two eldest took different roads, and the youngest remounted his wooden horse, and in a short time arrived at the palace of his beloved white cat, who received him with the greatest joy, while the trunkless hands helped him to dismount, and provided him with immediate refreshment. Afterwards the prince gave the white cat an account of the admiration which had been bestowed on the beautiful little dog, and informed her of the further injunction of his father.

" Make yourself perfectly easy, dear prince," said she ; " I have in my palace some cats who are perfect adepts in making such cambric as the king requires ; so you have nothing to do but to give me the pleasure of your company while it is making, and I will procure you all the amusement possible."

She accordingly ordered the most curious fireworks to be played off in sight of the window of the apartment in which they were sitting ; and nothing but festivity and rejoicing was heard throughout the palace for the prince's return. As the white cat frequently gave proofs of an excellent understanding, the prince was by no means tired of her company ; she talked with him of state affairs, of theatres, of fashions : in short, she was at a loss on no subject whatever ; so that when the prince was alone, he had plenty of amusement in thinking how it could possibly be, that a small white cat could be endowed with all the attractions of the very best and most charming of women.

The twelvemonth in this manner again passed insensibly away ; but the cat took care to remind the prince of his duty in proper time. " For once, my prince," said she, " I will have the pleasure of equipping you as suits your high rank." And, looking into the courtyard, he saw a superb car, ornamented all over with gold, silver, pearls, and diamonds, drawn by twelve horses as white as snow, and harnessed in the most sumptuous trappings ; and behind the car a thousand guards, richly apparelled, were waiting to attend on the prince's person. She then presented him with a nut : "You will find in it," said she, "the piece of cambric I promised you : do not break the shell till you are in the presence of the king your father." Then, to prevent the acknowledgments which the prince was about to offer, she hastily bade him adieu.

Nothing could exceed the speed with which the snow-white horses conveyed this fortunate prince to his father's palace, where his brothers had just arrived before him. They embraced each other, and demanded an immediate audience of the king, who received them with the greatest of kindness. The princes hastened to place at the feet of his majesty the curious present he had required them to procure. The eldest produced a piece of cambric so extremely fine, that his friends had no doubt of its passing through the eye of the needle, which was now delivered to the king, having been kept locked up in the custody of his majesty's treasurer all the time. But when the king tried to draw the cambric through the eye of the needle, it would not pass, though it failed but very little. Then came the second prince, who made as sure of obtaining the crown as his brother had done, but, alas! with no better success ; for though his piece of cambric was exquisitely fine, yet it could not be drawn through the eye of the needle. It was now the turn of the youngest prince, who accordingly advanced, and opening an elegant little box inlaid with jewels, took out a walnut and cracked the shell, imagining he should immediately perceive his piece of cambric ; but what was his astonishment to see nothing but a filbert! He did not, however, lose his hopes ; he cracked the filbert, and it presented him with a cherry-stone. The lords of the court, who had assembled to witness this extraordinary trial, could not, any more than the princes his brothers, refrain from laughing, to think he should be so silly as to claim the crown on no better pretensions. The prince, however, cracked the cherry-stone, which was filled with a kernel ; he divided

it, and found in the middle a grain of wheat, and in that
a grain of millet-seed. He was now absolutely confounded,
and could not help muttering between his teeth, " O white
cat, white cat, thou hast deceived me ! "   At this instant
he felt his hand scratched by the claw of a cat ; upon which
he again took courage, and opening the grain of millet-
seed, to the astonishment of all present, he drew forth a piece
of cambric four hundred yards long, and fine enough to be
threaded with perfect ease through the eye of the needle.

When the king found he had no pretext left for
refusing the crown to his youngest son, he sighed deeply,
and it was easy to be seen that he was sorry for the prince's
success.

" My sons," said he, " it is so gratifying to the heart
of a father to receive proofs of his children's love and
obedience, that I cannot refuse myself the satisfaction of
requiring of you one thing more.   You must undertake
another expedition.   That one of you, who, by the end of
a year, brings me the most beautiful lady, shall marry
her and obtain my crown."

So they again took leave of the king and of each other,
and set out without delay ; and in less than twelve hours,
our young prince arrived, in his splendid car, at the palace
of his dear white cat.   Everything went on as before till
the end of another year.   At length only one day remained
of the year, when the white cat thus addressed him :
" To-morrow, my prince, you must present yourself at the
palace of your father, and give him a proof of your
obedience.   It depends only on yourself to conduct thither
the most beautiful princess ever yet beheld, for the time is
come when the enchantment by which I am bound may be
ended.   You must cut off my head and tail," continued
she, " and throw them into the fire."

" I ! " said the prince, hastily—" I cut off your head
and tail !   You surely mean to try my affection, which,
believe me, beautiful cat, is truly yours."

"You mistake me, generous prince," said she ; "I do not doubt your regard ; but if you wish to see me in any other form than that of a cat, you must consent to do as I desire, when you will have done me a service I shall never be able sufficiently to repay."

The prince's eyes filled with tears as she spoke, yet he considered himself obliged to undertake the dreadful task ; and the cat continuing to press him with the greatest eagerness, with a trembling hand he drew his sword, cut off her head and tail, and threw them into the fire. No sooner was this done, than the most beautiful lady his eyes had ever seen stood before him : and ere he had sufficiently recovered from his surprise to speak to her, a long train of attendants, who, at the same moment as their mistress, were changed to their natural shapes, came to offer their congratulations to the queen, and inquire her commands. She received them with the greatest kindness, and ordering them to withdraw, thus addressed the astonished prince :

"Do not imagine, dear prince, that I have always been a cat, or that I am of obscure birth. My father was the monarch of six kingdoms ; he tenderly loved my mother, and left her always at liberty to follow her own inclinations. Her prevailing passion was to travel ; and a short time before my birth, having heard of some fairies who were in possession of the largest gardens filled with the most delicious fruits, she had so strong a desire to eat some of them, that she set out for the country where they lived. She arrived at their abode, which she found to be a magnificent palace, on all sides glittering with gold and precious stones. She knocked a long time at the gates ; but no one came, nor could she perceive the least sign that it had any inhabitant. The difficulty, however, did but increase the violence of my mother's longing ; for she saw the tops of the trees above the garden-walls, loaded with the most luscious fruits. The queen, in despair, ordered her attendants to place tents close to the door of the palace; but, having waited six weeks without seeing any one pass the gates, she fell sick of vexation, and her life was despaired of.

"One night, as she lay halr asleep, she turned herself about, and, opening her eyes, perceived a little old woman, very ugly and deformed, seated in the easy-chair by her bed-side. 'I and my sister fairies,' said she, 'take it very ill that your majesty should so obstinately persist in getting some of our fruit; but since so precious a life is at stake, we consent to give you as much as you can carry away, provided you will give us in return what we shall ask.' 'Ah! kind fairy,' cried the queen, 'I will give you anything that I possess, even my very kingdoms, on condition that I eat of your fruit.' The old fairy then informed the queen that what they required was, that she should give them the child she was going to have, as soon as it should be born; adding, that every possible care should be taken of it, and that it should become the most accomplished princess. The queen replied that, however cruel the conditions, she must accept them, since nothing but the fruit could save her life. In short, dear prince," continued the lady, "my mother instantly got out of bed, was dressed by her attendants, entered the palace, and satisfied her longing. Having eaten her fill, she ordered four thousand mules to be procured and loaded with the fruit, which had the virtue of continuing all the year round in a state of perfection. Thus provided, she returned to the king my father, who, with the whole court, received her with rejoicings, as it was before imagined she would die of disappointment. All this time the queen said nothing to my father of the promise she had made to give her daughter to the fairies; so that when the time was come that she expected my birth, she grew very melancholy; till at length, being pressed by the king, she declared to him the truth. Nothing could exceed his affliction when he heard that his only child, when

born, was to be given to the fairies. He bore it, however, as well as he could, for fear of adding to my
mother's grief; and also believing he should find some
means of keeping me in a place of safety, which the fairies
would not be able to approach. As soon, therefore, as I
was born, he had me conveyed to a tower in the palace, to
which there were twenty flights of stairs, and a door to
each, of which my father kept the key, so that none came
near me without his consent. When the fairies heard of
what had been done, they sent first to demand me; and
on my father's refusal, they let loose a monstrous dragon,
which devoured men, women, and children, and which, by
the breath of its nostrils, destroyed everything it came
near, so that even the trees and plants began to die. The
grief of the king was excessive; and, finding that his
whole kingdom would in a short time be reduced to
famine, he consented to give me into their hands. I was
accordingly laid in a cradle of mother-o'-pearl, ornamented
with gold and jewels, and carried to their palace, when the
dragon immediately disappeared. The fairies placed me
in a tower, elegantly furnished, but to which there was no
door, so that whoever approached was obliged to come by
the windows, which were a great height from the ground:
from these I had the liberty of getting out into a delightful garden, in which were baths, and every sort of cooling
fruit. In this place was I educated by the fairies, who
behaved to me with the greatest kindness; my clothes
were splendid, and I was instructed in every kind of
accomplishment; in short, prince, if I had never seen
any one but themselves, I should have remained very
happy. One day, however, as I was talking at the
window with my parrot, I perceived a young gentleman
who was listening to our conversation. As I had never
seen a man but in pictures, I was not sorry for the
opportunity of gratifying my curiosity. I thought him a
very pleasing object, and he at length bowed in the most

respectful manner, without daring to speak, for he knew that I was in the palace of the fairies. When it began to grow dark, he went away, and I vainly endeavoured to see which road 'he took. The next morning, as soon as it was light, I again placed myself at the window, and had the pleasure of seeing that the gentleman had returned to the same place. He now spoke to me through a speaking-trumpet, and informed me he thought me a most charming lady, and that he should be very unhappy if he did not pass his life in my company.

"I resolved to find some means of escaping from my tower, and was not long in devising the means for the execution of my project : I begged the fairies to bring me a netting-needle, a mesh, and some cord, saying I wished to make some nets to amuse myself with catching birds at my window. This they readily complied with, and in a short time I completed a ladder long enough to reach to the ground. I now sent my parrot to the prince, to beg he would come to the usual place, as I wished to speak with him. He did not fail ; and finding the ladder, mounted it, and quickly entered my tower. This at first alarmed me, but the charms of his conversation had restored me to tranquillity, when all at once the window opened, and the Fairy Violent, mounted on the dragon's back, rushed into the tower. My beloved prince thought of nothing but how to defend me from their fury ; for I had had time to relate to him my story, previous to this cruel interruption ; but their numbers overpowered him, and the Fairy Violent had the barbarity to command the dragon to devour my lover before my eyes. In my despair, I would have thrown myself also into the mouth of the horrible monster ; but this they took care to prevent, saying, my life should be preserved for greater punishment. The fairy then touched me with her wand, and I instantly became a white cat. She next conducted me to this palace, which belonged to my father, and gave

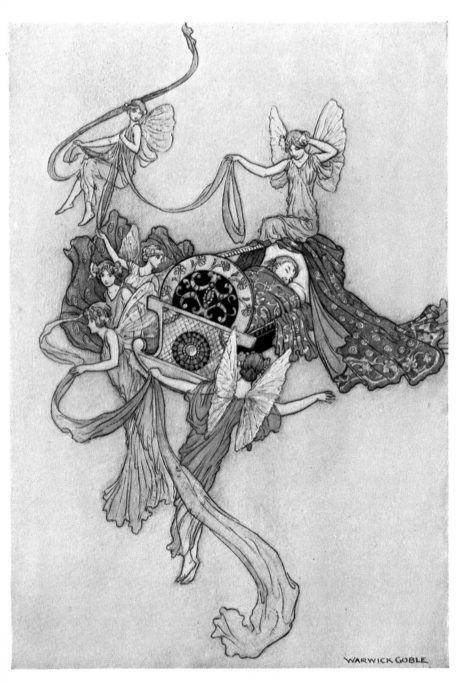

"'I was accordingly laid in a cradle of mother-of-pearl, ornamented with gold and jewels.'"

me a train of cats for my attendants, together with the twelve hands that waited on your highness. She then informed me of my birth and the death of my parents, and pronounced upon me what she imagined the greatest of maledictions : that I should not be restored to my natural figure until a young prince, the perfect resemblance of him I had lost, should cut off my head and tail. You are that perfect resemblance ; and accordingly you ended the enchantment. I need not add, that I already love you more than my life ; let us therefore hasten to the palace of the king your father, and obtain his approbation to our marriage."

The prince and princess accordingly set out side by side, in a car of still greater splendour than before, and reached the palace just as the two brothers had arrived with two beautiful princesses. The king, hearing that each of his sons had succeeded in finding what he had required, again began to think of some new expedient to delay the time of his resigning the crown ; but when the whole court were with the king assembled to pass judgment, the princess who accompanied the youngest, perceiving his thoughts by his countenance, stepped majestically forward and thus addressed him :

"It is a pity that your majesty, who is so capable of governing, should think of resigning the crown ! I am fortunate enough to have six kingdoms in my possession ; permit me to bestow one on each of the eldest princes, and to enjoy the remaining four in the society of the youngest. And may it please your majesty to keep your own kingdom, and make no decision concerning the beauty of three princesses, who, without such a proof of your majesty's preference, will no doubt live happily together ! "

The air resounded with the applauses of the assembly : the young prince and princess embraced the king and next their brothers and sisters : the three weddings immediately took place, and the kingdoms were divided as the princess had proposed.

PRINCE CHERRY

LONG ago there lived a monarch, who was such a very honest man that his subjects entitled him the Good King. One day, when he was out hunting, a little white rabbit which had been half killed by his hounds, leaped right into his majesty's arms. Said he, caressing it: "This poor creature has put itself under my protection, and I will allow no one to injure it." So he carried it to his palace, had prepared for it a neat little rabbit-hutch, with abundance of the daintiest food, such as rabbits love, and there he left it.

The same night, when he was alone in his chamber, there appeared to him a beautiful lady. She was dressed neither in gold, nor silver, nor brocade ; but her flowing robes were white as snow, and she wore a garland of white roses on her head. The Good King was greatly astonished at the sight ; for his door was locked, and he wondered how so dazzling a lady could possibly enter : but she soon removed his doubts.

" I am the Fairy Candide," said she, with a smiling and gracious air. " Passing through the wood, where you were hunting, I took a desire to know if you were as good as men say you are. I therefore changed myself into a white rabbit, and took refuge in your arms. You saved me ; and now I know that those who are merciful to dumb beasts will be ten times more so to human beings. You merit the name your subjects give you : you are the Good King. I thank you for your protection, and shall be always one of your best friends. You have but to say what you most desire, and I promise you your wish shall be granted."

"Madam," replied the king, "if you are a fairy, you must know, without my telling you, the wish of my heart. I have one well-beloved son, Prince Cherry : whatever kindly feeling you have towards me, extend it to him."

"Willingly," said Candide. "I will make him the handsomest, richest, or most powerful prince in the world : choose whichever you desire for him."

"None of the three," returned the father. "I only wish him to be good—the best prince in the whole world. Of what use would riches, power, or beauty be to him if he were a bad man?"

"You are right," said the fairy ; "but I cannot make him good : he must do that himself. I can only change his external fortunes ; for his personal character, the utmost I can promise is to give him good counsel, reprove him for his faults, and even punish him, if he will not punish himself. You mortals can but do the same with your children."

"Ah, yes!" said the king, sighing. Still, he felt that the kindness of a fairy was something gained for his son, and died not long after, content and at peace.

Prince Cherry mourned deeply, for he dearly loved his father, and would have gladly given all his kingdoms and treasures to keep him in life a little longer. Two days after the Good King was no more, Prince Cherry was sleeping in his chamber, when he saw the same dazzling vision of the Fairy Candide.

"I promised your father," said she, "to be your best friend, and in pledge of this take what I now give you" ; and she placed a small gold ring upon his finger. "Poor as it looks, it is more precious than diamonds ; for whenever you do ill it will prick your finger. If, after that warning, you still continue in evil, you will lose my friendship, and I shall become your direst enemy."

So saying, she disappeared, leaving Cherry in such amazement, that he would have believed it all a dream, save for the ring on his finger.

He was for a long time so good that the ring never pricked him at all ; and this made him so cheerful and pleasant in his humour that everybody called him, "Happy Prince Cherry." But, one unlucky day, he was out hunting and found no sport, which vexed him so much that he showed his ill temper by his looks and ways. He fancied his ring felt very tight and uncomfortable, but as it did not prick him, he took no heed of this : until, re-entering his palace, his little pet dog, Bibi, jumped up upon him, and was sharply told to get away. The creature, accustomed to nothing but caresses, tried to attract his attention by pulling at his garments, when Prince Cherry turned and gave it a severe kick. At this moment he felt in his finger a prick like a pin.

"What nonsense!" said he to himself. "The fairy must be making game of me. Why, what great evil have I done ? I, the master of a great empire, cannot I kick my own dog ? "

A voice replied, or else Prince Cherry imagined it, "No, sire; the master of a great empire has a right to do good, but not evil. I—a fairy—am as much above you as you are above your dog. I might punish you, kill you, if I chose ; but I prefer leaving you to amend your ways. You have been guilty of three faults to-day —bad temper, passion, cruelty : do better to-morrow."

The prince promised, and kept his word awhile ; but he had been brought up by a foolish nurse, who indulged him in every way, and was always telling him that he would be a king one day, when he might do as he liked in all things. He found out now that even a king cannot always do that ; it vexed him, and made him angry. His ring began to prick him so often that his little finger was continually bleeding. He disliked this, as was natural; and soon began to consider whether it would not be easier to throw the ring away altogether than to be constantly annoyed by it. It was such a queer thing for a king to have always a spot of blood on his finger! At last, unable to put up with it any more, he took his ring off, and hid it where he would never see it; and believed himself the happiest of men, for he could now do exactly what he liked. He did it, and became every day more and more miserable.

One day he saw a young girl, so beautiful that, being always accustomed to have his own way, he immediately determined to espouse her. He never doubted that she would be only too glad to be made a queen, for she was very poor. But Zelia—that was her name—answered, to his great astonishment, that she would rather not marry him.

"Do I displease you?" asked the prince, into whose mind it had never entered that he could displease anybody.

"Not at all, my prince," said the honest peasant-maiden. "You are very handsome, very charming; but you are not like your father the Good King. I will not be your queen, for you would make me miserable."

At these words the prince's love seemed all to turn to hatred: he gave orders to his guards to convey Zelia to a prison near the palace; and then took counsel with his foster-brother, the one of all his ill companions who most incited him to do wrong.

"Sir," said this man, "if I were in your majesty's place, I would never vex myself about a poor silly girl. Feed her on bread and water till she comes to her senses; and if she still refuses you, let her die in torment, as a warning to your other subjects should they venture to dispute your will. You will be disgraced should you suffer yourself to be conquered by a simple girl."

"But," said Prince Cherry, "shall I not be disgraced if I harm a creature so perfectly innocent?"

"No one is innocent who disputes your majesty's authority," said the courtier, bowing ; "and it is better to commit an injustice than allow it to be supposed you can ever be contradicted with impunity."

This touched Cherry on his weak point—his good impulses faded : he resolved once more to ask Zelia if she would marry him, and, if she again refused, to sell her as a slave. Arrived at the cell in which she was confined, what was his astonishment to find her gone ! He knew not who to accuse, for he had kept the key in his pocket the whole time. At last, the foster-brother suggested that the escape of Zelia might have been contrived by an old man, Suliman by name, the prince's former tutor, who was the only one who now ventured to blame him for anything that he did. Cherry sent immediately, and ordered his old friend to be brought to him, loaded heavily with irons. Then, full of fury, he went and shut himself up in his own chamber, where he went raging to and fro, till startled by a noise like a clap of thunder. The Fairy Candide stood before him.

"Prince," said she, in a severe voice, "I promised your father to give you good counsels, and to punish you if you refused to follow them. My counsels were forgotten, my punishments despised. Under the figure of a man, you have been no better than the beasts you chase : like a lion in fury, a wolf in gluttony, a serpent in revenge, and a bull in brutality. Take, therefore, in your new form the likeness of all these animals."

Scarcely had Prince Cherry heard these words, than to his horror he found himself transformed into what the fairy had named. He was a creature with the head of a lion, the horns of a bull, the feet of a wolf, and the tail of a serpent. At the same time he felt himself transported to a distant forest, where, standing on the bank of a stream, he saw reflected in the water his own frightful shape, and heard a voice saying :

PRINCE CHERRY

"Look at thyself, and know thy soul has become a thousand times uglier even than thy body."

Cherry recognised the voice of Candide, and in his rage would have sprung upon her and devoured her ; but he saw nothing, and the same voice said behind him :

"Cease thy feeble fury, and learn to conquer thy pride by being in submission to thine own subjects."

Hearing no more, he soon quitted the stream, hoping at least to get rid of the sight of himself ; but he had scarcely gone twenty paces when he tumbled into a pitfall that was laid to catch bears ; the bear-hunters, descending from some trees hard by, caught him, chained him, and, only too delighted to get hold of such a curious-looking animal, led him along with them to the capital of his own kingdom.

There great rejoicings were taking place, and the bear-hunters, asking what it was all about, were told that it was because Prince Cherry, the torment of his subjects, had just been struck dead by a thunderbolt—just punishment of all his crimes. Four courtiers, his wicked companions, had wished to divide his throne between them ; but the people had risen up against them, and offered the crown to Suliman, the old tutor whom Cherry had ordered to be arrested.

All this the poor monster heard. He even saw Suliman sitting upon his own throne, and trying to calm the populace by representing to them that it was not certain Prince Cherry was dead ; that he might return one day to re-assume with honour the crown which Suliman only consented to wear as a sort of viceroy.

"I know his heart," said the honest and faithful old man ; "it is tainted, but not corrupt. If alive, he may reform yet, and be all his father over again to you, his people, whom he has caused to suffer so much."

These words touched the poor beast so deeply that he ceased to beat himself against the iron bars of the cage in

183

which the hunters carried him about, became gentle as a lamb, and suffered himself to be taken quietly to a menagerie, where were kept all sorts of strange and ferocious animals — a place which he had himself often visited as a boy, but never thought he should be shut up there himself.

However, he owned he had deserved it all, and began to make amends by showing himself very obedient to his keeper. This man was almost as great a brute as the animals he had charge of, and when he was in ill humour he used to beat them without rhyme or reason. One day, while he was sleeping, a tiger broke loose, and leaped upon him, eager to devour him. Cherry at first felt a thrill of pleasure at the thought of being revenged ; then, seeing how helpless the man was, he wished himself free, that he might defend him. Immediately the doors of his cage opened. The keeper, waking up, saw the strange beast leap out, and imagined, of course, that he was going to be slain at once. Instead, he saw the tiger lying dead, and the strange beast creeping up, and laying itself at his feet to be caressed. But as he lifted up his hand to stroke it, a voice was heard saying, " Good actions never go unrewarded " ; and, instead of the frightful monster, there crouched on the ground nothing but a pretty little dog.

Cherry, delighted to find himself thus metamorphosed, caressed the keeper in every possible way, till at last the man took him up into his arms and carried him to the king, to whom he related this wonderful story, from beginning to end. The queen wished to have the charming little dog : and Cherry would have been exceedingly happy, could he have forgotten that he was originally a man and a king. He was lodged most elegantly, had the richest of collars to adorn his neck, and heard himself praised continually. But his beauty rather brought him into trouble, for the queen, afraid lest he might grow too large for a pet, took advice of dog-doctors, who ordered that he should be fed entirely upon bread, and that very sparingly ; so poor Cherry was sometimes nearly starved.

One day, when they gave him his crust for breakfast, a fancy seized him to go and eat it in the palace garden ; so he took the bread in his mouth, and trotted away towards a stream which he knew, and where he sometimes stopped to drink. But instead of the stream he saw a splendid palace, glittering with gold and precious stones. Entering the doors was a crowd of men and women, magnificently dressed ; and within there was singing and dancing, and good cheer of all sorts. Yet, however grandly and gaily the people went in, Cherry noticed that those who came out were pale, thin, ragged, half-naked, covered with wounds and sores. Some of them dropped dead at once ; others dragged themselves on a little way and then lay down, dying of hunger, and vainly begged a morsel of bread from others who were entering in— who never took the least notice of them.

Cherry perceived one woman, who was trying feebly to gather and eat some green herbs. " Poor thing ! " said he to himself ; " I know what it is to be hungry, and I want my breakfast badly enough ; but still it will not kill me to wait till dinner-time, and my crust may save the life of this poor woman."

So the little dog ran up to her, and dropped his bread at her feet ; she picked it up, and ate it with avidity. Soon she looked quite recovered, and Cherry, delighted, was trotting back again to his kennel, when he heard loud cries, and saw a young girl dragged by four men to the door of the palace, which they were trying to compel her to enter. Oh, how he wished himself a monster again, as when he slew the tiger !—for the young girl was no other than his beloved Zelia. Alas ! what could a poor little dog do to defend her ? But he ran forward and barked at the men, and bit their heels, until at last they chased him away with heavy blows. And then he lay down outside the palace-door, determined to watch and see what had become of Zelia.

Conscience pricked him now. " What ! " thought he, " I am furious against these wicked men, who are carrying her away ; and did I not do the same myself ? Did I not cast her into prison, and intend to sell her as a slave ? Who knows how much more wickedness I might not have done to her and others, if heaven's justice had not stopped me in time ? "

While he lay thinking and repenting, he heard a window open, and saw Zelia throw out of it a bit of dainty meat. Cherry, who felt hungry enough by this time, was just about to eat it, when the woman to whom he had given his crust snatched him up in her arms.

" Poor little beast ! " cried she, patting him, " every bit of food in that palace is poisoned : you shall not touch a morsel."

And at the same time the voice in the air repeated again, " Good actions never go unrewarded " ; and Cherry found himself changed into a beautiful little white pigeon. He remembered with joy that white was the colour of the Fairy Candide, and began to hope that she was taking him into favour again.

So he stretched his wings, delighted that he might now have a chance of approaching his fair Zelia. He flew up to the palace-windows, and, finding one of them open, entered and sought everywhere, but he could not find Zelia. Then, in despair, he flew out again, resolved to go over the world until he beheld her once more.

He took flight at once, and traversed many countries, swiftly as a bird can, but found no trace of his beloved. At length in a desert, sitting beside an old hermit in his cave, and partaking with him his frugal repast, Cherry saw a poor peasant-girl, and recognised Zelia. Transported with joy, he flew in, perched on her shoulder, and expressed his delight and affection by a thousand caresses.

She, charmed with the pretty little pigeon, caressed it in her turn, and promised it that, if it would stay with her, she would love it always.

"What have you done, Zelia?" said the hermit, smiling; and while he spoke the white pigeon vanished, and there stood Prince Cherry in his own natural form. "Your enchantment ended, prince, when Zelia promised to love you. Indeed, she has loved you always, but your many faults constrained her to hide her love. These are now amended, and you may both live happy if you will, because your union is founded upon mutual esteem."

Cherry and Zelia threw themselves at the feet of the hermit, whose form also began to change. His soiled garments became of dazzling whiteness, and his long beard and withered face grew into the flowing hair and lovely countenance of the Fairy Candide.

"Rise up, my children," said she; "I must now transport you to your palace, and restore to Prince Cherry his father's crown, of which he is now worthy."

She had scarcely ceased speaking when they found themselves in the chamber of Suliman, who, delighted to find again his beloved pupil and master, willingly resigned the throne, and became the most faithful of his subjects.

King Cherry and Queen Zelia reigned together for many years, and it is said that the former was so blameless and strict in all his duties, that though he constantly wore the ring which Candide had restored to him it never once pricked his finger enough to make it bleed.

LITTLE SNOWDROP

ONCE upon a time, in the middle of winter, when the flakes of snow fell like feathers from the sky, a queen sat at a window set in an ebony frame, and sewed. While she was sewing and watching the snow fall, she pricked her finger with her needle, and three drops of blood dropped on the snow. And because the crimson looked so beautiful on the white snow, she thought, " Oh that I had a child as white as snow, as red as blood, and as black as the wood of this ebony frame ! "

Soon afterwards she had a little daughter, who was as white as snow, as red as blood, and had hair as black as ebony. And when the child was born, the queen died.

After a year had gone by, the king took another wife. She was a handsome lady, but proud and haughty, and could not endure that any one should surpass her in beauty. She had a wonderful mirror, and whenever she walked up to it, and looked at herself in it, she said :

> " Little glass upon the wall,
> Who is fairest among us all ? "

Then the mirror replied :

> " Lady queen, so grand and tall,
> Thou art the fairest of them all."

And she was satisfied, for she knew the mirror always told the truth. But Snowdrop grew ever taller and fairer, and at seven years old was beautiful as the day, and

more beautiful than the queen herself.   So once, when the
queen asked of her mirror :

> "Little glass upon the wall,
> Who is fairest among us all ? "

it answered :

> " Lady queen, you are grand and tall,
> But Snowdrop is fairest of you all."

Then the queen was startled, and turned yellow and
green with envy.   From that hour she so hated Snowdrop,
that she burned with secret wrath whenever she saw the
maiden.   Pride and envy grew apace like weeds in her
heart, till she had no rest day or night.   So she called a
huntsman and said, " Take the child out in the forest, for
I will endure her no longer in my sight.   Kill her, and
bring me her lungs and liver as tokens that you have done
it."

The huntsman obeyed, and led the child away ; but
when he had drawn his hunting-knife, and was about to
pierce Snowdrop's innocent heart, she began to weep, and
said, " Ah ! dear huntsman, spare my life, and I will run
deep into the wild forest, and never more come home."

The huntsman took pity on her, because she looked
so lovely, and said, " Run away then, poor child ! "—
" The wild beasts will soon make an end of thee," he
thought ; but it seemed as if a stone had been rolled from
his heart, because he had avoided taking her life ; and as
a little bear came by just then, he killed it, took out its
liver and lungs, and carried them as tokens to the
queen.   She made the cook dress them with salt, and
then the wicked woman ate them, and thought she had
eaten Snowdrop's lungs and liver.   The poor child was
now all alone in the great forest, and she felt frightened
as she looked at all the leafy trees, and knew not what to
do.   So she began to run, and ran over the sharp stones,
and through the thorns ; and the wild beasts passed close

to her, but did her no harm. She ran as long as her feet could carry her, and when evening closed in, she saw a little house, and went into it to rest herself. Everything in the house was very small, but I cannot tell you how pretty and clean it was.

There stood a little table, covered with a white table-cloth, on which were seven little plates (each little plate with its own little spoon)—also seven little knives and forks, and seven little cups. Round the walls stood seven little beds close together, with sheets as white as snow. Snowdrop being so hungry and thirsty, ate a little of the vegetables and bread on each plate, and drank a drop of wine from every cup, for she did not like to empty one entirely.

Then, being very tired, she laid herself down in one of the beds, but could not make herself comfortable, for one was too long, and another too short. The seventh, luckily, was just right; so there she stayed, said her prayers, and fell asleep.

When it was grown quite dark, home came the masters of the house, seven dwarfs, who delved and mined for iron among the mountains. They lighted their seven candles, and as soon as there was a light in the kitchen, they saw that some one had been there, for it was not quite so orderly as they had left it.

The first said, "Who has been sitting on my stool?"

The second, "Who has eaten off my plate?"

The third, "Who has taken part of my loaf?"

The fourth, "Who has touched my vegetables?"

The fifth, "Who has used my fork?"

The sixth, "Who has cut with my knife?"

The seventh, "Who has drunk out of my little cup?"

Then the first dwarf looked about, and saw that there was a slight hollow in his bed, so he asked, "Who has been lying in my little bed?"

The others came running, and each called out, "Some one has also been lying in my bed."

But the seventh, when he looked in his bed, saw Snowdrop there, fast asleep. He called the others, who flocked round with cries of surprise, fetched their seven candles, and cast the light on Snowdrop.

"Oh, heaven!" they cried, "what a lovely child!" and were so pleased that they would not wake her, but let her sleep on in the little bed. The seventh dwarf slept with all his companions in turn, an hour with each, and so they spent the night. When it was morning, Snowdrop woke up, and was frightened when she saw the seven dwarfs. They were very friendly, however, and inquired her name.

"Snowdrop," answered she.

"How have you found your way to our house?" further asked the dwarfs.

So she told them how her stepmother had tried to kill her, how the huntsman had spared her life, and how she had run the whole day through, till at last she had found their little house.

Then the dwarfs said, "If thou wilt keep our house, cook, make the beds, wash, sew and knit, and make all neat and clean, thou canst stay with us, and shalt want for nothing."

"I will, right willingly," said Snowdrop. So she dwelt with them, and kept their house in order. Every morning they went out among the mountains, to seek iron and gold, and came home ready for supper in the evening.

The maiden being left alone all day long, the good dwarfs warned her, saying, "Beware of thy wicked stepmother, who will soon find out that thou art here; take care that thou lettest nobody in."

The queen, however, after having, as she thought, eaten Snowdrop's lungs and liver, had no doubt that she was again the first and fairest woman in the world; so she walked up to her mirror, and said :

THE FAIRY BOOK

> "Little glass upon the wall,
> Who is fairest among us all?"

The mirror replied:

> "Lady queen, so grand and tall,
> Here, you are fairest of them all;
> But over the hills, with the seven dwarfs old,
> Lives Snowdrop, fairer a hundredfold."

She trembled, knowing the mirror never told a falsehood; she felt sure that the huntsman had deceived her, and that Snowdrop was still alive. She pondered once more, late and early, early and late, how best to kill Snowdrop; for envy gave her no rest, day or night, while she herself was not the fairest lady in the land. When she had planned what to do, she painted her face, dressed herself like an old pedlar-woman, and altered her appearance so much, that no one could have known her. In this disguise she went over the seven hills, to where the seven dwarfs dwelt, knocked at the door, and cried, "Good wares, cheap! very cheap!"

Snowdrop looked out of the window and cried, "Good-morning, good woman: what have you to sell?"

"Good wares, smart wares," answered the queen— "bodice laces of all colours"; and drew out one which was woven of coloured silk.

"I may surely let this honest dame in!" thought Snowdrop; so she unfastened the door, and bought for herself the pretty lace.

"Child," said the old woman, "what a figure thou art! Let me lace thee for once properly." Snowdrop feared no harm, so stepped in front of her, and allowed her bodice to be fastened up with the new lace.

But the old woman laced so quick and laced so tight, that Snowdrop's breath was stopped, and she fell down as if dead. "Now I am fairest at last," said the old woman to herself, and sped away.

WARWICK GOBLE

"They were very friendly, however, and inquired her name. 'Snowdrop,' answered she."

LITTLE SNOWDROP

The seven dwarfs came home soon after, at eventide, but how alarmed were they to find their poor Snowdrop lifeless on the ground! They lifted her up, and, seeing that she was laced too tightly, cut the lace of her bodice; she began to breathe faintly, and slowly returned to life. When the dwarfs heard what had happened, they said, "The old pedlar-woman was none other than the wicked queen. Be careful of thyself, and open the door to no one if we are not at home."

The cruel stepmother walked up to her mirror when she reached home, and said :

> "Little glass upon the wall,
> Who is fairest among us all ?"

To which it answered, as usual :

> "Lady queen, so grand and tall,
> Here, you are fairest of them all ;
> But over the hills, with the seven dwarfs old,
> Lives Snowdrop, fairer a hundredfold."

When she heard this, she was so alarmed that all the blood rushed to her heart, for she saw plainly that Snowdrop was still alive.

"This time," said she, "I will think of some means that shall destroy her utterly"; and with the help of witchcraft, in which she was skilful, she made a poisoned comb. Then she changed her dress and took the shape of another old woman.

Again she crossed the seven hills to the home of the seven dwarfs, knocked at the door, and cried, "Good wares, very cheap !"

Snowdrop looked out and said, "Go away—I dare let no one in."

"You may surely be allowed to look !" answered the old woman, and she drew out the poisoned comb and held it up. The girl was so pleased with it that she let herself be cajoled, and opened the door.

When the bargain was struck, the dame said, "Now let me dress your hair properly for once." Poor Snowdrop took no heed, and let the old woman begin; but the comb had scarcely touched her hair before the poison worked, and she fell down senseless.

"Paragon of beauty!" said the wicked woman, "all is over with thee now," and went away.

Luckily, it was near evening, and the seven dwarfs soon came home. When they found Snowdrop lifeless on the ground, they at once distrusted her stepmother. They searched, and found the poisoned comb; and as soon as they had drawn it out, Snowdrop came to herself, and told them what had happened. Again they warned her to be careful, and open the door to no one.

The queen placed herself before the mirror at home and said :

> "Little glass upon the wall,
> Who is fairest among us all?"

But it again answered :

> "Lady queen, so grand and tall,
> Here, you are fairest of them all;
> But over the hills, with the seven dwarfs old,
> Lives Snowdrop, fairer a thousandfold."

When she heard the mirror speak thus, she quivered with rage. "Snowdrop shall die," she cried, "if it costs my own life!"

Then she went to a secret and lonely chamber, where no one ever disturbed her, and compounded an apple of deadly poison. Ripe and rosy-cheeked, it was so beautiful to look upon, that all who saw it longed for it; but it brought death to any who should eat it. When the apple was ready, she painted her face, disguised herself as a peasant-woman, and journeyed over the seven hills to where the seven dwarfs dwelt. At the sound of the knock, Snowdrop put her head out of the window, and said, "I cannot open the door to anybody, for the seven dwarfs have forbidden me to do so."

"Very well," replied the peasant-woman ; "I only want to be rid of my apples. Here, I will give you one of them !"

"No !" said Snowdrop, "I dare not take it."

"Art thou afraid of being poisoned?" asked the old woman. "Look here ; I will cut the apple in two, and you shall eat the rosy side, and I the white."

Now the fruit was so cunningly made, that only the rosy side was poisoned. Snowdrop longed for the pretty apple ; and when she saw the peasant-woman eating it, she could resist no longer, but stretched out her hand and took the poisoned half. She had scarcely tasted it, when she fell lifeless to the ground.

The queen, laughing loudly, watched her with a barbarous look, and cried, "O thou who art white as snow, red as blood, and black as ebony, the seven dwarfs cannot awaken thee this time !"

And when she asked the mirror at home :

> "Little glass upon the wall,
> Who is fairest among us all ?"

the mirror at last replied :

> "Lady queen, so grand and tall,
> You are the fairest of them all."

So her envious heart had as much repose as an envious heart can ever know.

When the dwarfs came home in the evening, they found Snowdrop lying breathless and motionless on the ground. They lifted her up, searched whether she had anything poisonous about her, unlaced her, combed her hair, washed her with water and with wine ; but all was useless, for they could not bring the darling back to life. They laid her on a bier, and all the seven placed themselves round it, and mourned for her three long days.

Then they would have buried her, but that she still looked so fresh and life-like, and had such lovely rosy cheeks. "We cannot lower her into the dark earth," said they; and caused a transparent coffin of glass to be made, so that she could be seen on all sides, and laid her in it, writing her name outside in letters of gold, which told that she was the daughter of a king. Then they placed the coffin on the mountain above, and one of them always stayed by it and guarded it. But there was little need to guard it, for even the wild animals came and mourned for Snowdrop : the birds likewise—first an owl, and then a raven, and afterwards a dove.

Long long years did Snowdrop lie in her coffin unchanged, looking as though asleep, for she was still white as snow, red as blood, and her hair was black as ebony. At last the son of a king chanced to wander into the forest, and came to the dwarfs' house for a night's shelter. He saw the coffin on the mountain with the beautiful Snowdrop in it, and read what was written there in letters of gold. Then he said to the dwarfs, "Let me have the coffin! I will give you whatever you like to ask for it."

But the dwarfs answered, "We would not part with it for all the gold in the world."

He said again, "Yet give it me; for I cannot live without seeing Snowdrop, and though she is dead, I will prize and honour her as my beloved."

Then the good dwarfs took pity on him, and gave him the coffin. The prince had it borne away by his servants. They happened to stumble over a bush, and the shock forced the bit of poisoned apple which Snowdrop had tasted out of her throat. Immediately she opened her eyes, raised the coffin-lid, and sat up alive once more. "Oh, heaven!" cried she, "where am I?"

The prince answered joyfully, "Thou art with me," and told her what had happened, saying, "I love thee

196

more dearly than anything else in the world. Come with me to my father's castle, and be my wife."

Snowdrop, well pleased, went with him, and they were married with much state and grandeur.

The wicked stepmother was invited to the feast. Richly dressed, she stood before the mirror, and asked of it :

> "Little glass upon the wall,
>   Who is fairest among us all ? "

The mirror answered :

> "Lady queen, so grand and tall,
>   Here, you are fairest among them all ;
>   But the young queen over the mountains old,
>   Is fairer than you a thousandfold."

The evil-hearted woman uttered a curse, and could scarcely endure her anguish. She first resolved not to attend the wedding, but curiosity would not allow her to rest. She determined to travel, and see who that young queen could be, who was the most beautiful in all the world. When she came, and found that it was Snowdrop alive again, she stood petrified with terror and despair. Then two iron shoes, heated burning hot, were drawn out of the fire with a pair of tongs, and laid before her feet. She was forced to put them on, and to go and dance at Snowdrop's wedding—dancing, dancing on these red-hot shoes till she fell down dead.

THE BLUE BIRD

A POWERFUL and wealthy king, having lost his wife, was so inconsolable, that he shut himself up for eight entire days, in a little cabinet, where he spent his time in knocking his head against the wall, until the courtiers were afraid he would kill himself! They accordingly placed stuffed mattresses over every wall, and allowed all his subjects, who desired, to pay him a visit, trusting that something would be said to alleviate his grief. But neither grave nor lively discourse made any impression upon him; he scarcely heard what was spoken. At last there presented herself before him a lady, covered from head to foot in a long crape veil, who wept and sobbed so much that the king noticed her. She told him that she did not come, like the rest, to console him, but rather to encourage his grief. She herself had lost the best of husbands, and here she began to weep so profusely, that it was a wonder her eyes were not melted out of her head. The king began to weep in company, and to talk to her of his dear wife— she did the same of her dear husband : in fact they talked so much, that they talked their sorrow quite away. Then, lifting up her veil, she showed lovely blue eyes and dark eyelashes. The king noticed her more and more— he spoke less and less of the departed queen ; by and by he ceased to speak of her at all. The end was, that he courted the inconsolable lady in the black veil, and married her.

By his first marriage he had one daughter, called

THE BLUE BIRD

Florina, or the little Flora, because she was so fresh and lovely ; at the time of his second marriage she was quite fifteen years old. The new queen also had a daughter, who was being brought up by her godmother, the fairy Soussio—her name was Troutina, because her complexion was all spotted like a trout's back. Indeed, she was altogether ugly and disagreeable ; and when contrasted with Florina, the difference between the two made the mother so envious, that she and Troutina spared no pains to make the princess's life unhappy, and to speak ill of her to her father.

One day the king observed that both girls were now old enough to be married, and that he intended to choose for one of them the first prince who visited his court.

" Be it so," said the queen ; " and as my daughter is older, handsomer, and more amiable than yours, she shall have the first choice." The king disputed nothing ; indeed, he never did—the queen ruled him in all things.

Some time after, news came that King Charming would shortly arrive, and that he was as charming as his name. When the queen heard this news, she sent for milliners, dressmakers, jewellers, and decked Troutina from head to foot ; but to Florina she allowed not a single new frock. The poor princess had to put on her old one, which was very old and shabby indeed ; she was so much ashamed of it that she hid herself in a corner of the saloon, lest King Charming should see her. But he did not, being overwhelmed with the ceremonious reception given him by the queen, who presented to him Troutina, all blazing with jewels, yet so ugly that King Charming involuntarily turned away his eyes.

" But, madam, is there not another princess, called Florina ? "

They pointed to the corner where Florina was hidden, and she came out, blushing so much, that the young king was dazzled with her beauty, in spite of her shabby gown.

He rose, and made her a profound reverence, paying her besides so many elegant compliments, that the queen became very much displeased. King Charming took no heed, but conversed with Florina for three hours without stopping. Indeed, his admiration of her was so plain, that the queen and Troutina begged of the king that she might be shut up in a tower during the whole time of his visit ; so, as soon as she had returned to her apartment, four men in masks entered, and carried her off, leaving her in a dark cell, and in the utmost desolation.

Meantime King Charming eagerly awaited her reappearance, but he saw her no more ; and by the queen's orders, every one about him spoke all the evil they could of poor Florina, but he refused to believe one word. "No," said he, "nature could not have united a base nature to such a sweet innocent face. I will rather suppose that she is maligned by her stepmother and by Troutina, who is so ugly herself that no wonder she bears envy towards the fairest woman in the world."

Meanwhile Florina, shut up in her tower, lamented bitterly. "Ah, would I had been sent here before I saw this amiable prince, who was so kind to me! It is to prevent my meeting him again that the queen treats me so cruelly. Alas ! the little beauty I have has cost me sore !"

The queen, to win King Charming for her daughter, made him many presents ; among the rest an order of knighthood, a golden heart, enamelled in flame-colour, surrounded with many arrows, but pierced by one only, the motto being "*She alone.*" The heart was made of a single ruby, as big as an ostrich's egg. Each arrow was a diamond, a finger's length, and the chain was of pearls, each weighing a pound. When the young king received this very handsome present, he was much perplexed, until they told him it came from the princess whom he had lately seen, and who requested him to be her knight.

" Florina ! " cried he, enchanted.

" No, Troutina."

" Then I am sorry I cannot accept the honour,"
replied King Charming. " A monarch is surely at liberty
to form his own engagements. I know what is a knight's
duty to his lady, and should wish to fulfil it ; as I cannot
fulfil it to Troutina, I would rather decline the favour she
offers me than become unworthy of it."

Civil as this answer was, it irritated the queen and her
daughter exceedingly ; and when, since in all his audiences
with their majesties he never saw Florina, he at last
inquired where the younger princess was, the queen
answered fiercely, that she was shut up in prison, and
would remain there till Troutina was married.

" And for what reason ? " asked King Charming.

" I do not know ; and if I did, I would not tell you,"
replied the queen, more angrily than ever ; so that King
Charming quitted her presence as soon as ever he could.

When he was alone, he sent for one of his attendants,
whom he trusted very much, and begged him to gain
information from some court lady about the Princess
Florina. This scheme succeeded so well, that Florina
was persuaded to promise she would speak to him for a
few moments next night, from a small window at the
bottom of the tower. But the faithless lady-in-waiting
betrayed her to the queen, who locked her up in her
chamber, and determined to send her own daughter to
the window instead. The night was so dark that King
Charming never found out the difference, but made to
Troutina all the tender speeches that he meant for Florina,
offering her his crown and his heart, and ending by
placing his own ring on her finger, as a pledge of eternal
fidelity. He also made her agree to fly with him next
night, in a chariot drawn by winged frogs, of which a
great magician, one of his friends, had made him a present.
He thought she talked very little, and that little not in

THE FAIRY BOOK

quite so pleasant a voice as formerly ; still, he was too much in love to notice much, and departed very joyful in having obtained her promise.

Next night Troutina, thickly veiled, quitted the palace by a secret door. King Charming met her, received her in his arms, and vowed to love her for ever. Then he lifted her into the fairy chariot, and they sailed about in the air for some hours. But as he was not likely to wish to sail about for ever, he at last proposed that they should descend to earth, and be married. Troutina agreed with all her heart, but wished that the ceremony should be performed at her godmother's, the fairy Soussio. So they entered together into the fairy-palace, and she told her godmother privately how all had happened, and how she had won King Charming, begging the fairy to pacify him when he found out his mistake.

"My child," replied the godmother, "that is more easily said than done; he is too deeply in love with Florina."

Meantime the king was left waiting in a chamber with diamond walls, so thin and transparent, that through them he saw Troutina and Soussio conversing together. He stood like a man in a dream : "What! am I betrayed ? Has this enemy to my peace carried away my dear Florina ?"

How great was his despair, when Soussio said to him in a commanding voice, "King Charming, behold the princess Troutina, to whom you have promised your faith : marry her immediately ! "

"Do you think me a fool ? " cried the king ; "I have promised her nothing. She is——"

"Stop—if you show me any disrespect——"

"I will respect you as much as a fairy deserves to be respected, if you will only give me back my princess."

"Am not I she?" said Troutina. "It was to me you gave this ring ; to me you spoke at the window."

THE BLUE BIRD

"I have been wickedly deceived!" cried the king; "come, my winged frogs, we will depart immediately."

"You cannot," said Soussio; and, touching him, he found himself fixed as if his feet were glued to the pavement.

"You may turn me into stone!" exclaimed he; "but I will love no one, except Florina."

Soussio employed persuasions, threats, promises, entreaties. Troutina wept, groaned, shrieked, and then tried quiet sulkiness; but the king uttered not a word. For twenty days and twenty nights he stood there, without sleeping, or eating, or once sitting down—they talking all the while.

At length, Soussio, quite worn out, said, "Choose, seven years of penitence and punishment, or marry my god-daughter."

"I choose," answered the king; "and I will not marry your god-daughter."

"Then fly out of this window, in the shape of a Blue Bird."

Immediately the king's figure changed. His arms formed themselves into wings; his legs and feet turned black and thin, and claws grew upon them; his body wasted into the slender shape of a bird, and was covered with bright blue feathers; his eyes became round and beady; his nose an ivory beak; and his crown was a white plume on the top of his head. He began to speak in a singing voice, and then uttering a doleful cry, fled away as far as possible from the fatal palace of Soussio.

But, though he looked only a blue bird, the king was his own natural self still, and remembered all his misfortunes, and did not cease to lament for his beautiful Florina. Flying from tree to tree, he sang melancholy songs about her and himself, and wished he were dead many a time.

The fairy Soussio sent back Troutina to her mother, who was furious. "Florina shall repent having pleased

King Charming!" cried she; and dressing her own
daughter in rich garments, with a gold crown on her head,
and King Charming's ring on her finger, she took her to
the tower. "Florina, your sister is come to see and bring
you marriage presents, for she is now the wife of King
Charming."

Florina, doubting no more her lover's loss, fell down
in a swoon, and the queen immediately went to tell her
father that she was mad for love, and must be watched
closely lest she should in some way disgrace herself. The
king said, her stepmother might do with her exactly what
she pleased.

When the princess recovered from her swoon, she
began to weep, and wept all night long, sitting at the
open window of her tower. The Blue Bird, who kept
continually flying about the palace, but only at night time,
lest any one should see him, happened to come and perch
upon a tall cypress opposite the window, and heard her;
but it was too dark to see who she was, and at daylight
she shut the window. Next night, it was broad moonlight,
and then he saw clearly the figure of a young girl, weeping
sore, and knew that it was his beloved Florina.

When she paused in her lamentations, "Adorable
princess," said he, "why do you mourn? Your troubles
are not without remedy."

"Who speaks to me so gently?" asked she.

"A king, who loves you, and will never love any
other."

So saying he flew up to the window, and at first
frightened the princess very much, for she could not
understand such an extraordinary thing as a bird who
talked in words like a man, yet kept still the piping voice
of a nightingale. But soon she began stroking his beautiful
plumage, and caressing him.

"Who are you, charming bird?"

"You have spoken my name. I am King Charming,

condemned to be a bird for seven years, because I will not renounce you."

"Ah! do not deceive me. I know you have married Troutina. She came to visit me with your diamonds on her neck, and your ring on her finger, wearing the golden crown and royal mantle which you had given her, while I was laden with iron chains."

"It is all false," sang the Blue Bird, and told her his whole story, which comforted her so much that she thought no more of her misfortunes. They conversed till daybreak, and promised faithfully every night to meet again thus.

Meantime the princess could not sleep for thinking of her Blue Bird. "Suppose sportsmen should shoot him, or eagles and kites attack him, and vultures devour him just as if he were a mere bird and not a great king? What should I do if I saw his poor feathers scattered on the ground, and knew that he was no more?" So she grieved all day long.

The beautiful Blue Bird, hid in a hollow tree, spent the hours in thinking of his princess. "How happy I am to have found her again, and found her so engaging and so sweet." And as he wished to pay her all the attentions that a lover delights in, he flew to his own kingdom, entered his palace by an open window, and sought for some diamond ear-rings, which he brought back in his beak, and, when night came, offered them to Florina. So night after night he brought her something beautiful, and they talked together till day, when he flew back to the hollow tree, where he sang her praises in a voice so sweet that the passers-by thought it was not a bird but a spirit. Rumours went about that the place was haunted, and no one would go near the spot. Thus, for two years, Florina spent her time, and never once regretted her captivity. Her Blue Bird visited her every night, and they loved one another dearly. And though she saw nobody, and he lived in the hollow of a tree, they always found plenty to say to one another.

The malicious queen tried with all her might to get Troutina married, but in vain. Nobody would have her. "If it were Florina, now," said the kings, or the kings' ambassadors, "we should be most happy to sign the contract."

"That girl thwarts us still," said the queen. "She must have some secret correspondence with foreign suitors. But we will find her out and punish her."

The mother and daughter finished talking so late that it was midnight before they reached Florina's apartment. She had dressed herself as usual, with the utmost care, to please her Blue Bird, who liked to see her lovely ; and she had adorned herself with all the pretty things he had given her. He perched on the window-sill, and she sat at the window, and they were singing together a duet, which the queen heard outside. She burst the door open, and rushed into the chamber.

The first thing Florina did was to open her little window that the Blue Bird might fly away. But he would not. He had seen the queen and Troutina, and though he could not defend his princess, he refused to leave her. The two rushed upon her like furies. Her wonderful beauty and her splendid jewels startled them. "Whence came all these ornaments ? " cried they.

"I found them," replied Florina, and refused to answer more.

"Some one has given them to you that you might join in treason against your father and the kingdom."

"Am I likely to do this ? I, a poor princess, kept in captivity for two years, with you as my gaoler ? "

"In captivity," repeated the queen. "Why, then, do you dress yourself so fine, and adorn your chamber with flowers ? "

"I have leisure enough : I may just as well spend

some of it in adorning myself, instead of bemoaning my misfortune—innocent as I am."

"Innocent, indeed!" cried the queen, and began to search the room. In it she found all King Charming's presents—diamonds, rubies, emeralds, amethysts—in short, jewels without end. Meantime, from the window, the Blue Bird, who had the eye of a lynx, sang aloud, "Beware, Florina!"

"You see, madam," said Florina, "even the spirits of the air take pity upon me."

"I see that you are in league with demons; but your father shall judge you"; and, very much frightened, the queen left her, and went to hold counsel with Troutina as to what was to be done. They agreed to put in Florina's chamber a waiting-maid, who should watch her from morning till night. When the princess learnt this she was in great grief.

"Alas!" cried she, "I can no longer talk with my bird who loved me so; and our love was consolation for all our misfortunes. What will he do? What shall I do?" And she melted into floods of tears.

She dared not open the window, though she heard continually his wings fluttering round it. For more than a month she waited; but the serving-maid watched her night and day. At last, overcome with weariness, the girl fell asleep, and then Florina opened her little window, and sang in a low voice:

> "Blue Bird, Blue Bird,
> Come to my side."

The Blue Bird flew to the window-sill, and they lavished on one another a hundred caresses, and talked together till dawn. Next night it happened the same, till they began to hope that the waiting-maid, who seemed to enjoy her sleep so much, would sleep every night to come. But on the third night, hearing a noise, she wakened,

and saw by the light of the moon the Princess Florina
sitting at the window with a beautiful Blue Bird, who
warbled in her ear and touched her gently with his beak.
The spy listened and heard all their conversation, very
much astonished that a princess could be so fond of a
mere bird. When day came, she related all to the
queen and Troutina, who concluded that the bird could
be no other than King Charming. They sent the girl
back, told her to express no curiosity, but to feign sleep,
and to go to bed earlier than usual. Then the poor
deceived princess opened her little window, and sang her
usual song :

> "Blue Bird, Blue Bird,
> Come to my side."

But no Blue Bird appeared. The queen had caused sharp
knives to be hung outside the hollow of the tree : he flew
against them and cut his feet and wings, till he dropped
down, covered with blood.

"Oh, Florina, come to my help!" sighed he. "But
she is dead, I know, and I will die also."

At that moment, his friend, the magician, who, since
he had seen the chariot with flying frogs return without
King Charming, had gone eight times round the world in
search of him, made his ninth journey, and came to the
tree where the poor Blue Bird lay, calling out, "King
Charming, King Charming!"

The king recognised the voice of his best friend :
whereupon the magician took him out of the hollow
tree, healed his wounds, and heard all his history. He
persuaded King Charming that, overcome with fear and
cruel treatment, Florina must have betrayed him.

"Then do as you will with me!" cried the king.
"Put me into a cage and take me back with you. I shall
at least be safe there for the five years that are to be
endured."

"Stopping beside a fountain, she let her hair fall loose, and dipped her weary feet in the cool water."

THE BLUE BIRD

"But," said the enchanter, "can you remain five years in so undignified a position? And you have enemies who will assuredly seize on your kingdom."

"Why can I not return and govern it as before?"

"I fear," replied his friend, "that the thing is difficult. Who would obey a Blue Bird?"

"Ah, that is too true!" cried the king sadly. "People only judge by the outside."

Meantime Florina, overcome with grief, fell dangerously sick, and in her sickness she kept singing, day and night, her little song:

> "Blue Bird, Blue Bird,
> Come to my side."

But no one regarded her.

At last a sudden change took place in her fortunes. The king her father died, and the people, who knew she was his heir, began to inquire, with one accord, where was the Princess Florina? They assailed the palace in crowds, demanding her for their sovereign. The riot became so dangerous that Troutina and her mother fled away to the fairy Soussio. Then the populace stormed the tower, rescued the sick and almost dying princess, and crowned her as their queen.

The exceeding care that was taken of her, and her longing to live in order to see again her Blue Bird, restored Florina's health, and gave her strength to call a council and arrange all the affairs of her kingdom. Then she departed by night, and alone, to go over the world in search of her Blue Bird.

The magician, who was King Charming's friend, went to the fairy Soussio, whom he knew, for they had quarrelled and made it up again, as fairies and magicians do, many times within the last five or six hundred years. She received him civilly, and asked him what he wanted. He tried to make a bargain with her, but could effect

209   P

nothing, unless King Charming would consent to marry Troutina. The enchanter found this bride so ugly that he could not advise. Still, the Blue Bird had run so many risks in his cage : the nail it was hung upon had broken, and the king suffered much in the fall ; Minetta, the cat, had glowered at him with her green eyes ; the attendants had forgotten his hemp-seed and his water-glass, so that he was half dying of hunger and thirst ; and a monkey had plucked at his feathers through the wires as disrespectfully as if, instead of a king, he had been a linnet or a jay. Worse than all, his next heir spread reports of his death, and threatened to seize on his throne.

Under these circumstances the magician thought it best to agree with Soussio that King Charming should be restored to his kingdom and his natural shape for six months, on condition that Troutina should remain in his palace, and that he should try to like her and marry her. If not, he was to become again a Blue Bird. So he found himself once more King Charming, and as charming as ever ; but he would rather have been a bird and near his beloved, than a king in the society of Troutina. The enchanter gave him the best reasons for what had been done, and advised him to occupy himself with the affairs of his kingdom and people ; but he thought less of these things than how to escape from the horror of marrying Troutina.

Meanwhile the Queen Florina, in a peasant's dress, with a straw hat on her head, and a canvas sack on her shoulder, began her journey : sometimes on horseback, sometimes on foot, sometimes by sea, sometimes by land, wandering evermore after her beloved King Charming. One day, stopping beside a fountain, she let her hair fall loose, and dipped her weary feet in the cool water, when an old woman, bent, and leaning on a stick, came by.

"My pretty maiden, what are you doing here all alone ? "

"Good mother," replied the queen, "I have too many troubles to be pleasant company for anybody."

"Tell me your troubles, and I may be able to soften them."

Florina obeyed, and told her whole history, and how she was travelling over the world in search of the Blue Bird. The little woman listened attentively, and then, in the twinkling of an eye, became, instead of an old woman, a beautiful fairy.

"Incomparable Florina, the king you seek is no longer a bird ; my sister Soussio has restored him to his proper shape, and he reigns in his own kingdom. Do not afflict yourself; happiness will yet be yours. Take these four eggs, and whenever you are in trouble, break them, and see what ensues." So saying, the fairy vanished.

Florina, greatly comforted, put the eggs in her sack, and turned her steps towards the country of King Charming. She walked eight days and nights without stopping, and then came to a mountain made entirely of ivory, and nearly perpendicular. Despairing of ever climbing it, she sank down at the foot, prepared to die there, when she bethought herself of the eggs. "Let me see," said she, "if the fairy has deceived me or not." So she broke one, and inside it were little hooks of gold, which she fitted on her feet and hands, and by means of which she climbed the mountain with ease. Arrived at the summit she found new difficulties ; for the valley below was one large smooth mirror, in which sixty thousand women stood admiring themselves. They had need, for the charm of the mirror was that each saw herself therein, not as she was, but as she wished to be ; and the grimaces they made were enough to cause a person to die of laughter. Not one of them had ever gained the top of the mountain ; and when they saw Florina there, they all burst into angry outcries, "How has this woman got up the hill? If she descends upon our mirror her first footstep will crack it into a thousand pieces."

The queen, uncertain what to do, broke the second egg, and there flew out two pigeons harnessed to a fine chariot, in which Florina mounted, and descended lightly over the mirror to the valley's foot. "Now, my pretty pigeons," said she, "will you convey me to the palace of King Charming?" The obedient pigeons did so, flying day and night till they reached the city gates ; when the queen dismissed them with a sweet kiss, which was worth more than her crown.

How her heart beat as she entered, and begged to see the king ! "You !" cried the servants, mocking. " Little peasant-girl, your eyes are not half good enough to see the king. Besides, he is going to-morrow to the temple with the Princess Troutina, whom he has at last agreed to marry."

Florina sat down on a doorstep, and hid her face under her straw hat and her drooping hair. "Alas !" she cried, " my Blue Bird has forsaken me."

She neither ate nor slept, but rose with the dawn, and pushed her way through the guards to the temple, where she saw two thrones, one for King Charming, and the other for Troutina. They arrived shortly ; he more charming and she more repulsive than ever. Knitting her brows, Troutina exclaimed, " What creature is that who dares approach so near my golden throne ? "

"I am a poor peasant-girl," said Florina. " I come from afar to sell you curiosities." And she took out of her sack the emerald bracelets which the Blue Bird had given her.

" These are pretty trinkets," said Troutina ; and going up to the king she asked him what he thought of them. At sight of the ornaments he turned pale, remembering those he had given to Florina.

" These bracelets are worth half my kingdom ; I did

not think there had been more than one pair in the world."

"Then I will buy these," said Troutina; but Florina refused to sell them for money: the price she asked was permission to sleep a night in the Chamber of Echoes.

"As you will; your bargains are cheap enough," replied Troutina, laughing: and when she laughed she showed teeth like the tusks of a wild boar.

Now the king, when he was a Blue Bird, had informed Florina about this Chamber of Echoes, where every word spoken could be heard in his own chamber; she could not have chosen a better way of reproaching him for his infidelity. But vain were her sobs and complainings; the king had taken opium to lull his grief; he slept soundly all night long. Next day, Florina was in great disquietude. Could he have really heard her, and been indifferent to her sorrow; or had he not heard her at all? She determined to buy another night in the Chamber of Echoes; but she had no more jewels to tempt Troutina; so she broke the third egg. Out of it came a chariot of polished steel, inlaid with gold, drawn by six green mice, the coachman being a rose-coloured rat, and the postilion a grey one. Inside the carriage sat little puppets, who behaved themselves just like live ladies and gentlemen.

When Troutina went to walk in the palace garden, Florina awaited her in a green alley, and made the mice gallop, and the ladies and gentlemen bow, till the princess was delighted, and ready to buy the curiosity at any price. Again Florina exacted permission to pass the night in the Chamber of Echoes; and again the king, undisturbed by her lamentation, slept without waking till dawn.

The third day, one of the palace valets, passing her by, said, "You stupid peasant-girl, it is well the king takes opium every night, or you would disturb him by that terrible sobbing of yours."

"Does he so?" said the queen, now comprehending

213

all. "Then if you will promise to-night to keep the opium cup out of his way, these pearls and diamonds," and she took a handful of them out of her sack, "shall assuredly be yours."

The valet promised; and then Florina broke her fourth egg, out of which came a pie composed of birds, which, though they had been plucked, baked, and made ready for the table, sang as beautifully as birds that are alive. Troutina, charmed with this marvellous novelty, bought it at the same price as the rest, adding generously a small piece of gold.

When all the palace were asleep, Florina for the last time, hoping King Charming would hear her, called upon him with all sorts of tender expressions, reminding him of their former vows, and their two years of happiness. "What have I done to thee, that thou shouldst forget me and marry Troutina?" sobbed she; and the king, who this time was wide awake, heard her. He could not make out whose voice it was, or whence it came, but it somehow reminded him of his dearest Florina, whom he had never ceased to love. He called his valet, inquired who was sleeping in the Chamber of Echoes, and heard that it was the little peasant-girl who had sold to Troutina the emerald bracelet. Then he rose up, dressed himself hastily, and went in search of her. She was sitting mournfully on the floor, with her hair hiding her face, and her eyes swollen with tears; but he knew at once his faithful Florina. He fell on his knees before her, covered her hands with kisses, and they embraced and wept together. For what was the good of all their love when they were still in the power of the fairy Soussio?

But at this moment appeared the friendly enchanter, with a fairy still greater than Soussio, the one who had given Florina the four eggs. They declared that their united power was stronger than Soussio's, and that the lovers should be married without further delay.

THE BLUE BIRD

When this news reached Troutina, she ran to the Chamber of Echoes, and there beheld her beautiful rival, whom she had so cruelly afflicted.   But the moment she opened her mouth to speak, her wicked tongue was silenced for ever ; for the magician turned her into a trout, which he flung out of the window into the stream that flowed through the castle garden.

As for King Charming and Queen Florina, delivered out of all their sorrows, and given to one another, their joy was quite inexpressible, and it lasted to the end of their lives.

Note.—It will be seen that this tale, which is from the French, bears a curious resemblance to Grimm's story of "The Iron Stove," except that the latter retains a brevity and German simplicity, not found here.   This family likeness may be traced in the fairy tales of all countries.   I merely refer to it to show that the repetition of incidents was not unobserved or unintentional. —EDITOR.

THE SIX SWANS

Once upon a time, a king, hunting in a great forest, chased a wild boar so eagerly, that none of his people could follow him. When evening came, he stopped to look about him, and saw that he had lost himself. He sought everywhere for a way out of the wood, but could find none. Then he perceived coming towards him an old woman, whose head kept constantly shaking. She was a witch.

"My good woman," said he to her, "cannot you show me the way through the wood?"

"Oh yes, your majesty," answered she, "that I can, but only on one condition, and if you do not agree to it, you will never get out, and must die here of hunger."

"What is the condition?" asked the king.

"I have an only daughter," said the old woman, "she is as beautiful as any one you could find in the wide world, and well deserves to be your wife; if you will make her your queen, I will show you the way out of the wood."

The king, in the fear of his heart, consented, and the old woman led him to her house, where her daughter sat by the fire. She received the king as if she had expected him, and he saw that she was very beautiful; but still she did not please him, and he could not look at her without a secret shudder. After he had lifted up the maiden beside him on his horse, the old woman showed him the way, and the king arrived again at his royal castle, where the wedding was celebrated.

"The queen threw one of the shirts over each of them, and when the shirts touched their bodies,
they were changed into swans, and flew away over the wood."

THE SIX SWANS

He had been married once before, and had by his first wife seven children, six boys and a girl, whom he loved more than anything in the world. But, because he was afraid that the stepmother might not treat them well, or might even do them some harm, he took them to a lonely castle which stood in the middle of a wood. It was so hidden, and the road was so difficult to find, that he himself would not have found it, if a wise woman had not given him a wonderful skein of thread ; which, when he threw it down before him, unrolled of itself and showed him the way. The king went out so often to his dear children, that the queen noticed his absence, and was full of curiosity to know what business took him thus alone to the wood. So she gave his servants a sum of money, and they told her the secret, and also told her of the skein, which was the only thing that could show the way. After that she never rested till she had found out where the king kept the skein. Then she made some little white silk shirts, and as she had learned witchcraft from her mother, she sewed a spell into every one of them. And one day when the king was gone out to hunt, she took the little shirts and went into the wood, and the skein showed her the way.

The six brothers, who saw some one in the distance, thought their dear father was coming, and ran to meet him, full of joy. As they approached, the queen threw one of the shirts over each of them, and when the shirts touched their bodies, they were changed into swans, and flew away over the wood. The witch's daughter went home quite happy, and thought she had got rid of all her stepchildren ; but the one little girl had not run out with her brothers, and the queen knew nothing about her.

Next day, the king came joyfully to visit his children, but he found nobody except the little sister.

" Where are your brothers ? " asked he.

"Oh, dear father," she answered, "they are gone and have left me alone," and then she told him all that she had seen out of her window; how her brothers were turned into swans, and had flown away over the wood; she also showed him the feathers which they had dropped into the courtyard, and which she had picked up.

The king was grieved, but he never thought that the queen had done this wicked deed; however, because he dreaded lest the little girl would be stolen from him likewise, he wished to take her away with him. But she was afraid of the stepmother, and begged the king to let her stay one night more in the castle in the wood.

The poor little girl thought, "I cannot rest here any longer, I will go and look for my brothers."

And when the night came, she ran away, and went straight into the wood. She went on all through the night, and the next day too, till she was so tired that she could go no further. Then she saw a little house, and went in, and found a room with six little beds; she did not dare to lie down in any, but crept under one of them, laid herself on the hard floor, and meant to pass the night there. But when the sun was just going to set, she heard a rustling, and saw six swans come flying in at the window. They sat down on the floor, and blew at one another, and blew all their feathers off, and took off their swan's-skins like shirts. Then the little girl saw them and recognised her brothers, and was very glad, and crept out from under the bed.

The brothers were not less rejoiced when they saw their little sister, but their joy did not last long.

"You cannot stop here," said they to her, "this is a house belonging to robbers; if they come home, and find you, they will kill you."

"Cannot you protect me?" asked the little sister.

"No," answered they, "we can only take off our swan's-skins for a quarter of an hour every evening, and have our natural shape for that time, but afterwards we are turned into swans again."

The little sister cried and said, " Cannot you be released ? "

" Oh no ! " answered they, " the conditions are too hard. You must not speak or laugh for six years, and must make for us six shirts out of stitchweed during that time. If while you are making them a single word comes from your mouth, all your work will be of no use." When her brothers had said this, the quarter of an hour was over, and they turned into swans again, and flew out of the window.

But the little girl made a firm resolution to release her brothers, even if it cost her her life. She left the house, and went into the middle of the wood, and climbed up in a tree and spent the night there. Next morning she got down, collected a quantity of stitchweed, and began to sew. She could not speak to any one, and she did not want to laugh, so she sat, and only looked at her work.

When she had been there a long time, it happened that the king of the country was hunting in the wood, and his hunters came to the tree on which the little girl sat. They called to her, and said, " Who are you ? "

But she gave them no answer.

" Come down to us," said they, " we will not do you any harm."

But she only shook her head. As they kept teasing her with their questions, she threw them down her gold necklace, and thought they would be satisfied with that. But they did not leave off, so she threw her sash down to them, and as that was no good, she threw down her garters, and at last everything that she had on, and could spare ; so that she had nothing left but her shift. But the hunters would not be sent away, and climbed up the tree and brought down the little girl and took her to the king.

THE FAIRY BOOK

The king asked, "Who are you? what were you doing up in the tree?"

But she did not answer. He asked it in all the languages that he knew, but she remained as dumb as a fish. But, because she was so beautiful, the king's heart was moved, and he fell deeply in love with her. He wrapped his cloak round her, took her before him on his horse, and brought her to his castle. Then he had her dressed in rich clothes, and she shone in her beauty like bright sunshine; but they could not get a word out of her. He set her by him at the table, and her modest look and proper behaviour pleased him so much, that he said, "I will marry her, and no one else in the world," and after a few days he was married to her.

But the king had a wicked mother, who was not pleased with this marriage, and spoke ill of the young queen. "Who knows where the girl comes from," said she, "she cannot speak; she is not good enough for a king."

A year after, when the queen brought her first child into the world, the old mother took it away, and smeared her mouth with blood while she was asleep. Then she went to the king, and accused her of eating her child. The king would not believe it, and would not let any one do her any harm. And she always sat and sewed the shirts, and took no notice of anything else. Next time, when she had another beautiful baby, the wicked stepmother did the same as before; but the king could not resolve to believe what she said.

He said, "My wife is too pious and good to do such a thing; if she were not dumb, and if she could defend herself, her innocence would be made clear."

But when for the third time the old woman took away the new-born child, and accused the queen, who could not say a word in her own defence, the king could not help himself; he was forced to give her up to the court of justice, and she was condemned to suffer death by fire.

When the day came upon which the sentence was to be executed, it was exactly the last day of the six years, in which she might not speak or laugh ; and she had freed her dear brothers from the power of the spell. The six little shirts were finished, except that on the last one a sleeve was wanting. When she came to the place of execution, she laid the shirts on her arm, and when she stood at the stake, and the fire was just going to be lit, she looked round, and there came six swans flying through the air. Then her heart leaped with joy, for she saw that her deliverance was near.

The swans flew to her, and crouched down, so that she could throw the shirts over them ; as soon as the shirts were touched by them, their swan's-skins fell off, and her brothers stood before her. They were all grown up, strong and handsome ; only the youngest had no left arm, but instead of it a swan's wing.

They hugged and kissed their sister many times, and then the queen went to the king, and began to speak, and said, " Dearest husband, now I may speak, and declare to you that I am innocent and falsely accused " ; and she told him about the deceit of the old mother, who had taken away her three children, and hidden them.

However they were soon fetched safely back, to the great joy of the king ; and the wicked mother-in-law was tied to the stake, and burnt to ashes. But the king and queen, with their six brothers, lived many years in peace and happiness.

THE JUNIPER-TREE

ONE or two thousand years ago, there was a rich man who had a beautiful and pious wife ; they loved one another dearly, but they had no children. They wished and prayed for some night and day, but still they had none. In front of their house was a yard, where stood a Juniper-tree, and under it the wife stood once in winter, and peeled an apple, and as she peeled the apple she cut her finger, and the blood fell on the snow.

" Oh," said she, sighing deeply and looking sorrowfully at the blood, " if I only had a child as red as blood, and as white as snow ! "

While she spoke, she became quite happy ; it seemed to her as if her wish would surely come to pass. Then she went into the house ; and a month passed, and the snow melted ; and two months, and the ground was green ; and three months, and the flowers came up out of the earth ; and four months, and all the trees in the wood burst forth, and the green twigs all grew thickly together; the little birds sang so that the whole wood rang, and the blossoms fell from the trees. The fifth month passed, and she stood under the Juniper-tree, and it smelt so beautiful, and her heart leaped for joy. She fell upon her knees, but could not speak. When the sixth month was gone, the fruit was large and ripe, and she was very quiet ; the seventh month, she took the juniper berries, ate them eagerly, and was sick and sorrowful ; and the eighth month went by, and she called to her husband,

and cried and said, "If I die, bury me under the Juniper-tree."

After this she was quite comforted and happy, till the next month was past, and then she had a child as white as snow and as red as blood. When she beheld it, she was so glad, that she died.

Her husband buried her under the Juniper-tree, and began to mourn very much; but after a little time, he became calmer, and when he had wept a little more, he left off weeping entirely, and soon afterwards he took another wife.

The second wife brought him a daughter, but the child of the first wife was a little son, and was as red as blood, and as white as snow. When the wife looked at her daughter, she loved her; but when she looked at the little boy, she hated him, and it seemed as if he were always in her way, and she was always thinking how she could get all the property for her daughter. The Evil One possessed her so, that she was quite angry with the little boy, and pushed him about from one corner to another, and cuffed him here and pinched him there, until the poor child was always in fear. When he came home from school, he could not find a quiet place to creep into.

Once, when the woman went up to her room, her little daughter came up too, and said, "Mother, give me an apple."

"Yes, my child," said the woman, and gave her a beautiful apple out of the chest; and the chest had a great heavy lid, with a great sharp iron lock.

"Mother," said the little daughter, "shall not brother have one too?"

That vexed the woman, but she said, "Yes, when he comes from school."

And when she saw from the window that he was coming, it was just as if the Evil One came into her, and she snatched away the apple from her daughter, and said, "You shall not have one before your brother."

Then she threw the apple into the chest, and shut the

lid close down.   When the little boy came in at the door, the Evil One made her say kindly, " My son, will you have an apple ? "

Yet she looked so angry all the time, that the little boy said, " Mother, how dreadful you look ! Yes, give me an apple."

Then she felt that she must speak to him.   " Come with me," said she, and opened the lid ; " pick out an apple for yourself."

And as the little boy stooped over, the Evil One prompted her, and smash ! she banged the lid down, so that his head flew off and fell among the red apples. Then she was seized with terror, and thought, " Can I get rid of the blame of this ? "   So she went up to her room to her chest of drawers, and took out of the top drawer a white cloth, and placed the head on the neck again, and tied the handkerchief round it, so that one could see nothing, and set him before the door on a chair, and gave him the apple in his hand.

Soon after, little Margery came to her mother, who stood by the kitchen fire, and had a pot of hot water before her, which she kept stirring round.

" Mother," said little Margery, " brother sits before the door, and looks quite white, and has an apple in his hand ; I asked him to give me the apple, but he did not answer me, and I was frightened."

" Go to him again," said her mother, " and if he will not answer you, give him a box on the ear."

Then Margery went, and said, " Brother, give me the apple."

But he was silent, so she gave him a box on the ear, and the head fell down.

She was frightened, and began to cry and sob, and ran to her mother, and said, " Oh, mother, I have knocked my brother's head off ! " and cried and cried, and would not be comforted.

"Out of the fire flew a beautiful bird, who, singing deliciously, rose up high in the air."

"Margery," said her mother, "what have you done!
—but now be quiet, and no one will notice ; it cannot be
helped now—we will cook him in vinegar."

Then the mother took the little boy, and chopped him
in pieces, put him into the pot, and cooked him in vinegar.
But Margery stood by, and cried and cried, and all her
tears fell into the pot, so that the cookery did not want
any salt.

When the father came home, and sat down to dinner,
he said, "Where is my son?"

The mother brought a great big dish of black soup,
and Margery cried and cried without ceasing. Then the
father said again, "Where is my son?"

"Oh," said the mother, "he is gone into the country,
to see his uncle, where he is going to stay awhile."

"What does he want there? And he has not even
said good-bye to me!"

"Oh, he wished very much to go, and asked if he
might remain away six weeks ; he is well taken care of
there, you know."

"Well," said the father, "I am sorry ; for he ought
to have bade me good-bye."

After that he began to eat, and said, "Margery, what
are you crying for? Brother will be sure to come back.
Oh, wife," continued he, "how delicious this food tastes ;
give me some more." And the more he ate, the more he
wanted ; and he said, "Give me more, you shall not have
any of it ; I feel as if it were all mine." And he ate and
ate, throwing the bones under the table, till he had
finished it all.

But Margery went to her drawers, and took out of
the bottom drawer her best silk handkerchief, and fetched
out all the bones from under the table ; she tied them up
in the silk handkerchief, and took them out of doors, and
shed bitter tears over them. Then she laid them under
the Juniper-tree in the green grass ; and when she had

put them there, she felt all at once quite happy, and did not cry any more.

Soon the Juniper began to move, and the twigs kept dividing and then closing, just as if the tree were clapping its hands for joy. After that there went up from it a sort of mist, and right in the centre of the mist burnt a fire, and out of the fire flew a beautiful bird, who, singing deliciously, rose up high in the air. When he was out of sight, the Juniper-tree was just as it had been before, only the handkerchief with the bones was gone. But Margery felt quite pleased and happy, just as if her brother were still alive. And she went back merrily into the house to dinner.

The bird flew away, sat himself on a goldsmith's house, and began to sing :

> " My mother, she killed me ;
> My father, he ate me ;
> My sister, little Margery,
> Gathered up all my bones,
> Tied them in a silk handkerchief,
> And laid them under the Juniper-tree :
> Kywitt ! Kywitt ! what a beautiful bird am I ! "

The goldsmith sat in his workshop, making a gold chain, but he heard the bird, which sat on his roof, and sang, and he thought it very beautiful. He stood up, and as he went over the door-step he lost one slipper. But he went right into the middle of the street, with one slipper and one sock on ; he had on his leather apron ; in one hand he carried the gold chain, and in the other the pincers, while the sun shone brightly up the street. There he stood, and looked at the bird.

" Bird," said he, " how beautifully you can sing ! Sing me that song again."

" No," said the bird, " I do not sing twice for nothing. Give me that gold chain, and I will sing it again."

THE JUNIPER-TREE

"There," said the goldsmith; "you shall have the gold chain—now sing me that song once more."

Then the bird came and took the gold chain in his right claw, and went and sat before the goldsmith, and sang :

> My mother, she killed me ;
> My father, he ate me ;
> My sister, little Margery,
> Gathered up all my bones,
> Tied them in a silk handkerchief,
> And laid them under the Juniper-tree :
> Kywitt! Kywitt! what a beautiful bird am I!

Afterwards he flew away to a shoemaker's, and set himself on his roof, and sang :

> My mother, she killed me ;
> My father, he ate me ;
> My sister, little Margery, .
> Gathered up all my bones,
> Tied them in a silk handkerchief,
> And laid them under the Juniper-tree :
> Kywitt! Kywitt! what a beautiful bird am I!

When the shoemaker heard it, he ran out of his door in his shirt-sleeves, looked towards his roof, and had to hold his hand over his eyes, so that the sun should not dazzle him.

"Bird," said he, "how beautifully you can sing!" And he called in at his door, "Wife, just come out; there is a bird here which can sing so beautifully." Then he called his daughter and his workpeople, both boys and girls; they all came into the street, looked at the bird, and saw how handsome he was; for he had bright red and green feathers, and his neck shone like real gold, and his eyes twinkled in his head like stars.

"Bird," said the shoemaker, "now sing me that song again."

"No," replied the bird, "I do not sing twice for nothing; you must give me something."

THE FAIRY BOOK

"Wife," said the man, "go to the garret: on the highest shelf there stands a pair of red shoes—bring them here."

The wife went and fetched the shoes.

"There," said the man, "now sing me that song again."

Then the bird came and took the shoes in his left claw and flew back on the roof, and sang:

> My mother, she killed me;
> My father, he ate me;
> My sister, little Margery,
> Gathered up all my bones,
> Tied them in a silk handkerchief,
> And laid them under the Juniper-tree:
> Kywitt! Kywitt! what a beautiful bird am I!

And when he had finished, he flew away, with the chain in his right claw and the shoes in his left. He flew far away to a mill, and the mill went "Clipper, clapper, clipper, clapper, clipper, clapper." And in the mill there sat twenty millers, who chopped a stone, and chopped, "Hick, hack, hick, hack, hick, hack"; and the mill went, "Clipper, clapper, clipper, clapper, clipper, clapper."

The bird flew up, and sat in a lime-tree that grew before the mill, and sang:

> My mother, she killed me;

then one man stopped;

> My father, he ate me;

then two more stopped and listened;

> My sister, little Margery,

then four more stopped;

> Gathered up all my bones,
> Tied them in a silk handkerchief,

now only eight more were chopping,

228

THE JUNIPER-TREE

now only five,

now only one.

Laid them under

the Juniper-tree.

Kywitt! Kywitt! what a beautiful bird am I!

Then the last man stopped too, and heard the last word.
"Bird," said he, "how beautifully you sing! Please to sing me that song once more."
"No," answered the bird, "I do not sing twice for nothing; give me the millstone, and I will sing it again."
"Yes," said he, "if it belonged to me only, you should have it."
"Yes," cried all the others, "if he sings it again, he shall have it."
Then the bird came down, and all the twenty millers took poles, and lifted the stone up. The bird stuck his neck through the hole in the millstone, and put it on like a collar, and flew back to the tree, and sang:

> My mother, she killed me;
> My father, he ate me;
> My sister, little Margery,
> Gathered up all my bones,
> Tied them in a silk handkerchief,
> And laid them under the Juniper-tree:
> Kywitt! Kywitt! what a beautiful bird am I!

And when he had done singing, he opened his wings, and though he had in his right claw the chain, in his left the shoes, and round his neck the millstone, he flew far away to his father's house.
In the room sat the father, the mother, and little Margery at dinner; and the father said, "Oh, how happy I am! altogether joyful."
"For me," said the mother, "I feel quite frightened, as if a dreadful storm was coming."
But Margery sat, and cried and cried.

Then there came the bird flying, and as he perched himself on the roof, "Oh," said the father, "I feel so happy, and the sun shines out of doors so beautifully! It is just as if I were going to see an old friend."

"No," said the wife; "I am so frightened, my teeth chatter, and it feels as if there was a fire in my veins"; and she tore open her dress. But Margery sat in a corner, and cried, holding her apron before her eyes, till the apron was quite wet through.

The bird perched upon the Juniper-tree, and sang:

> My mother, she killed me;

Then the mother stopped up her ears, and shut her eyes tight, and did not want to see or hear; but there was a roaring in her ears like the loudest thunder, and her eyes burned and flashed like lightning—

> My father, he ate me;

"Oh, wife," said the man, "look at that beautiful bird!—he sings so splendidly. And the sun shines so warm, and there is a smell like real cinnamon!"

> My sister, little Margery,

Then Margery laid her head on her knee, and sobbed out loud; but the man said, "I shall go out—I must look at the bird quite close."

"Oh, do not go," said the wife; "it seems to me as if the whole house shook, and was in flames."

But the man went out and watched the bird, which still went on singing:

> Gathered up all my bones,
> Tied them in a silk handkerchief,
> And laid them under the Juniper-tree:
> Kywitt! Kywitt! what a beautiful bird am I!

After that, the bird let the gold chain fall, and it fell

THE JUNIPER-TREE

right on to the man's neck, fitting exactly round it.   He
went in and said, "See what a beautiful bird that is—it
has given me such a splendid gold chain !"
But the wife was frightened, and fell flat down on the
floor, and her cap dropped off her head.
Then the bird sang again :

> My mother, she killed me ;

"Oh, that I were a thousand feet under the earth, so
that I might not hear !"

> My father, he ate me,

Then she fell down, as if she was dead.

> My sister, little Margery,

"Oh !" said Margery, "I will go out too, and see if
the bird will give me anything."

> Gathered up all my bones,
> Tied them in a silk handkerchief,

And the shoes were thrown down.

> And laid them under the Juniper-tree :
> Kywitt ! Kywitt ! what a beautiful bird am I !

Then Margery was very joyful ; she put on the new
red shoes, and danced and jumped about. "Oh," said
she, "I was so unhappy when I came out, and now I am
so happy ! That is a wonderful bird ; he has given me a
pair of red shoes."
"For me," cried the wife, and jumped up, and her hair
stood on end like flames of fire, "I feel as if the world
were come to an end ; I will go out—perhaps I shall feel
easier."
But as she went out of the door—smash !—the bird
threw the millstone on her head, and she was crushed to
pieces.

THE FAIRY BOOK

The father and Margery heard it, and rushed out to see what had happened : there was a great flame and smoke rising up from the place, and when that was gone, there stood the little brother all alive again—as if he had never died. He took his father and Margery by the hand, and they were all three quite happy, and went into the house to dinner.

THE END